DISRUPTION

THE CAMBRIDGE FILES

STEVEN WHIBLEY

Published by Steven Whibley Publishing
Victoria, British Columbia
www.stevenwhibley.com

Publisher: Steven Whibley Publishing
Editing: Maya Packard; Ricki Ewings
Cover Design: Pintado (rogerdespi.8229@gmail.com)
Interior Layout and Design: Tammy Desnoyers (www.tammydesign.ca)

Library and Archives Canada Cataloguing in Publication

Whibley, Steven, 1978-, author
    Disruption / Steven Whibley.

(The Cambridge files ; bk. 1)
Issued in print and electronic formats.
ISBN 978-1-927905-03-6 (bound).--ISBN978-1-927905-05-0 (pbk.).--
ISBN 978-1-927905-04-3 (pdf)

    I. Title. II. Series: Whibley, Steven, 1978- . Cambridge files ; bk. 1.

PS8645.H46D57 2014   jC813'.6   C2014-900207-6
                                              C2014-900208-4

For Isaiah and Aubree

– Steven Whibley

DISRUPTION

THE CAMBRIDGE FILES

STEVEN WHIBLEY

CHAPTER 1

Every year, Marksville Middle School's graduating class puts on a farewell talent show, and every year there are dorks who sing, dorks who dance, and dorks who juggle or do magic. Some of the really dorky dorks recite poetry or act out scenes from something stupid and Shakespearean.

The show was a tradition that me and the other non-dork students had to endure. For three years, we'd sat on the gym's bleachers and watched as untalented fourteen-year-olds performed and thought they were special. But there we were, at the last talent show I'd ever have to sit through. There was only one thing I needed to do to this tradition before I left.

Destroy it.

My best friend, Jason and I stood like rock stars, bumping fists, and making hand signs at the crowd in front of us. We wanted to start already, but clearly Principal Barlett needed a bit more time to realize his attempt at a humorous introduction to the talent show was failing. It didn't matter because no one was going to remember his monologue after we were done. He cleared his throat and glanced over his shoulder at us to see if we were ready.

Jason held his cardboard guitar in the air to signal that we were.

"I've made you all wait long enough," Principal Bartlett said into the microphone. "I present the first act by two of your graduating eighth graders, Jason Cole and Matt Cambridge!"

The kids in the bleachers erupted with cheers, and Jason nodded to the seventh grader at the control box. A rock song I'd never heard blasted through the speakers, and Jason and I started jumping around pretending to sing along.

Fifteen seconds in, just as we'd planned, I dropped to one knee, lit the match that had been taped to the back of my cardboard guitar, and dropped it into the bucket.

Before I'd taken three steps back, there was a whoosh, and a funnel of thick white smoke rose up from the bucket like a giant twisting snake. Everyone in the gym went silent, then all the teachers suddenly lurched to their feet. I stopped moving and gave Jason an *is it supposed to do that?* look.

When the smoke column hit the ceiling of the gym and spread out into a giant cloud, the cheers of the student body were reignited. The teachers looked around at their colleagues, uncertain, it seemed, as to whether they should evacuate or sit back down. That uncertainty lasted only a few more seconds.

The heavy white cloud hovering below the ceiling thirty feet above us started to fall. At first, people thought it was fun. Quite a few started cheering. But then they started to cough, and the cheers became screams and cries for help.

"I can't breathe!" someone screamed, which was stupid since you need to breathe in order to scream. The smoke didn't sting my eyes or throat, and it wasn't so thick that you couldn't see. Still, that bit of panic, combined with the white smoke circulating through the air, was enough to send the entire place into a frenzy.

Panic, in that tightly packed gym, spread like flames, and in seconds, students rushed for the exits in a mad stampede, which caused even more panic. Everywhere I looked people were running or crying or both. And just when I thought it couldn't get any worse, the fire alarm clanged overhead and the sprinklers burst to life.

Jason stepped up beside me and after a few moments of watching the mayhem, said, "This isn't going *exactly* like we'd planned."

By then the sprinklers had managed to pull the remaining smoke out of the air, and a milky liquid dripped off everything around us.

I took a deep breath and sighed as the mob thinned out and the remaining students hobbled for the exits.

"Yeah," I said, "we might have overshot a bit."

We thought our prank would simply end the talent show and that we'd all be sent home. We really hadn't intended to hurt people. But people *were* hurt, and the police showed up and hauled us to the station to call our parents. Jason's dad showed up first with a couple of lawyers in tow. Jason and I sat outside the conference room and watched through the windows as the adults in suits and the men in uniform talked it out. "It'll be okay," Jason said.

And it was ... sort of. I'm not sure what Jason's dad said, but he's disgustingly rich, and I guess the kids of rich people get away with stuff. The fact that I was *with* a rich kid meant I got away with stuff too.

My mom showed up at the station a few minutes after we'd been released. She talked to the officer in charge and then marched me to the car. She didn't speak to me the whole way home, though she tried to a couple of times. Her mouth would open, and she'd inhale, but then her lips would become thin lines and she wouldn't speak. That's how my mom was. She never yelled and never lost her temper. She taught first graders; maybe that was why she always seemed to have so much patience.

She pulled the car into the driveway and shut off the engine. I could tell by the way she was breathing that I wasn't supposed to get out yet.

She turned. "I'm so disappointed in you," she said finally. Moisture had gathered in her eyes, and I thought she might actually cry.

My stomach knotted. "We didn't think—"

"That's right," she snapped. "You didn't think. You didn't think at all." She unbuckled her seatbelt and took a long, slow breath. "Go to your room. I don't want to see you right now."

When my dad came home later that evening, things really went downhill. My dad was a janitor for a company called Sledge Industries. He was bald and nearly six feet tall, with thick arms and broad shoulders. He always walked a bit hunched, not like he had bad posture, more like he was always a second away from charging at something. My friends said that in another life my dad had probably been one of those Italian mob enforcers—you know, the guy you get to break legs or threaten people. Usually Dad was a pretty peaceful guy, unless I did something wrong. Then he became a rottweiler.

As he stood in the doorway of my room, I realized that he actually kind of looked like a rottweiler too—only scarier. He spent the better part of an hour screaming at me about stupidity and damages and recklessness, and then he just stopped.

And that was it. For nearly two days.

I'd said I was sorry. And I was kind of sorry. I mean, no one had been seriously hurt. It was all just skinned knees and a few bruises. Yes, a few kids had asthma flare-ups, but they'd be fine. I *was* sorry, but

I also felt like everyone was kind of overreacting. It was just smoke.

So when my dad stepped into my room on that last day and told me what my punishment was, I wasn't sure how to react.

"It's going to strengthen my moral compass?" I asked. "What kind of Kool-aid-drinking camp is it?"

"I told you not to speak," my dad said in a low warning tone. "Don't argue. Don't whine. Don't say anything. Or I swear, Matt, I'll send you to Alaska. It's this camp, or it's Alaska with your aunt, because clearly we're not getting through to you."

I swallowed. I'd seen my dad angry before. He'd even threatened to send me to my aunt's place in Alaska before, but this was different. This was some kind of angry desperation I'd never seen before.

"You'll go to this camp," he said. "You'll listen. You'll learn. Because it wasn't easy getting you into this place." He rubbed the back of his neck and looked away from me, almost as if he was ashamed about something. "You're not... exactly supposed to be there. So for three weeks, just blend in."

"Blend in how? What does that even m—"

His fist slammed against the surface of my desk, knocking everything on it to the floor. "Do. Not. Talk."

I put my lips together.

"You leave the day after tomorrow." He shook his head, then turned and stepped out of the room looking very tired.

And as much as I didn't like the idea of losing three weeks of summer to this stupid camp, I liked the idea of Alaska even less. It could've been worse.

I was such an idiot.

CHAPTER 2

"Summer camp?" Jason asked while we walked home after school. "I mean, *that's* your punishment? Camp? And you thought my parents were soft."

I rolled my eyes at him. "It's not going to be a sit-around-the-campfire-and-eat-marshmallows kind of camp," I said. "It's probably some kind of military camp. My dad keeps saying I basically tried to kill a couple hundred middle schoolers." I hadn't told Jason about my dad acting weird about it, or warning me to blend in. If there was a chance he could get in trouble over it, I figured it would be better if I didn't tell anyone else.

Jason laughed. "Please. We did everyone a favor, and we made the last week of school a memorable one."

He held out his fist and I bumped it with mine.

"The good news," Jason added, "is I did some digging online, and there's only a handful of camps just outside the city. They're all your run-of-the-mill, let's-hold-hands-and-sing-Kumbaya type places. So I don't think you're gonna be doing any marching drills."

"I sincerely doubt that," I said. "Not if it was my dad's idea." No way he'd let me off that easy. "He's really mad," I said after a few minutes. "He just keeps telling me that if I mess up at camp, he's sending me to live with my aunt next year. In Alaska."

Jason nodded. "He probably means it this time. Better just fly under the radar, Matt. Make a tie-dyed T-shirt, shoot some arrows, and learn what a moose turd looks like. Then get back here so we can plan some pranks for high school."

I laughed. "Moose turd?"

"I know what goes on in those summer camps," Jason said. "It's a bunch of dorks running around the woods smelling animal turds."

I laughed again. "And if it *is* a military camp?"

"Then shoot some guns and learn how to do military stuff." He kicked a stone. "Then come back and teach me."

"Deal," I said.

"While you're gone," Jason said, "I'll think up some truly epic pranks for us to pull when you get back. Things we've never done. Things that will make grown men weep."

"That might be tough," I said with a smile. "We've done a lot."

"If there's one thing I've learned from TV," Jason said, "it's that there's always something bigger and better. Maybe we can finally pull that train-station one."

I laughed. The train-station prank was an ongoing plan of ours that involved a boatload of fireworks and a train station. It wasn't a real detailed plan.

Jason reached into his backpack. "Hey, that reminds me. Here." He pulled out a small black object and tossed it over to me. "It's just a cell phone. I know your parents won't let you have one, but at least you can use this while you're gone."

"You got me a phone?"

"It's my old one."

Jason's old phone was about a million times better than most people's new ones.

13

"Just don't pocket-dial me while you're having a sing-along." He pretended to vomit into a bush.

"Thanks, man."

He waved his hand. "It's not a big deal. Hey, what time do you leave tomorrow?"

I groaned. "Buses leave at six o'clock."

"In the morning?"

I nodded.

He grimaced. "Maybe it *is* an army camp."

CHAPTER 3

Dad pulled the car into an alley, just close enough for me to see the parking lot in the distance and the five yellow school buses parked in the lot. Dozens of kids marched around loading suitcases and backpacks into the storage compartments and hugging parents goodbye. The ones I could see looked like total losers. Their idiotic smiles and almost comically awestruck expressions made me shake my head. I had a feeling it was going to be a very long summer.

Dad put his hand on my shoulder. "Follow instructions at camp, Matt. Don't get into trouble. And try to learn something."

"Yeah, yeah," I said. "Or you'll send me to Alaska. I get it."

Dad sighed. "Matt, these kids come from wealthy families, successful families who can give them all the advantages in life. You could really benefit from what they can teach you."

"Clearly not if *I'm* going to the camp too," I said. I knew my comment would hurt him, but I didn't care.

Dad closed his eyes and took a deep breath. Then he gripped my shoulder tighter. "Son, don't mess up. There's a lot riding on your ability to fly under the radar in there. Plus, you know your mom will be disappointed if you don't take advantage of this opportunity."

I nodded. *Mom* would be disappointed? Either he realized it wouldn't be much of a deterrent to tell me *he'd* be disappointed, or he was already as disillusioned as he could get.

15

It had taken my mom the better part of an hour to say goodbye to me. She'd sniffled and wiped her eyes as if I were going off to war. I glanced up the street at the parking lot again. Unless war was being fought by a bunch of nerdy kids, I wasn't going to be on any front lines.

"I get it, Dad. I'll blend in." I gestured out of the car. "Do you think I haven't noticed how far away we are? I get that you don't want them to see that I'm your kid."

"That's not it, Matt," my dad said. "This camp is associated with my work. It's only supposed to be for the children of executives. It's not a camp we'd be able to afford."

I raised my eyebrows. "And yet here I am, about to go in."

There was more to this story. My dad looked genuinely ashamed, and the fact that he was telling me any of this meant he was worried.

"Look, Matt ... You need to take this seriously. There's a lot on the line." He turned and looked out the window. "I didn't *exactly* get permission to send you to this camp," he said. "I had to pull some strings."

Strings? What kind of strings could you pull?

"Just don't wreck this opportunity, Matt. If you blow this, if they kick you out, or if you run away ..."

"Uh-huh, I know. Alaska." I reached for the handle. "I'll do my best not to embarrass you."

I pushed open the door and was about to get out when my dad grabbed my arm.

"Matt," he said. "I'm not trying to threaten you. You're just not making good choices. You're getting involved in things that could send you down a road your mother and I don't want for you." He shook his head. "This is your chance, son. Please don't throw it away."

I brushed his hand off my arm and got out of the car. "I already said I'd blend in, didn't I?" I grabbed my bag from the back seat, slammed the door, and started walking toward the buses.

"Matt!" Dad called.

I turned.

"We love you, son."

"Great. Lucky me." I turned again and started walking.

"See you in a few weeks!" he called after me.

I didn't turn back this time. I just kept walking. I hoped ignoring him would make him feel guilty for sending me away for three weeks of summer. But that was dumb. I was going to camp, not prison. I glanced over my shoulder. My dad was still there, watching me. What kind of camp was this going to be? If it was a camp for rich kids, then it wasn't going to be the military camp I'd imagined. Rich kids got cushy camps, didn't they? It might be one for future business leaders, though, and the only activities we'd have would involve calculators and discussions on the economy. I shuddered.

That would be worse than military camp.

"Fit in," I said, repeating my dad's words. "Fit in or you're going to Alaska." I gritted my teeth, took a breath, and forced a smile. This was going to be a long three weeks.

CHAPTER 4

I headed toward a large man standing in front of the buses. He stood rigid, with that perfect posture you see only in movies about military camps. Beside him stood a very petite woman, or perhaps a woman who only looked petite because she stood beside such a giant. Either way, they both had clipboards, and they scrutinized the kids as they walked by, probably checking off little boxes beside questions like, "Is the camper wearing a sweater vest?" *Check.* "Does the camper have his pants pulled up to his armpits?" *Check.*

"Name?" the man asked when I stepped up to them. He was well over six feet tall and as thick as a WWE wrestler. He had a square, clean-shaven face and reddish-blond hair, cropped very short. He wore one of those safari vests, the kind with a thousand pockets; each of his bulged. I wondered if one of the pockets contained a list or maybe a diagram to tell him what was in the other pockets.

"Matt," I said.

He lowered his clipboard and glared at me as if trying to burn holes in my face. He spoke each word like it was its own sentence. "Matt. What."

I hadn't noticed when he first spoke, but he had a slight accent. We had a substitute teacher from South Africa once, and this guy sounded the same. I rolled my eyes at him, and the woman smiled.

"Matt *Cambridge*," I said.

The muscles in his jaw clenched, and he turned back to his

clipboard. He slid the pencil down the page and stopped, presumably at my name. His brow furrowed, and then he looked back at me. "You're Matthew Cambridge?"

I put my arms out to the side. "In the flesh. But please, no autographs."

The woman smiled again and made another note on her clipboard.

Safari Man glanced over my shoulder and looked right, then left. "Where are your parents?"

"My dad just dropped me off."

"He *what*?" The man's face flushed, and his knuckles whitened around his pencil. "He's gone? Parents are supposed to check their kids in before leaving."

I shrugged.

The woman made more notes on her clipboard, which seemed to have a calming effect on Safari Man. Another man, this one wearing dress pants and a dress shirt with rolled-up sleeves, strolled over, and Safari Man tapped the clipboard with his pencil.

The man in the dress shirt glanced at him casually and then turned back to me and smiled. "Welcome to camp, Matthew. Is everything okay?"

"I don't know," I said. "Maybe you should ask the Crocodile Hunter here. Apparently, he thought my dad was coming to camp with me."

Safari Man's pencil snapped in his hand, and the woman at his side chuckled.

"Ms. Sani," the second man said, his tone cool and even. "Most of our campers are ... less outspoken than Mr. Cambridge."

The woman waved her hand. "Save it, Mr. Dalson." She turned to me. "Matt, is it?"

I nodded.

"Are you looking forward to camp, Matt?"

19

"Oh yeah." I rubbed my hands together. "Maybe I'll get a cabin with a kid who farts too much or maybe I'll swim in a lake filled with leeches or eat some disgusting food that makes the cafeteria at my old school look like fine dining."

She laughed some more and then scribbled something at the bottom of the page. Then she pulled the paper from her clipboard and handed it to the man she had called Mr. Dalson.

He took the sheet, but for a moment kept his gaze fixed on me. His eyes were gray, like the sky before a storm. My usual scoff-at-authority attitude shrank.

I could almost hear Dad's voice in the back of my mind. *Way to go, son. Not even at the camp yet and already completely ignoring the one thing I asked of you—blend in. Make sure you pack your parka. Alaska's cold this time of year.*

Dalson's gaze lowered and settled on the paper. Then he blinked. "I don't understand." He turned back to the woman. "We're approved? You made it seem like it could take a while. Weeks maybe."

She pointed at the paper. "It's a preliminary approval. I'll stop by toward the end of the summer and reassess." Dalson glanced back at the page, and she added, "Relax. It's just a formality." She gestured around the parking lot. "You have dozens of counselors, far more than the minimum requirement. Your campers look happy. The parents I've spoken to seem satisfied, and the camp is probably one of the nicest ones on the west coast."

That was a relief.

"The only thing you were missing," she continued, "was campers like Matt."

Dalson looked at me and then back at the woman. Safari Man

looked doubly confused.

The woman sighed. "Do you know how many camps I look into, Mr. Dalson?" She tapped her clipboard. "Dozens and dozens every year." She swept her hand behind her at the kids getting sorted onto buses. "And do you know how many of those have campers as wholeheartedly enthusiastic as yours?"

Dalson shook his head.

"None," she said. "I was starting to get a very bad feeling about this place until this kid came along." She smiled at me and then picked up her briefcase. "All camps have kids who don't want to be there. Kids whose parents make them go." She pointed at me. "You're not here because you want to be, are you?"

I shook my head. "Nope."

"Punishment?" she asked.

I nodded. "Yep."

"What did you do?"

I shrugged. "I nearly killed a gymnasium full of middle-school kids."

Her eyebrows rose, and then she smiled and looked at Mr. Dalson. "See? He's the one I was waiting to see. If you have one, you'll have more than one." She nodded at me. "Have fun, Matt Cambridge. Perhaps I'll see you when I come for the final check."

"Yeah, sure," I said.

She smiled, then nodded at Mr. Dalson and Safari Man, walked straight to a white car with a rusted bumper, and drove away.

"Nicely done, Matt. We weren't sure why she was taking so long with our approval. We'll have to work on camper appearance." He extended his hand. "I'm Dalson." He nodded to Safari Man. "And this is Smith."

"You will call me *sir*," Smith added roughly. He glanced in the direction the woman had driven. "That was pretty gutsy. I thought you were blowing the whole thing. I was this close to throttling you." He held up his thumb and forefinger an inch apart.

Throttling me? I swallowed. Was he seriously telling me that he had been seconds away from strangling me? I shook my head. It must mean something different in whatever country he was from. The two men stood there staring at me for a moment, so I said, "Um, no problem."

"We were wondering who you were, Matt," Dalson said. "We saw your name on the list as a late registration. Your rankings are pretty impressive. I guess after that, I understand why." He looked at Mr. Smith. "A real outside-the-box thinker, wouldn't you say?"

Mr. Smith grunted approvingly.

"Well, it took real guts to talk to her like that," Dalson continued. "And talk to Smith like that." He frowned and looked me up and down, then said, "You'll be a Delta, of course. We were going to have five this year anyway."

I had no idea what they were talking about, but the way they spoke made me think they expected me to understand completely. "Er, thank you."

Mr. Smith pointed at the buses. "You're on Bus Two, Matt Cambridge."

I nodded, then turned and headed for my ride. Dad had said there'd be things I wouldn't understand, but I was getting the distinct impression he had understated that point considerably. The other kids seemed confident and excited.

No more mouthing off, I decided. I hadn't even gotten to the camp yet, and I'd already almost been throttled by a counselor. I suddenly realized I didn't know if they were camp counselors or camp directors—Mr. Smith could be the camp nurse for all I knew. But from now on, I was going to stay in the background. Blend in and just get through these few weeks.

CHAPTER 5

I slipped into an empty seat toward the middle of the bus. There were about a dozen kids already on board. Some looked like they might be a year or two older than me, and others looked like they might be as young as ten. The first thing I noticed, though, was that they weren't smiling the way they had been outside. Some scowled, while others wore expressions like blocks of concrete. Even the kids who looked a couple years younger than me looked like they weren't to be messed with. I wondered if Dad had inadvertently snuck me into a camp for rich kids with bipolar disorder. I'd heard people like that can have unexpectedly drastic mood changes.

I lowered my head and pretended not to notice.

I hadn't been sitting more than a minute when a kid my age, maybe a year older, marched from somewhere in the back of the bus and stopped in the aisle beside me.

"You're in my seat, fish." He was bigger than me, but not by much. His blond hair was cropped short, and he had dark eyes. Brown probably, but they looked almost black.

I'd seen enough prison movies to know that "fish" was something you called the new guy, but I'd never heard another kid use it. I decided to ignore him.

"Hey." He poked me in the arm. "I'm talking to you, newbie."

I sighed and stood up. "Your seat?"

He nodded. "Yeah, that's right."

"Fine." I grabbed my bag and heaved it across the aisle.

"That's my seat too," he said.

"C'mon, Chase," a thin but tough-looking boy said from a few seats back. "Leave the new kid alone. We haven't even gotten to camp yet."

"Best behavior until we're on the bus," Chase said. He spoke like he was reciting a rule. He waved his hand around like a magician who'd just conjured his surroundings. "We're on the bus now, wouldn't you say?"

I was getting tired of this kid. I pointed behind him. "What about that seat? Is it yours too?"

He stared at me and nodded with an evil smirk that, combined with his overly dark eyes, made him look like one of those demon-human hybrids you see on late-night TV. I took a slow breath and could feel the collective gaze of everyone on the bus. I wasn't interested in fighting this kid. He looked tougher than me. But I knew bullies. In elementary school there had been one in my class, Benjamin Bertem. He used to pick on a bunch of us until one day when we waited for him after school and beat him up, five against one. Yeah, yeah, it wasn't a fair fight. We were all hauled down to the principal's office and had to write letters of apology to Ben. But after that, he never bothered us again.

Bullies are like hyenas. They pick out the weak one in the group and attack. If you make it known you're not going to put up with it, they move on.

I rolled my shoulder and thought, *Sorry, Dad*, then turned and glared at Chase.

"Well if that's your seat," I shifted my weight from my heels to the balls of my feet, "maybe you should have a seat." I lunged at him full force, arms stretched out. I figured I'd probably get a bit of a beating, so I wanted this hit to count.

I'm not entirely sure what happened. He moved, or maybe I slipped, but one second I was rushing into him, and the next I was upside down, my face pressed against the floor between two seats across the aisle. Chase gripped one of my legs, holding it up so I couldn't right myself, and with his free hand, he pounded me in the ribs over and over. His fist felt like it had been dipped in cement. I yelped and squirmed, thrashing around like a hooked fish.

"C'mon, Chase," I heard someone say. "Let 'im go."

Chase laughed and shouted something I couldn't make out, but as he did, he stopped hitting me long enough for me to twist my hips and place my hands on the floor beside my face. I drew the knee of my free leg up to my chest and lunged back as hard as I could. I hit him, he dropped my leg, and I landed on the floor of the bus. I pulled myself to my feet, spun around, and swung my fist where I imagined Chase's face would be.

My fist slammed into the palm of a very large hand owned by a guy wearing a safari vest. My mouth and eyes widened in the same instant.

"What are you two doing?" Mr. Smith snapped. He stood between me and Chase, one hand clenched around my fist and the other hand on Chase's chest, holding him back. Blood trailed from Chase's nose. "That woman from the accreditation association hasn't been gone five minutes." His voice was as rough as sandpaper, and his grip tightened with each syllable. "What if she'd come back? What if she'd seen you two?" He glared murderously at Chase, then me. "You know what's at stake. This is your future we're building, and I have no patience for little brats who want to sabotage this organization. Understood?"

Chase sighed. "Yes, sir."

I blinked. I guessed there was only so much bloodshed allowed before accreditation was rejected. That, or Smith was really worried about lawsuits. It's a camp for rich punks, I remembered; they'd probably sue for too much pulp in their orange juice.

Smith glared at me, and his grip coiled tighter over my fist. "Well?" I winced. "Y—yes, sir."

He gave us both a shove and said, "Sit down and shut up. Unauthorized violence is not permitted. Not here. Not at camp." He glared at us again, and when he spoke next, it was through clenched teeth. "Break that rule and I'll see to it you're both kicked out of the program. *Capisce?*"

Chase paled, then nodded and sulked back to his seat. Smith turned to me, and I quickly grabbed my bag and slipped back into my original seat. I'd only been part of this camp for ten minutes, and already I had half a dozen questions rattling around my skull. None of them made much sense. *No unauthorized violence?* Did that mean there would be *authorized* violence at the camp? I wasn't looking forward to that. I was never any good at wrestling or boxing. Why had Smith and Dalson seemed so pleased with my sarcastic comments to the lady in the parking lot? Was this some kind of comedy camp? If so, I'd be golden. And what was the deal with these campers? One minute they were practically skipping around the buses holding hands and braiding each other's hair, and the next they looked like a group therapy session for kids with anger management issues. Probably not a comedy camp, then.

"That was a lucky kick." The voice came from over my shoulder, and I turned to see a girl staring back at me. She had light blue eyes and dark hair pulled back into a ponytail. Her skin was the color of toffee. "Still," she added with a grin, "it was nice to see Chase take a shoe to the side of the head."

I shrugged. "Thanks. I guess."

"I'm Rylee." She reached over the seat and held her hand out. "I kind of pride myself on knowing who's who, and I don't think we've met."

"I'm Matt," I said shaking her hand. "And no, we haven't met. This is my first time."

She nodded. "That explains it."

"What?"

"Why you tried to fight Chase." She glanced over her shoulder. "You didn't know better."

I felt my brow furrow.

"He's a Delta. He's not going to make things very comfortable for you. My advice?" She leaned closer to my seat. "Either hope another Delta picks you, or make yourself scarce for the next three weeks and hope Chase forgets your name." She made a face at me. "But if I'm being honest, I think you might be in real trouble." She smiled again. "Don't sweat it. Maybe another Delta will pick you."

"I don't have a clue what you're talking about," I said. I glanced over Rylee's shoulder. Chase was eyeing me the way a Rottweiler would eye a squirrel. "What's his problem, anyway?"

"The last three camps, he's come in second in team challenges." Her eyes shifted back and forth. "Second. Three times in a row. So he takes that anger out on others. Especially new kids. Plus, he's a sociopath." If she was joking, she needed to do some work on her delivery. The way she said it made me think not only that she was serious, but that being a sociopath was entirely normal. "It's good to have at least one sociopath on each team. You never know when a team challenge might require you to do something someone with a conscience might have a problem with."

"Yeah," I said, "sure. Makes total sense." She was messing with me. Cute *and* sarcastic. I was liking this girl more and more by the second.

"But since he's the Delta, it means he has the power to be dangerous rather than just annoyingly unpredictable."

I shook my head. "I've dealt with his kind before," I said. "He'll get over it."

She laughed and then stopped abruptly. "Oh, you were being serious." She bit her lip. "I know him. Or, at least, I've seen him pick on people before. Trust me; your best bet is to get picked by a different Delta. It's a long shot, but ..."

Okay, now she seemed really sincere, and that just made me nervous. But I remembered that Dalson guy saying something about how I was going to be a Delta. I almost mentioned it to Rylee, but stopped myself. I wasn't sure what it was to be a Delta, and clearly I was supposed to know.

"What about you?" I asked. "Are you a Delta too?"

A boy from across the aisle looked up from his laptop and laughed. "Her? A Delta?" He laughed again. "Not likely." He had a tangle of orange hair and pasty skin that looked almost translucent. If he hadn't been on the bus, I'd have thought his skin had never seen sunlight.

Rylee frowned. "Shut it, wire-head." She looked back at me. "He's a techie. He knows very little about anything outside of computers." He shook his head and turned back to his computer, and Rylee straightened. "Chase has been a Delta for at least six camps now, so he's going to be named a Delta. I could probably guess who the others will be, but no one *really* knows until they're called."

The kid hunched over his keyboard snickered.

"It could happen," she whispered. Then she looked back at me. "I haven't been one yet. But if I were picked, I'd be brilliant." She leaned forward. "I have my team all picked out."

The frizzy-haired kid sighed.

Rylee glared. "Keep it up and I'll take you off my list."

"All right," I said under my breath, "there are teams, and the Deltas are like the captains? What sport are we playing?"

"Wow, you *are* new," Rylee said. "Which is really weird since you're so old."

"Old?"

"You know what I mean."

I didn't have a clue what she meant, but for the hundredth time that morning, I had a feeling I should. "What kind of competition is it?" I asked. "How do the teams compete?"

Rylee fished an iPod from her pocket and put one of the earbuds in her ear. "You're asking the wrong questions, Matt." She nodded toward the back of the bus. "You should be working out a plan to avoid Chase." She slipped the other earbud in place and leaned forward. "And that's not something I'm interested in getting involved in." She pressed a button on her iPod and closed her eyes.

I turned back around in my seat and stared straight ahead. I wasn't actually worried about Chase. He was a bully, and I'd deal with him if I had to. I was more worried about the fact that my dad had asked me to blend in, and instead of doing that, I'd somehow landed a spot as a Delta—a team captain. Maybe I could still fake it if I knew what sport we'd be playing or what was expected of me as a team captain, but I didn't have a clue, and I had a feeling I was going to have a very hard time when we got to camp.

Alaska wasn't always cold, was it? I wasn't really a fan of the cold.

I rubbed the side of my chest where Chase had pounded me and turned my attention to the road.

Dad, what have you gotten me into?

CHAPTER 6

At the beginning of eighth grade, my science class had taken a field trip, and in two hours on the bus, three fights had broken out, one boy had been taped to the emergency exit, and another had been stuffed under a seat. The trip to the camp was more like an hour and a half, but in that time, no one did anything that could've been seen as *bad*. And it wasn't that they were good either. In fact, with a few exceptions, everyone on the bus had these icy expressions. Mess with any one of them, and I was reasonably certain you'd end up with a sharpened toothbrush in your spleen.

Maybe this camp was for criminally insane youth, and my dad had sent me here because he saw these campers as my peers. One little prank goes wrong, and everyone thinks you're a dangerous criminal. Give me a break! I shook my head. No, he'd said it was for rich kids. Not that rich kids couldn't be dangerous criminals, yet somehow I doubted there'd be a camp for that sort of thing.

"Five minutes," the driver yelled. I jumped because until that moment he hadn't uttered a single word, and hearing an adult's voice caught me by surprise. "You're to head directly to the soccer field. Deltas will be named, and selections will commence immediately."

Everyone straightened in their seats and clutched their backpacks against their chests. Rylee wasn't kidding about Delta being a big deal. The more I watched, the more I realized these kids weren't like other kids, at least no kids I knew. They were disciplined, but not in the cadet-at-military-camp way. I had friends who were in Junior ROTC, and they said bus trips were as wild as ever. Plus, the only supervision on the bus was the driver, and yet, with the single exception of what had happened before we left, no one had gotten out of hand.

I craned my head over the back of the seat to ask Rylee if there was anything else I needed to know before we got off the bus, but she shook her head before I could speak. She pressed her finger to her lips and whispered, "Just follow me when we get off the bus. And for Pete's sake, stay away from Chase."

The bus turned off the highway and followed a narrow road for a few minutes, then turned again, this time onto an even narrower dirt road. The branches clawed at the windows of the bus until they thinned and finally fell back. Before long the trees disappeared behind rolling hills that stretched out around us. A moment later we passed through a wooden gate with a large crossbeam high overhead that said CAMP FRIENDSHIP.

"Camp Friendship," I muttered, holding back a laugh. "You've got to be kidding me." The kids looked like criminals. The staff looked like soldiers. That name had to be a joke.

The camp came into view a couple seconds later. Manicured lawns dotted with red-roofed cabins stretched out on both sides of the gravel driveway. I spotted an archery range a short distance down a small grassy hill, and on the other side of the bus, I noticed a row of dirt-bikes lined up beside a course that disappeared into the woods, only to re-emerge a short distance later and then weave back in.

I'd never been to camp before, but this was exactly what I'd expected. In fact, the entire place could have been designed from images taken out of every clichéd after-school special I'd seen on TV.

I half expected to see a camera crew standing by to film us when the bus skidded to a stop. There wasn't one.

"Out!" the driver yelled.

I squeezed in front of Rylee as everyone shuffled down the aisle. The doors folded open and a cloud of dust was sucked into the bus, reminding me of one of those Vietnam War movies where soldiers jump out of a helicopter, only to get blasted before they hit the ground.

"Move it, Matt," Rylee whispered, nudging me out the door. I hit the ground and jogged after the rest of the kids, who all seemed to know exactly where to run. Rylee jogged beside me and ushered me to the right, between rows of cabins. "Chase will be front and center," she said. "Just stay on the outer edge and maybe he won't notice you."

"I don't think this is necessary," I said. "He wasn't that mad. I've been in bigger fights."

"Yeah, you looked like you were handling yourself just fine," Rylee said sarcastically. "If you want to take your chances, go ahead. I don't care. Go stand beside him and hold his hand for all I care."

I quickly decided it wasn't the smartest move to alienate the one person who'd talked to me. If the kids on my bus were any indication, Camp Friendship seemed, ironically, like the least likely place to make friends. "Nah, you're right," I said. "Sorry, didn't mean to sound ungrateful. Do you really think I should go over and hold Chase's hand?"

She laughed. "Yeah, you should. Maybe he's so mean because he didn't get enough hugs as a baby."

"That's just what I was thinking," I said.

She laughed again and then came to an abrupt stop. She pointed at my chest. "Just so you know, I'm not your friend, or your asset. Don't try to make me one. This isn't a Level One camp. I earned my spot."

Huh? I stood there, staring dumbly back at her, trying to make sense of what she'd said. I couldn't.

She glared at me for another moment and then smiled. "Now c'mon. If they call my name for Delta, I want to be there."

We rounded another cabin and came up on a large soccer field. There had to be at least two hundred campers crammed together on the field and dozens of others standing on the sidelines. Rylee and I wove through the mob until we were standing near the front, but on the far left of the group.

Mr. Smith and Mr. Dalson stood side by side on a large platform in front of us, and a row of stern-faced adults stood behind them. Dalson looked relaxed and even had a half smile, which put me at ease a bit. The others, including Mr. Smith, looked like angry gym teachers who were looking forward to tormenting a fresh batch of students.

"Welcome to Camp Friendship." Dalson spoke in the same friendly tone he'd used in the parking lot, and he paced casually along the front of the platform. "I see a few new faces and would like to extend a special welcome to you. Delta selections for this year were scheduled to begin after Week One, but we had a bit of luck this morning with our temporary accreditation." He drew in a breath and held it while he cast his gaze over the crowd. "As such, Delta selections will begin ... immediately."

Rylee drew in a quick breath and chewed her lip. Whatever it was to be a Delta, she wanted it. Bad.

"I want to be clear," Dalson continued, "that even though we might have temporary accreditation and not be under the same scrutiny as we had expected, surprise visits are always a possibility. I expect you all to follow proper protocol and remain proper *campers* at all times."

Campers sounded like a code word. I glanced at the people around me, but none of them seemed to notice, or if they did, they didn't care. This was one strange place.

"Let's not waste any time," he added. He gestured behind him at the line of adults. "You'll get to know most of these counselors during your stay, and your team counselors will introduce themselves at some point before competitions begin." He turned to Mr. Smith and nodded.

Mr. Smith took a step forward. When he spoke it was in stark contrast to Mr. Dalson's friendly tone. "This year," he began, "we will have five Delta teams."

"Five?" Rylee muttered. "Last camp I went to only had four." She looked straight ahead when she spoke. I figured she was probably talking to herself. I really hoped she *would* be picked to be a Delta. She could have my spot. Maybe I'd misunderstood what Dalson and Smith had said in the parking lot. Maybe I was worried about nothing.

While Rylee chewed on her lip and stood on her tiptoes to see over the couple kids in front of us, I took a second to study the faces of the other kids nearby. They looked like just a regular bunch of kids, except for the overly serious expressions. There were small scrawny kids, and there were fat kids, and kids who looked like jocks, but most of them just looked like average, everyday kids like me. If they did call my name, I really hoped it would turn out that we'd be doing a sport I was good at, like soccer or baseball.

"When I call the names of this year's Deltas, you are to present front and center," Mr. Smith continued in his marching-order tone. "When all Deltas have been named, team selection will begin." He turned and said something to the adults behind him.

"They're not going to tell us what sport we're playing?" I whispered.

Rylee swatted my arm. "Shut up, and stop trying to be funny. You sound stupid."

I grimaced—I wasn't trying to be. That's when it hit me, and I suddenly felt like an idiot. We were standing on a soccer field. Maybe Camp Friendship was some kind of super-serious soccer camp or something. I should have realized that as soon as I saw the field. I smiled as a wave of relief washed over me. Soccer I could do. It might even be fun. I glanced at the kids around me again, hoping to spot a few I'd like to use on my team—if they did call me up as a Delta. But as I looked around, I was struck yet again by how average most of the campers were.

Soccer camps were for jocks. The kid to my right was shorter than me and had to be about two hundred pounds. I bet if they searched his pockets they'd find a dozen Twinkies ... or at least a dozen wrappers. Plus, on the bus Rylee had said she had a team all sorted out, and that the computer geek from the bus had been on it. He did not look like a soccer player either.

No. It had to be something else. My stomach flipped. Maybe they wouldn't call me.

Mr. Smith finished speaking with the other adults and now faced the campers, looking down at his clipboard. He glanced up, paused for a beat, and said, "Team Octopus will be led by ... Dexter Miller."

"Octopus?" If I hadn't been so nervous, I probably would have laughed.

"All kids' camps have cutesy names for teams," Rylee whispered. "It would be a pretty big red flag if the names were more appropriate, don't you think?"

"Yeah," I said, doing my best to mask my confusion, "sure would. Total red flag." Total red flag for *what*, I had no clue.

"Not a big surprise they'd pick him to be a Delta," Rylee said.

"Dexter has won a number of smaller competitions in lower-level camps on the east coast."

Dexter was a tall, dark-skinned boy of about sixteen or seventeen. He pushed out of the crowd and stood to the right of Mr. Smith. His expression was about as friendly as a cobra's.

"For Team Hyena," Mr. Smith said next, "Becca Plain."

Rylee groaned. "I hate her. She better not pick me."

Becca Plain looked about the same age as me and had short red hair and a small pointy nose that made her face look very serious. She scanned the crowd when she took her position at the front, and I could actually feel her gaze as she sized up people in the crowd. She was at least a foot shorter than Dexter but looked mean and tough.

"For Team Squirrel," Smith said, "Chase Erickson."

I tensed at the name and noticed a couple kids around me do the same. Chase strolled up to the front, smiling like he didn't have a care in the world. He nodded at a few kids in the crowd, and then his gaze flicked straight to me. He'd known exactly where I was the whole time. He glared at me in a way that validated what Rylee had been talking about. He had me in his crosshairs, and he intended to pull the trigger. It went against everything I knew about bullies. I'd stood up to him. I'd proven myself not to be an easy target, but he was still targeting me. What a jerk. I was officially worried but decided not to show it. I glared back.

"You're just going to make it worse," Rylee said.

"Team Arctic Fox will be led by ..." Mr. Smith paused to consult his clipboard and then looked up. "Alexander Bratersky."

Alexander Bratersky was the meanest-looking kid I'd seen so far. Way meaner than Chase. At best, he was sixteen, but I'd have bet he was actually only fifteen or maybe even fourteen. He had close-cropped blond hair and tattoos that crawled up his arms and disappeared under the sleeves of his dark T-shirt, only to reappear at his neck. Even though his sunglasses hid his eyes, his gaze felt ice-cold, or perhaps his presence cooled the area. Either way, I suddenly wished I had a sweater.

"One more," Rylee whispered. "C'mon, c'mon ..." She bit her lip and rubbed her hands together. I looked up at the sky and silently prayed that I'd misunderstood what Dalson had said in the parking lot. I didn't want to be a captain. I just wanted to survive this stupid camp and go home.

"Delta for Team Grizzly will be ..."

Rylee's hands clenched and opened, then clenched and opened again while Mr. Dalson checked the clipboard. At least a dozen other kids that I could see were acting similarly nervous. My stomach did one final flip as Mr. Smith announced the last name.

"Matthew Cambridge."

CHAPTER 7

I don't think Rylee breathed as I moved forward. I glanced back once as I stepped out of the crowd, and her eyes were like giant orbs staring back above a gaping mouth. I did my best to seem confident as I made my way up to the platform.

I positioned myself beside Alexander Bratersky. He'd seemed large from a distance, but up close, he wasn't much taller than me, an inch or two tops. I quickly realized it was his stance that made him seem bigger. He stood with a rigid posture except for a slight tilt of his head. It made him look like he wasn't standing at his full height, even though he was. I wondered if that was something he did consciously. I took a mental snapshot. It might come in handy back in my real life.

Chase was at the other end of the line and looked as though someone had just forced gym socks into his mouth, which was about the only silver lining to this whole thing. I wondered if my dad had any idea where he'd sent me. I also wondered what he'd said, or written on my application, that would have made Mr. Smith and Mr. Dalson think I was captain—no, Delta—material. I had a passing thought that this whole thing was some really elaborate joke designed to teach me a lesson, but not even Jason's dad had the money to make a hoax as elaborate as that happen.

"Your Deltas," Mr. Smith announced to the gathering. I half expected cheers, but none came. Mostly, when I looked out over the crowd, I saw a mixture of disinterest, dread, and ... hostility.

Dalson took a step forward and clapped his hands together once. "Excellent. Now, Deltas, it's time to choose your teams. There are five Deltas, and you'll each pick five teammates. Standard rules apply at this camp. Deltas have discretion on whom to cut from the program." A visible wave of discomfort passed through the crowd, and Dalson paused as if to accent that piece of information. "But there will be no substitutions, and any major lapses in judgment will result in your immediate dismissal."

Alexander Bratersky and Chase Erickson didn't react to that warning, but the other two Deltas shifted their weight uneasily from one foot to the next. Whatever it was about this place, it seemed no one wanted to get kicked out.

Mr. Smith rolled his shoulder and drew in a deep breath. "Deltas, when your name is called, you will name your first teammate." His gaze passed over the line of Deltas like a burning fuse until it landed on me, and I felt like I was about to explode. "Matt Cambridge."

I felt sweat pop out on my forehead. I didn't want to go first. Why did I have to go first? I had no clue what I was doing. What was I building a team *for*? My mind suddenly flashed to the conversation I'd had with Rylee on the bus. She'd said she had the perfect team all picked out.

"Rylee." My voice came out rough, and I pointed at the girl for good measure.

Rylee made her way up on stage just as Mr. Smith called, "Alexander Bratersky."

"Derek Anderson," Alexander said without hesitation.

"You're a Delta?" Rylee whispered as she stepped beside me.

39

"Why didn't you tell me? Were you testing me? Why'd you pick me first?"

"Becca Plain," Mr. Smith called out.

"Kari Martins," the redheaded Delta said from farther down the line. I knew my turn was coming again. "Rylee, who should I pick next?"

"Huh? Why are you asking me?"

"Dexter Miller," Mr. Smith called.

"Ali Donaldson," Dexter said.

"C'mon," I urged. "You said you had a team all sorted. Now tell me who to pick."

"Chase Erickson."

Chase's voice boomed from the end of the line. "Bryce Foul."

This time Mr. Smith didn't say my name, but he looked down the line at me with an expression that clearly implied, "Make your next selection."

"Just give me a name, Rylee." The desperation in my voice must've registered because Rylee suddenly looked very worried.

"Just call Angie Salt," Rylee whispered.

"Angie Salt," I said.

A girl stepped out of the crowd as the other Deltas continued with their selections. She was a few pounds more than "curvy" and had a smile that looked practiced. Her hair was bleached blonde and stopped just above her shoulders.

"All right," I whispered. "Who do I call next?"

"Um ..." Rylee licked her lips and glanced over the crowd. "If you'd have told me I was going to be on your team, I would have had more time to come up with some names."

"You *said* you already had the perfect team sorted out," I reminded her. "Who's next?"

Rylee squared her shoulders and lifted her chin. "Pick Amara Ubeku."

Chase had just called out his next selection, and Mr. Smith's gaze turned back to me.

"Amara Ubeku," I said.

Amara was a tall, skinny guy who looked at least a year older than me. He had dark skin and a shaved head. He adjusted his thin-rimmed glasses as he stepped out of the crowd and stared at me just long enough to make me uncomfortable. He crossed the platform with long, wiry strides and took a post next to Angie. He looked intelligent and mean. Not mean in the *I'm going to mug you in a dark alley* sort of way. More of a *say or do something I don't like and I will make bad things happen to you* sort of way.

I turned to Rylee, and she whispered another name as my turn came again.

"Junosuke Tagai," I said, repeating her suggestion.

Junosuke was Asian and about the same height as me. He had thick dark hair and walked with a sort of swagger.

"It's Juno," he said as he joined the group. "Everyone just calls me Juno."

Rylee tilted her head toward me. "Pick Yaakov Katz next."

I repeated the name when my turn came again. Yaakov Katz turned out to be the kid who had been buried in his laptop on the bus. He was at least a full head shorter than me and had arms like coat hangers. Not exactly the kind of person you'd pick for a sports team, but I'd pretty much given up on that idea. I just hadn't firmed up my next theory yet.

When the final name had been called, Mr. Smith turned to the remaining kids. "Team and cabin assignments will be located on the bulletin board outside the first-aid station in the next few minutes. You have the rest of the morning to get squared away. Remember," he added, "that the quadrant you've been assigned is specific to a team. That team's Delta can use you as they see fit. Is that clear?"

The campers nodded without making a sound. It was eerie.

Dalson stepped forward and cast his gaze around the crowd and nodded approvingly. Then he turned to the Deltas. "I suggest you take the day, get your teams settled in your cabins. A hint for the competitions that'll start next week: strategy and finesse will get you more points than will muscle and fire."

I had no idea what he was talking about, but I tried to make my expression as icy as those around me so it would at least appear as though I knew what was going on.

"Why are you making that face?" Rylee asked. "You look constipated."

I groaned.

"Preliminary rankings will begin later today." Dalson's expression turned serious. "One last thing." He pointed at us Deltas and then gestured over all the other campers. "This is a camp for kids. Just a regular summer camp. At all times and in all places, you will adopt the persona of a regular camper. Only when you and your team are executing a plan during a competition will that change."

Weird to weirder. I needed to figure this place out. Now. What kind of camp has to tell their campers to act normal? A military camp? A drama camp? A camp for kids who were so maladjusted that they needed to be reminded that they're normal?

Dalson nodded to Mr. Smith, and the large man shouted, "Dismissed!"

The campers turned and headed off, presumably to wait for their cabin assignments. I, on the other hand, wasn't quite able to get my mind to communicate with my body well enough to move. Instead, I looked at my teammates' faces. Each of them gazed at me with expressions somewhere between confusion and concern.

"Well?" Angie asked. "What'll you have us do, Captain Cambridge?" She chuckled. "Captain Cambridge. That sounds like a cereal that should have colorful marshmallow boats in it or something."

I glanced at Rylee with a raised brow.

"She's not as crazy as she seems," Rylee said. "Well actually," she said, wincing just a bit, "she kind of is."

Angie seemed buoyed by the comment and lifted her chin.

I sighed. "Anyone know where our cabins are?"

CHAPTER 8

The Delta cabins were positioned on the outer edges of the camp's grounds. Rylee explained they were all spaced well enough apart to make cheating more of a challenge. The way she said it made me think that cheating wasn't against the rules and might even be encouraged.

Our cabin was blue with a red roof and at least twice the size of the other cabins we passed along the way. Inside was an open living area with wide-planked wooden floors and rough timber on the walls. The roof was supported by thick beams so dark they almost looked charred. Six narrow cots, like the kind you see in army movies, were positioned around the room. At the foot of each was a large plastic storage bin the color of dirt.

Six beds? "We're all together?" I asked.

"What do you mean?" Angie asked. She tucked a strand of hair behind her ear. "You don't want us in the same cabin as you?"

"Well ..." I gestured to her and Rylee. "You're girls."

Juno and Yaakov laughed.

"At least you're observant," Amara said. His voice was deep, and he spoke with an accent I'd never heard before. He took a breath and let it out with a sigh that made it clear he thought I had no business leading the five of them to a bathroom, let alone in the upcoming competitions. He walked across the room and put his bag on one of the beds against the far wall.

"And modest, too," Angie said with a grin. She threw her stuff on the bed closest to the door. "Don't worry, Captain, sharing a room with a girl isn't nearly as scary as you think."

"I was just ... I mean ..." My cheeks burned, and I decided to drop it.

Juno sat on the edge of the bed he'd claimed and looked at me like I was a Rubik's Cube he couldn't figure out.

There was one bed across the room positioned under a window. I claimed it and tossed my bag into the trunk. I decided to throw the phone Jason had given me in with my bag and reached into my pocket. What I pulled out was a phone with a crack right down the screen and half the keypad. I cursed. It must've happened when Chase and I had fought on the bus. There went my connection to the outside world, for the next three weeks anyway.

I cursed again and dropped the busted phone into the storage bin and then smacked the lid closed. When I looked up, Juno was staring at me. I glared back for a moment, hoping he'd look away, but he didn't. He just kept right on staring, tilting his head one way, then the other.

Lighten up, Cambridge, I told myself. *If you're going to make this camp work, you're going to need some friends.* I drew a deep breath and let it out slowly as I straightened.

I met Juno's gaze again, only this time I imagined I was looking at one of my friends from school. "Yes?" I asked finally.

"Why us?" Juno asked. "You're a Delta, and that's fine, you can pick who you want. But I don't recognize you, so I don't think we've ever been at the same camps before." He glanced around the room. "I know these guys. None of us have ever been picked for Delta teams before. Why'd you pick us?"

The others moved around the room sorting their belongings, but

45

they did so in such a silent way it was clear they were all listening, waiting for my answer. I shrugged and then gestured to Rylee, who was putting her clothes in the bin beside the bed she'd picked. "Rylee recommended you guys."

Rylee groaned from her cot across the room.

Amara turned to Rylee. "So you know this guy?"

"I don't *know* him," Rylee said. "He was just on my bus."

"She was running her mouth," Yaakov said. "Talking about how if she were a Delta she'd know who to pick to win the whole thing."

Amara turned back to me. "And you believed her? You believed some girl you'd only just met on a bus? She's never been on a Delta team before, you know."

"Neither have I," I said.

"What?" everyone in the room said in rapid succession.

"This is your first command?" Juno asked.

"You gotta be kidding me," Yaakov said.

Command? So this *was* some kind of military camp. That, or these guys took camp activities way too seriously.

Juno looked around the room. "Someone please tell me this is a joke. Tell me we're not all on a Delta team commanded by a greenie." When I didn't say anything, he locked his fingers behind his head and looked up at the ceiling. "Oh, come *on!*"

Angie laughed. "Well, I'm thrilled. I've always wanted to be on a Delta team. But it is weird that you trusted Rylee. She's cute, sure, but not cute enough to risk getting booted out of the program."

Rylee rolled her eyes but didn't respond.

Angie leaned forward and placed her elbows on her knees. "What's really going on here, Captain Cambridge?" She narrowed her eyes and tapped her glossy lips. "Who are you, really?"

I glanced over at Rylee. She was nervously chewing her lip but looked at me with the same perplexed expression as everyone else— well, almost everyone else. Yaakov had turned his full attention to his laptop and was tapping away at his keyboard.

I didn't know enough about this place to fake it. They were my teammates, and it seemed they all really wanted to be on a Delta team, so maybe they'd be okay with the truth. Not the full truth, obviously. I couldn't tell them my dad had got me into this place somehow, or that he'd clearly done a lot more than that to make Smith and Dalson think I was Delta material.

Just the basics, I decided. "Look. This camp is a punishment for me. My dad signed me up thinking it would straighten me out or something. I don't want to be your Delta. I don't want to be here. But I am, and we are in this together, so let's just get through it."

No one reacted for several seconds. Then Angie said, "Punishment for what?"

I shook my head. "It's stupid."

She widened her eyes and gave me an expression that said, *Spill already.*

I sighed. "I pulled a stupid stunt the last week of school that damaged the gym and, according to some people, nearly killed everyone inside."

Rylee, Yaakov, and Juno shot each other worried glances. Amara and Angie pursed their lips and nodded almost approvingly, though I couldn't tell what exactly they approved of—my being punished for endangering a bunch of kids or my apparent attempt at mass murder.

Rylee huffed and then turned to Yaakov and cleared her throat.

Yaakov snapped out of his trance, glanced down at his computer and then back to Rylee, and shook his head.

Amara caught their exchange. "You know something." He pointed at Yaakov. "You figured something out on your little computer, didn't you?"

Yaakov shrugged.

"C'mon, you little nerd," Juno said. "Tell us already."

Yaakov gave me a nervous look and then glanced back to Rylee. Then he shook his head.

"He's scared," Angie said.

"I'm not *scared*," Yaakov said. He lowered his voice. "I'm cautious."

Angie looked back at me, one brow raised. "He's scared."

"Of what?" I asked. "Me?" I laughed. "I didn't *actually* kill anyone." I cast my gaze around the room. "No one died, not even the kids with breathing problems." I lowered my voice and mumbled, "The ones who got trampled in the stampede turned out okay." I shook my head. "I wasn't actually *trying* to kill anyone."

"You heard Dalson," Angie said. "Deltas can kick teammates out of the program at any time, for any reason. Yaakov, the techno-nerd over there, must know something about you, something he thinks you don't want other people to know. He thinks sharing it with the group will land him out on his butt."

I looked at Yaakov. The way his face was buried in his laptop all the time, it wasn't hard to sort out he was probably some kind of hacker, but what could he possibly have looked up about me? My grades? I shook my head. I didn't care if they knew I was garbage at math. Maybe that I'd gotten suspended for stealing some beakers from the science lab last year?

I looked at Yaakov. "What do you think you know?"

He shifted his glasses but said nothing.

"I'm not going to kick anyone off the team."

"Or out of the program?" Angie asked.

"Or out of the program," I added, not really knowing what that meant anyway. Yaakov hesitated, chewed his lip for a moment, and then said, "It's just ... I've been trying to hack into the camp's surveillance so we can get a look at our competition, and sometimes hacking means getting access to one system at a time—"

"Oh, get on with it already," Angie said. "Nobody cares how you figured it out. Just tell us something juicy about our little captain here."

Yaakov blew out a breath. "His scores." He looked at me. "I accessed records and, um, stumbled upon your scores, for past missions.... They're, well, they're really good. Not the best in the whole camp, but really good. I mean, they're better than Chase's, and his are *really* good too."

"What?" I heard myself say it along with everyone else in the room. Their heads snapped around to stare at me in the same instant.

"Let me see that," Rylee said.

She was joined at Yaakov's bedside by the rest of the team, who murmured until I elbowed my way in and looked at the screen. It was a scan of what looked like a sign-up roster for the camp. My name was there. I even recognized my dad's handwriting. But the numbers that filled the boxes beside my name were lower than almost all the numbers beside other names. When I looked up, my team was staring back at me. Rylee, more than the others, looked particularly dumbfounded. Her mouth gaped, and she kept glancing at Yaakov's computer and then at me and then back to the computer. The others looked puzzled too ... well, everyone except Angie. Angie had a huge grin and looked at me as if I was some big piece of chocolate.

"I have no idea what those numbers mean," I said, "but look at them. My scores, if that's what those are, are worse than almost everyone's, not higher."

"Um, yeah," Angie said. "Those numbers are errors. Higher numbers mean more errors. You hardly have any. You messed up less than everyone else." She leaned over and examined the screen. "This isn't your first camp, Matt Cambridge. In fact, I bet this isn't even your first command."

Rylee started in on me next, grumbling about how I'd lied to her and how it didn't make any sense. However, I wasn't really listening. I just kept shaking my head. Low numbers were good? It was suddenly very obvious what had happened. When my dad put my name on the roster, he must've seen the other kids' scores and thought he'd help me fly under the radar by giving me scores that would be below average.

"Blend in, Matt," Dad had said when he dropped me off. *Yeah, thanks, Dad. Not enough that you put me in this situation to begin with, but now you've made it so I'm expected to be an overachiever. Great, just great.*

I turned back to my team. In the time it had taken for me to consider my dad's lies, they'd gone back to unpacking. They kept glancing at me, as if each of them had a question they wanted to ask, but no one spoke.

I opened my mouth to say something, yet words didn't come. What could I say? That my dad had manipulated some records to get me into this camp and screwed up? I'd already told the truth that this was my first camp and it was part of my punishment to be here, so they must've thought I'd lied about at least one thing already. Besides, I didn't know these guys. Even if I trusted them, and even if I managed to convince them of the truth, I still had to consider the possibility they'd tell someone in the camp. Then maybe that person would tell someone else, and before long it would get back to whoever was in charge—probably Dalson—and I'd be kicked out. I wasn't sure what would happen to my dad if I got booted from camp—until that moment I wasn't entirely sure I'd cared—but I guess I didn't actually want him getting fired or anything.

Pull yourself together, Matt.

Expectations are high, but who cares? It's a camp. A weird camp, with strange rules and bizarre campers, but it's just a camp. I probably was better than most of these freaks anyway. If I had gone to a bunch of camps, I probably would've gotten better scores. Besides, it was this or Alaska. I took a deep breath and blew it out in a single breath.

It was just a camp. I could do this.

CHAPTER 9

We spent the next hour or so unpacking.

Angie, who had seemed like such a laid-back and free-spirited girl, became almost compulsive with the way she transferred her belongings into the plastic chest. She even had cardboard dividers so she could keep things organized. In contrast, Juno just unzipped his bag and shook the contents into the bin, and Yaakov, well, he didn't unpack anything. He just put his whole bag into the plastic bin. I think he might have been copying me. Poor kid, no one at this camp should use me as a role model.

There was a sharp rap at the door.

"Sir?" a girl's voice called.

Everyone in the room looked at me. I guessed I was the *sir*.

I cleared my throat. "Um, come in."

The door swung open, and a girl a year or two younger than me and about as thin as a javelin stood in the opening. Her bony arms were pressed firmly to her sides, and a serious expression was etched into her face. She had brown hair pulled back in a ponytail and a red T-shirt with a graphic picture of a bear on the chest and the words CAMP FRIENDSHIP written below it. *Please tell me those aren't our team uniforms*, I thought.

"Captain," she said, her words coming out in a quick burst, "I'm to tell you that the preliminary rankings challenge will begin in ten minutes at the soccer pitch." She glanced around the room. "It's a Delta event."

Preliminary rankings? Delta event? I was pretty sure "soccer pitch" was another way of saying "soccer field," otherwise I wouldn't have understood much of what the girl said.

"Fine," I said.

"Ten minutes," the girl said again.

"I heard you," I snapped.

She recoiled a step and then swallowed and forced herself straight again.

I sighed. "Sorry. Thank you for delivering the message. I'll be there."

She nodded, then turned on her heel and jogged away.

I turned back to my team and found them all staring at me.

"*Sorry?*" Amara asked.

"What?" I said.

"Deltas don't apologize if they accidentally stab you in the throat," Juno said. He pointed out the door. "And you apologize for raising your voice?"

"You're not like other Deltas, are you, Cambridge?" Angie asked.

I shrugged and then pointed at the door. "You guys coming?"

"Didn't you hear the runner?" Rylee asked. "It's a Delta event."

I felt my forehead crease and my eyebrows draw together. "Then ..."

Angie stood up from her bed and strolled across the space between us. "You're on your own, *mein Spielführer.*" I had no idea what *Spielführer* was, but she patted me on the back, so I decided to believe it was a good thing. "Make us proud."

I made a mental note to take Rylee aside and ask her why these guys were so special. They seemed like a bunch of misfits to me.

"Remember," Amara called behind me as I stepped out of the cabin, "don't get killed. You die, and we all get kicked out of the program."

I waved away his sarcasm and didn't look back.

In retrospect, I probably should have realized that Amara wasn't the joking type and doing my best not to get killed was probably sound advice.

CHAPTER 10

Dalson stood on the sidelines and lifted his chin at me as I approached the field.

"Ah, Mr. Cambridge, we've been expecting you."

A shorter man with gray hair and a tall, slender woman with brown curls stood together just a few yards to the right of Dalson. Three other adults were positioned around the field's perimeter. They all looked like angry linesmen, only, rather than flags, they carried clipboards, and each stood, pen in hand, ready to take notes. Presumably the notes would be on whatever I was about to do.

"Cambridge," a deep unmistakable voice said from behind me. I spun to see Mr. Smith towering over me and jumped back in alarm. Someone that big should not be able to sneak up on anything. He didn't smile, but his eyes glinted with pride. I imagined he was pleased that his presence elicited such a response.

I looked between Mr. Smith and Mr. Dalson. "Um," I began, "I was told I had some kind of Delta challenge?"

"That's right," Dalson said breezily. He turned and looked out at the soccer field and brought his hands to his hips. He reminded me of a sailor standing on the bow of a ship, looking out over the ocean.

"Do you see that ball?" he asked.

The field was completely deserted except for an official-looking soccer ball positioned about ten or fifteen yards from the goal. It was difficult to miss.

"Uh, yeah," I said, "I see it."

"Your test is quite simple. Put the ball into the net."

I laughed and then stopped myself abruptly when I realized that neither Dalson nor Mr. Smith was smiling. "That ball?" I pointed at the only item on the field and felt dumb for doing so, but I thought there must be a trick.

"That's the one," Dalson said.

I didn't know what to say. All the kids seemed at least reasonably healthy. Some looked like straight-up jocks. If it weren't for that, I'd have thought maybe this was a camp for children with disabilities that made simple tasks, like kicking a ball, a challenge. But no one in my cabin seemed especially challenged in that department. This test had to be more than just kicking a ball into an empty net.

Mr. Smith spoke next. "You'll be scored by how well you accomplish the task. Do you understand?"

I nodded. Though I didn't understand at all.

"Do you have any objections?"

I shook my head.

Mr. Smith raised his hand over his head. There was a whoosh as green tarps were raised in overlapping segments around the field. Suddenly everything and everyone outside the tarps were cut off.

"Listen carefully," Dalson said, "because you'll get this clue only once." He paused for a beat. "This challenge can set the tone of the whole session. You may use anything in the confines of the wall to accomplish your task. You'll be judged on a number of things, but in the end, speed counts above all else."

He raised a single eyebrow, and I got the impression he was giving me a chance to speak. I stared back. I couldn't think of anything to say that wouldn't make me look like I was completely clueless.

"Very well," he continued. "Your time begins as soon as you take a step."

Speed counts above all else.

I considered the possibility that that's all this really was, just some test to see how fast I was. I wasn't really worried. I once put a cherry bomb in one of the jack-o'-lanterns at a Halloween display in the mall and had to run away from three surprisingly fit security guards, so I knew how to move.

But then maybe it was something else. The time would start when I took my first step, so I tried to take in the entire scene. I studied the observers around the field and peered at the ball and then the net, looking for some sign this wasn't entirely straightforward. With the exception of the fabric walls around the field, nothing looked ... weird.

I blew out a breath and told myself not to overthink it. It *was* a test of speed, and the winner probably got a new set of cleats or a pair of gloves for the team goalie. I gave a quick nod and then sprinted forward. I made it ten or so feet before something clicked under my foot. I figured I'd stepped on a sprinkler head and didn't look back, at least I didn't until I heard something burst behind me and felt something splatter against my back. I whipped around.

A device about the size of a hockey puck sat on the grass, and a cone of red paint marked the grass behind me. I wiped at the wetness on my back and my hand came back covered in the same red paint sprayed on the grass.

"What the ..." I stepped back. Another click from under my foot, and I instinctively stepped away. I watched as another hockey puck–like object popped out of the grass. When it was about chest high, a blast of yellow paint burst out and covered me from chest to thigh.

I glanced over my shoulder at the sidelines. Mr. Smith and Mr. Dalson watched me curiously while the people with clipboards jotted notes at a blurry pace.

"Paint land mines?" I stood there for another second and added, "Cool."

Energy surged in my chest. The point was obviously to kick the ball into the net while getting splattered with the fewest colors. I narrowed my gaze at the soccer ball down the field and took off at a mad sprint. Each time I felt a click under my foot, I'd dart to the right or to the left, and I managed to avoid the other bursts entirely. The little paint poppers were everywhere.

I reached the ball running full speed and kicked it as hard as I could toward the net. As it left its place on the ground, three mines popped off the ground. I didn't have a lot of time to think. Less than a second, I imagined. But I figured each mine was aimed a different direction so there was only one way to avoid the blast. I dropped and flattened myself to the ground.

Boom! Boom! Boom!

The explosions happened in quick succession and echoed in my ears. Heat, like a giant beast made of flames, lashed out with blazing limbs and scorched the back of my neck, arms, and legs. Flooded with disorientation, I rolled onto my back and blinked at the cloud of black smoke hovering just above my body. A gust of wind spun the smoke into evil shapes before pulling it apart and clearing the air.

I pushed myself up onto my elbows and coughed. Bits of twisted metal and singed grass surrounded me.

"It blew up?" I muttered. I coughed again. That wasn't a paint bomb. The weight of what had just happened hit me all at once. In a frantic rush, I ran my hands over my body checking for injuries, and glanced at my arms and hands, expecting to see them caked with blood. They weren't. With the exception of the ringing inside my head and some burned hair, I wasn't injured. I collapsed back onto the grass and heaved one breath after the next, trying to will my heart to stop hammering out of control. I didn't succeed.

Dalson suddenly stood over me, blocking out the sun. He looked like a shadowy superhero with his hands fisted at his hips and the sun forming a halo around his head. He leaned over, grabbed me by my arm, and heaved me to my feet.

I gestured at the bits of debris and choked on my words.

"Don't worry," he said, "all the rest are deactivated. You can step freely now." He didn't sound upset, but then his voice was tinny and weak through the ringing in my ears.

I took a step back, but when I moved, it seemed the ground moved too, and I staggered a couple paces to my right. I managed to stay on my feet, barely, and to will the earth to stop spinning. Dalson clamped a firm hand on my shoulder and steadied me.

I drew a couple deep breaths, and the ringing lessened to a dull buzz. I scanned the field. A woman, one of the linesmen I'd seen before, sprayed the path I'd made across the field with something that was turning the paint-splattered grass green again. The other linesmen compared notes, and Smith crouched on the field where I'd started. He had what looked like a fisherman's tackle box beside him and held up one of the land mines, no doubt trying to sort out if any of the other ones were as defective as the last ones I'd triggered. He snatched another hockey-puck mine out of the tackle box and carefully placed it in the grass.

"He's resetting them." I meant it as a question, but it came out like a statement and sort of sounded like I was tattling on the beefy counselor.

Mr. Dalson's grip on my shoulder tightened. I glanced up. He eyed me carefully, but not the way you'd expect if he were trying to see if I needed medical attention. Instead, he stared at me like a damaged toy, deciding whether he should fix me.

I just stood there dumbly as another series of questions jolted through me. Why wasn't anyone panicking? Why weren't they yelling? A mine had just exploded and very nearly cut me in half. Why wasn't the camp medic rushing across the field? Why were the fabric walls still up?

Dalson gave me a gentle shove and guided me back across the field. "I shouldn't say this," he said in a low voice, "but well done."

"W-what?" I rubbed my ears. No way had I heard him correctly. "Well done?"

He grinned when we got to the sidelines. "The ringing won't last long. You're free to go get cleaned up. There won't be any more challenges for you today."

I didn't respond. I couldn't. My mouth gaped like the fish I was. I now understood why they used that name for newbies. Newbies stood around with their mouths hanging open like mine.

He looked around and then brought his head close to mine. "Between you and me, Cambridge, how'd you know the mines around the ball were real? What gave it away?"

I blinked trying to understand the question.

"You couldn't have known just by looking at them." He nudged my shoulder. "C'mon, how'd you know?"

I didn't answer. I couldn't. I felt like the explosion had knocked me into some alternate reality. One where a kid almost getting blown to bits was grounds for congratulations and where camp leaders seemed surprised when their campers survived challenges. The fact that my hands shook as though I'd just downed a gallon of Red Bull didn't help matters.

Dalson nodded even though I hadn't spoken, and then tapped his ear. He locked eyes with me and spoke, mouthing each word carefully. "Well done." He raised his hand and brought it down in a quick movement. The fabric wall around the field dropped in a blink, and a dozen or so campers who had been near the barrier scattered back to their cabins like startled cockroaches.

I glanced at the field. It was as though I'd never set foot on the turf. There were no signs of paint explosions or burned grass. There were no bits and pieces of debris, at least none that I could see. The only thing on the field was an official-looking soccer ball, on the exact spot it had been when I had arrived.

What was going on here?

CHAPTER 11

My senses trickled back as I trudged toward the cabin.

At home, Jason and I used to watch all kinds of reality shows about SWAT teams and prison guards. I remembered a few episodes where they used things called flashbangs and stun grenades to take care of criminals. Flashbangs are essentially really loud bangs accompanied by bright flashes of light. The idea is to disorient without hurting anyone. Jason and I had wanted to get a couple to set off in school during study hall, but they're surprisingly hard to come by. Even for a kid with as much money as Jason.

I wondered if the mines under the soccer ball had been flashbangs. In the TV shows I'd watched, I was pretty sure they'd called them harmless. My hand went to my head, and the singed ends of my hair crunched. I'd been torched. There was nothing harmless about getting torched.

Still, the reaction from Dalson and the linesmen had made it clear they'd intended those mines to go off that way, which meant they were okay with the possibility I wouldn't have ducked and so ... what? They had waited until I was clear before setting them off? Otherwise, they were okay with the possibility that I'd be killed or, at the very least, maimed.

I cursed my dad for sneaking my name onto a camp roster without checking it out first. What kind of parent does that? I thought about it for a second and then considered the possibility that he *had* looked into it and had decided to send me anyway. That thought morphed out of control, and by the time I was halfway back to the Delta cabin, I had concocted a massive conspiracy where Dad had taken out a major life insurance policy on me and was looking to rid himself of his troubled kid once and for all. Not sure Mom would be happy with that, but then again, she *had* been wanting to remodel the kitchen.

"Focus, Matt," I told myself. Obviously, this camp wasn't what it seemed; I'd had that much sorted out before the first challenge. Now, though, I was starting to realize just how different it really was. I clenched my fists and reminded myself that if things got any worse, I'd just bolt. I'd find a way to call Jason, he'd help me get back home, and if it cost my dad his job, so be it.

But there was something else. Something tickled the back of my mind, and it was a feeling I knew I wouldn't be able to ignore—curiosity. This camp was different—crazy different. And that made me want, no, *need* to figure it out more. They had competitions where kids could get blown up. I wasn't even beginning to make sense of everything, but I had to try. There was something more to this place. I just had to stay alive until I figured out what it was.

It was like when Jason and I were little and some older kids told us about the bogeyman who lived in closets. Jason believed them and decided night-lights were the answer, but even though I mostly believed them, too, I wasn't satisfied with night-lights. If there was some crazy monster in my closet, I had to know for sure. Jason took some convincing, but eventually he was on board, and together we spent the next few weekends having sleepovers where we'd try to bait that sucker out of our closets with food, shiny things, or money. Twice Jason and I even used each other as bait while the other waited with an aluminum baseball bat. It scared us half to death, but I just had to know.

Yaakov gave a frightened yelp when I pushed open the cabin door. The others, who were hunched over his bed, turned sharply in my direction and jumped to their feet, forming a human wall in front of the bed.

An awkward second passed, and then Rylee said, "Matt?"

"Captain?" Angie asked. "Is that you?" One of her thin eyebrows rose, and she laughed. "Look at you. Was the challenge some kind of art project? You're filthy."

The others didn't smile.

"What happened?" Rylee asked.

"It didn't go well," I grumbled.

"Clearly," Juno said. "Just tell us we're not starting out with the lowest ranking."

"How would he know how everyone else ranked?" Rylee snapped. "It was a *preliminary* challenge." She turned to Yaakov; his gaze was fixated on his computer screen. "Yaakov?"

"I'm already on it," he said.

"What happened?" Rylee asked again. This time her voice was much less agitated.

"I just want to take a shower." I plodded my way to my storage bin and pulled a set of clean clothes from my bag.

When I turned around, Amara was blocking my path. I tried to move around him, but he grabbed my shoulder and held me in place. His eyes narrowed as he scanned me up and down, all the while muttering in a language I couldn't understand and was pretty sure I'd never heard before.

"Land mines," he said finally. "Right? Poppers, probably. Modified to disperse paint, obviously."

"That's ... that's right," I said. "Probably. Except—"

"Except for a couple of them," Amara cut in. "Your hair looks singed."

He ran a thumb over my eyebrow, and I smacked it away. Then he touched my hair, and I smacked his hand away again.

"A couple of them were only directionally modified," he said.

"Not a couple," I snapped. "Three. And I don't know what they were, but if I hadn't been on the ground when they exploded I could've been ... really hurt." I hesitated to say "killed" because I didn't want to seem dramatic, yet that's what I was thinking.

"Hurt?" Yaakov asked without looking up. "Don't you mean killed?"

"Not likely," Angie said. "Probably just maimed."

"Oh, that's loads better," I said fiercely.

"How big were they?" Amara asked.

I couldn't tell if they were just giving me a hard time or if they were serious. I also wasn't sure which would be worse, their trying to scare me, or being unaffected that I'd nearly died.

Juno sidled up beside Amara. "I'm with Angie; he'd have been maimed. Now, seriously, how big were the mines?"

I groaned. "The size of a hockey puck, I guess."

"Hockey puck?" Amara asked. He made a circle with his hands as if I had no idea how big a hockey puck was.

I nodded, and Juno whistled.

"I've seen those in other camps," Juno said. "They're pretty messy if they hit you right." He grimaced, and I had a sick feeling he wasn't talking about paint when he said *messy*.

"Argh," Yaakov growled at the computer. "You think you're so smart I can't get around that?" He hunched over his computer, and his fingers became a blur on the keyboard.

While he had the attention of the rest of the team, I slipped around Amara and Juno and crept for the door.

"Hurry up, Yaakov," Juno said. "I know hackers who'd already be in and out without leaving a footprint."

Yaakov gave an annoyed sigh. "No, you don't. You have no idea the system they have in place. We're talking quadruple redundancies, state-of-the-art anti-hacking programs, and tracker bots that could find an infiltration in a trillionth of a second. I've already set up a—" He glanced up at what I'm sure were blank expressions from the rest of the team and shook his head. "You know what? If anyone else were doing this, they'd have already been discovered and would probably be dead."

I cringed at the second mention of death and slipped through the door. The sound of the bickering vanished when I was a dozen feet away from the cabin. I made it twice that distance before Rylee called my name and jogged up from behind me.

"Sorry about that," she said. "I know it's rough when a challenge doesn't go as well as you'd hoped."

"What would you know about it, Rylee?" I snapped without slowing down. "When were you ever on a Delta team? Huh? Try never." I wasn't sure if I was angrier that I'd almost been killed, or that I'd likely made a fool out of myself for not knowing there was more to the challenge than just kicking a ball.

Rylee kept pace with me and didn't seem taken aback in the least by my anger. "Don't worry about it, Matt. If we start out in last place, who cares? We'll make up for it. I'm telling you, we have a good team."

I stopped abruptly and pointed toward the cabin. "*That's* a good team? Them? In what universe are they good? This is the first time any of them have been on a Delta team. If they were so great, why haven't they been picked before?"

Rylee eyed me carefully. "You said you've never been to one of these camps before, but your scores say you're a liar." I opened my mouth to speak, but she continued before I got a word out. "Your body language says you're not a liar, and your questions make me think you're really sincere in your ignorance." She waved her hand. "You're an enigma, Matt Cambridge. But that's an asset here, so let me put your mind at ease about your team." Rylee held up one finger. "Juno is a fighter. A really great fighter. There's no one in camp who will be able to beat him. I promise. He's been training since he was crawling." She lifted another finger. "Amara is an explosives genius. He can make them, and he can disarm them. Trust me, he'll be useful." A third finger went up. "Yaakov doesn't look it, but he's the best hacker in the camp. Better than any of the instructors, I bet. If we need to hack into something, he's the one to do it." She put her hand against her chest. "I am really good at reading people. My friends back home call me Six because they think I have a sixth sense."

I rolled my eyes. "A sixth sense? Give me a break." I gestured back to the cabin. "And don't get me started on those weirdos. They seem like a bunch of punks."

Rylee shrugged. "They are. But they'll be good in competitions when the time comes. You can trust them."

"What about Angie?"

Rylee's face scrunched up. "Angie's a bit ... different."

"Meaning?"

"She's a sociopath." She frowned. "Or maybe a psychopath, depending on who you ask."

"I'm asking you."

Rylee waved her hand. "Do I look like a psychologist? Just know that when the time comes, she's the person you want on your team because she'll do ... anything. She doesn't really have a ... well, a conscience."

I shook my head. I wasn't in the mood to be teased, or played, or whatever it was that Rylee was doing to me. I might not have known a lot about the camp, but I knew Angie was no psychopath. She couldn't be, because kids can't be psychopaths. My chest hurt when I breathed, and I could feel the paint drying on my arms and face. "I need a shower."

I headed for the bathrooms, and Rylee called out behind me. "Just don't get bummed out about the preliminary rankings. They don't usually count for much anyway."

Anger flashed inside me. I'd nearly been blown up, and Rylee thought I was *bummed out*? I turned around to really give her a piece of my mind, but she was already jogging back to the cabin. I considered hollering after her, but what was the point? I stormed into the showers and slammed the door behind me.

My face, neck, and forearms were burned pink; scrubbing them wasn't an option. I put my head against the wall of the shower and let the water clean the dirt and paint off my skin and soothe the nicks and scratches that must've been caused by shrapnel.

Shrapnel. The word made my entire body tense.

I told myself over and over that the land mine couldn't have been lethal. But there was a rolling in the pit of my stomach that wouldn't go away. This camp had to be military. No one else would use explosives. There weren't uniforms, though; no saluting, no people with ranks. I didn't know a lot about army camps for kids, but I was pretty sure they didn't look like Camp Friendship. Where were the marching drills and push-ups and KP duty I'd heard about? Camp Friendship didn't seem to have any of that.

Plus, why had Dalson told everyone to treat this place like a regular camp? I couldn't think of a single explanation for why anyone would say that. Under what circumstances would a camp want to look like a regular camp, but not *be* a regular camp?

For a half second, I thought about calling Dad to see if he'd consider bringing me home. But no—he'd be disappointed in me, and I'd probably end up in Alaska. A three-week camp experience was a lot better than a year in Alaska, no matter what happened. Plus, the longer I stood under the shower, the more my curiosity bloomed. Questions piled on top of questions. I cursed myself again for the broken cell phone. If I could call Jason, he would help me figure things out.

It was only Day One, and already I'd been beaten up and nearly blown sky-high.

By the time I'd toweled off and put on clean clothes, I had made two resolutions. First, to do whatever it took to get to the bottom of this place, and second, to devise a plan of escape—a backup plan—just in case this turned out to be a camp of near-death experiences.

CHAPTER 12

I'd barely taken half a dozen steps out of the shower building when I heard, "Captain Cambridge, sir."

I turned. A round-faced boy with short blond hair, who was at least six inches shorter than me, stared back. I guessed he was about ten or eleven years old. A boy and a girl, about the same ages, stood a step behind him and had similarly blank expressions.

"It's, um, Matt," I said. "You can call me Matt."

The boy shrugged. "Of course, Captain. I mean Matt." He gestured to the camp. "I keep forgetting we're supposed to be getting into the habit of being regular campers. I'll call you Matt from now on."

I gave him a look that I hoped said, *What do you want?*

"Sorry," he continued. "My name's Rob Tendres." He gestured behind him to his friends. "This is Alexis Greenwood and Duncan Brooks."

The girl had short, inky-black hair and seashell-white skin. The boy beside her had a shaved head and coffee-colored skin. He also had a scar at least an inch long that ran just beneath his left eye. Neither of them spoke.

"We're on Team Grizzly," Rob added. He touched the figure of a bear on his T-shirt as if it were a piece of identification. I must've looked confused, because he added, "Your team, sir, I mean, Matt."

"Right," I said with a sigh. "I know what team I'm on. It's wonderful to meet you. But I was nearly blown up a few minutes ago, so if you'll excuse me ..." I turned and started to walk away.

"Wait, sir, I mean, Matt." He caught up to me and kept pace. "Could we talk to you for a second?"

I stopped and looked up at the sky. This kid didn't seem the type to give up. "Fine." I turned. The trio stood shoulder to shoulder with stiff soldier-like postures. It made my skin crawl to see a bunch of preteens acting with such discipline.

Rob glanced at his two friends, and they gave almost indistinguishable nods. Then he turned back to me and blurted out, "We'd like to be involved in the challenges."

I thought about almost getting blown up on the soccer field and forced a laugh. "No offense, kid, but you don't know what you're asking."

"I know we're young," he added quickly, "but we're a lot more experienced than some of the fifteen- or sixteen-year-olds. We've been to a lot of these camps, sir; a lot. We could be really useful. More useful than people give us credit for."

"I'll keep it in mind, kid," I said.

Rob sighed and turned to his friends.

"Sir," Alexis said, "we just want to be utilized. We've been coming to these camps for years, participating in the same training exercises year after year, but we know we won't be taken seriously until we participate as members of a Delta team."

"Years?" I asked. "You're not even teenagers, and you've been coming here for years?"

The three of them looked at me as if I'd just said a made-up word.

"Not *here*," Alexis said hesitantly. "Camps *like* this one."

Rob nodded toward a group of cabins to his right. "This is the first year for Camp Friendship, sir."

This was my chance. I had to be smart about it, but if I could get these kids to tell me more about this camp or others like it, I'd be able to figure out what I was involved in better.

I drew in a breath and straightened, doing my best to look captain-like. "All right, tell me what training exercises you've done."

Duncan cleared his throat. "We've been mostly limited to the standard ones," he said. "But we've excelled in those."

I lifted my chin. "And the standard ones would be ..."

Duncan looked at me like he wasn't sure I was serious. Then he shrugged and said, "Tactical firearms, principles of dynamic entry, barricade situations, and defensive tactics. Plus, we've had our share of the standard surveillance and counter-surveillance. You know, just the standard stuff."

I wasn't even sure I knew the words he was saying, let alone what he meant by them. I was once again reminded of the SWAT shows I watched back home on TV and thought for sure some of those terms he'd used were ones I'd heard on those shows.

"It's just," Rob continued, "you can't learn, or *do* the cool stuff, unless you're on a Delta team. No one considers you until you're older."

I considered my team and wondered if that was why none of them had been on Delta teams before. Because they were still pretty young.

"Of course not," I said, trying my best to sound like I knew what I was talking about. A dozen questions sprang to mind, but I forced them back. I needed to sound like a leader. I didn't need any rumors about how clueless I was getting back to Dalson or Smith. I decided I could ask them one more thing. "And if I were to ask you who runs this camp, what would you say?"

"Well," Rob began, "obviously the agency runs—"

Alexis lunged out and punched Rob before he could finish his sentence. He spun around glaring and then seemed to realize he'd said something wrong.

"Idiot," Alexis muttered. "He was testing you. We're supposed to be *regular* campers. What would regular campers say?"

Rob turned back to me and sighed. "I'm sorry, sir. I wasn't sure what you were asking." He cleared his throat. "Camp Friendship is run by a group dedicated to cultural awareness and friendship."

The Agency? Which agency was he talking about? The teach-kids-to-avoid-land-mines agency? Or was this some kind of camp run by social services? At least that might explain why all the kids looked so mean, but it wouldn't explain why the adults tried to blow them up on soccer fields.

I was just about to ask Rob more about the agency when Alexander Bratersky came into view down the path. He had a towel over his shoulder and a few clothes in his hand. I smiled, thinking at least I wasn't the only one who needed a shower after the soccer ball challenge. But any notion of a smile wilted when I caught a glimpse of the Arctic Fox Delta. He had paint on only one part of his body: his face. It was the color of blood and splattered in such a way it actually looked like war paint; he looked absolutely murderous.

I knew better, of course. He'd obviously been blasted by one of the mines.

He gave me a careful up and down look as he neared, as if he were assessing my level of risk to him. On a scale of one to ten, if I were being really generous about myself, I'd be a risk factor two. And that would only be the case if I landed a couple lucky punches.

Bratersky grunted something as he shoved past and disappeared through the shower doors. I wondered what position he'd been in to get splattered across the face like that, but maybe more importantly, how he had managed the challenge with only one hit.

"Captain," Rob said, pulling me back into the conversation, "all we're asking is that you use us. And then tell people you used us."

They must've seen my confusion because Alexis added, "If you win, and people know we helped you, next year we'll be picked for full Delta team members."

"Or at least we'll have a better chance," Rob added.

Nothing at this place made any sense, and all I wanted to do was call Jason and pick his brain. He'd be able to help me figure it out. A couple hours on his computer and he'd probably know everything there was to know about this place. I cursed Chase for the fight on the bus. Because of him, my cell phone was useless.

"A cell phone," I said suddenly.

Rob nodded. "They're supposed to be turned in to the directors before camp. It's not easy to find one here."

"But not impossible," Alexis added.

"So you can get one?" I asked.

Rob nodded. "Some campers keep 'em despite the rules. We could find out who has one and get it for you."

I nodded. "Great. Do that. Consider it a test."

"Any team in particular you want it from?" Alexis asked.

I smiled. "Yeah, Squirrel."

Rob smiled. "I thought you'd say that."

Clearly word had spread of my fight with Chase on the bus. I decided not to care.

"We do this," Alexis said, "and you'll use us for real missions? And you'll tell people that you used us?" Her eyes narrowed, and she took a step closer. I drew back. For a little girl, she was sure aggressive.

"Get me a phone," I said forcefully, "and I'll think about it."

I turned again and started off toward the cabin. I expected more badgering, maybe one of them jumping on my ankle and throwing a fit, like any number of kids I'd seen who didn't get their way, but after a dozen steps in silence, I glanced over my shoulder to see them heading in the opposite direction.

They looked younger from this far, and guilt twisted my gut for taking advantage of such little kids. I really shouldn't have asked them to steal. I decided to cancel that order the next time I saw them.

There was something else that bothered me. They hadn't been fazed by my request. It was like stealing from someone on another team was entirely expected. Rylee had said cheating was difficult, not that it wasn't allowed; maybe the same went for stealing. I made a mental note not to leave anything valuable in my cabin.

CHAPTER 13

My team was once again huddled on Yaakov's bed when I walked into the cabin. Their heads snapped up just like they did before. I wasn't covered in paint this time, but still they eyed me like I had a riddle written on my forehead. Then, one by one, starting with Angie, they smiled. Amara didn't smile, but he looked undeniably happy.

I glanced in the mirror by the door, thinking a few rogue splatters of paint must've survived my shower. My face was clean. I turned back to the group and started toward my bed. "What's wrong with you guys?"

"We're impressed," Juno said. "Very impressed."

"You did good," Rylee added.

I dumped my towel and toiletries on my bed. "Impressed with what? That I managed to get all the paint off me? Gee, thanks."

Angie smirked. "Humble, too. Not a quality I've ever seen in a Delta." She gave an approving nod. "I have to admit, Captain, I thought we'd pulled the short straw getting you as our team leader. Don't get me wrong, I was going to make the most of it, but even though you had some pretty good scores from previous camps, you just gave off an aura of ..." She tapped her chin. "What's the best term to use?"

"Inexperience?" Amara asked.

"Ignorance," Juno suggested.

My mouth tightened.

"I was going to say fear," Angie said. "Pure, monster-under-my-

76

bed, blubbering-schoolgirl fear." She flicked her hand at Amara and Juno. "But theirs work too."

"Well, I'm thrilled to have somehow proven you wrong. What, pray tell, did I do to redeem myself?"

Yaakov turned his computer so the screen faced me. "We watched the challenge."

"They recorded it?" I took a couple quick steps across the room to Yaakov's bed. "And you guys saw it?"

I felt my cheeks heat up as everyone nodded. Then Rylee reached down and pushed a button. A movie played out in half speed. I leaned closer and realized I was watching myself.

On screen I dodged my way across the field toward the soccer ball. Dark objects popped up behind me and blasted cones of paint. To my credit, I didn't look half bad, and as I continued down the field, I actually started looking pretty athletic.

I booted the soccer ball, and three dark objects popped off the ground. My on-screen self dropped to my stomach. I cringed at what was about to happen. There was no sound on the playback, but in an instant, a burst of flame consumed me. Black smoke lingered for a moment, only to be whisked away by a breeze. An oblong of singed grass surrounded me, and bits and pieces of shrapnel littered the area.

Juno let out an excited whoop and slapped my back.

I felt strangely detached from what I was seeing. For a moment I even felt sorry for the kid on screen who'd very nearly been killed.

As the feed cut out and the screen darkened, I realized that the vantage point of the filming had been from above.

"Who recorded that?" I asked. "I didn't see anyone. I sure didn't notice a helicopter or anything."

"Very funny," Yaakov said. "If only there were some kind of high-tech hardware the Agency could put in space. If such a thing were ever invented, I propose we call them *satellites*. It would be the invention of the century, and the Agency could access them for their youth-training protocols." He rolled his eyes. "Wouldn't that be something?"

"Satellites?" I said. "Youth-training protocols?"

"Porcupines," Angie said with a smirk. "Skunks. Waterboarding." She looked at me with raised eyebrows. "What? Are you the only one who gets to say random words?"

Yaakov and Juno laughed and then abruptly stopped when there was a sharp knock at the door. Yaakov tapped his keyboard, and the screen went blank just as the door swung open. I swallowed as a woman only a couple inches taller than me entered the room. She had her dark hair pulled back into a ponytail and a thin face with pointy features. One hand held a clipboard at her side, and the other was behind her back. She wore a foul, tight-lipped expression that made me think of an exterminator who'd just discovered a cabin full of rats and was now contemplating the very best way to kill them all.

"Team Grizzly!"

Her voice was like a cannon, and I jumped. Then I realized everyone was looking at me. I wasn't exactly sure what kind of response she wanted, though. It's not like she'd asked a question. I settled on, "*Um, yes, ma' am?*"

"Um, yes, ma'am?" the woman repeated. She took a step closer and narrowed her eyes at me. "That's how you're going to speak to me? Like a frightened, stuttering schoolgirl?"

Under normal circumstances, I probably wouldn't have backed down. I'd gone toe-to-toe with teachers or other figures of authority, but that was because I knew that when push came to shove, they couldn't really do anything to me. I was just a kid. What were they going to do—call my parents? Oh, well. If this woman had been one of my teachers at school, I would have said something smart-alecky. But this wasn't school, and just a couple hours ago, I'd nearly been blown up. For all I knew, being a smart aleck at Camp Friendship meant I'd be hanging from my fingernails in a cellar somewhere. Plus, she glared at me like her favorite hobby was kid-killing.

"Sorry, ma'am," I said.

The woman forced a breath through her nose. Then she smiled and relaxed her stance. In an instant she'd gone from looking like she might skin us all alive to looking like she'd be right at home in a kindergarten. When she spoke again, her tone was as pleasant as an aunt talking with her favorite nieces and nephews.

"Did you see what I did there?" she asked. "Make a slight adjustment to your body language, add a smile, and you transform your entire demeanor. You can come across as tough as concrete or as pleasant as a summer's day." She licked her lips. "Remember, this is a kids' summer camp. My number one priority is to make sure you all understand that you're expected to act accordingly."

Juno and Rylee instantly adopted a more relaxed posture. Angie was already as calm as she could be, and Yaakov remained as nervous as ever. Amara seemed to try to relax too. He even dropped a shoulder a bit and forced a grin, but all it did was make him look like a creepy kid who couldn't stand up straight.

The woman patted his shoulder. "We'll work on it."

She took a step back and addressed the group. "My name is Elizabeth Clakk. I'm your camp counselor. I'll answer questions, address concerns, set up your Delta training modules, and most importantly, should you make it to Week Two, I'll be the one who approves event strategies."

"What are the modules?" Rylee asked.

"Normally you'd get to pick your modules," Clakk said, "but with the exception of Matt, all of you are new to being on a Delta team."

With the exception of me? I clenched my jaw.

Dad, how many lies have you told them?

"As such," she continued, "your modules are picked for you." She slid several papers from her clipboard and handed them out. "Make note of time and location. Memorize the list, then destroy it in the usual fashion. The next time you find yourself on a Delta team, you'll have your pick. Unless, of course, you win, in which case you won't have to come back here." She laughed and then said, "I'm not joking. Win, and you move on—and so do I." She looked up at the ceiling and muttered, "Oh, what I'd give to not have to be surrounded by little brats every summer." She paused a moment and turned to me. "But that's unlikely, isn't it? You've picked a Delta team of rookies, Matt Cambridge. Any particular reason for that?"

I shook my head. "Um, no reason. Just, er, thought they looked like an interesting group."

"Interesting?" Clakk asked. "Really? Interesting trumps experienced?"

"I think we'll do all right," I said. She was easier to talk back to when she looked pleasant, but not so easy that I wanted to risk sarcasm. Besides, I didn't know why, but I had a sudden pang of defensiveness over my crew.

"You're not like other Deltas I've met, Matt. Apparently the Agency hasn't even released your full records yet. Do you know how unusual that is?"

I shrugged. "Very?"

"Indeed," she said, "very." She stared at me for an awkward moment and then slid another sheet from her clipboard and handed it to me. "Your training modules are mostly predetermined as well, Matt. There were one or two electives, but I picked the ones I thought would be most advantageous given your scores from previous camps."

Great. So I had gotten a bunch of things my dad said I was good at, but which I probably hadn't even heard of.

"If there's something you feel you must change, let me know now and I'll see what I can do."

I glanced at the page. The title read CT/SERE and was followed by Archery, Swimming, Orienteering, Basic Self-Defense, and Arts and Crafts.

Those were not the activities I had expected to see. Not after what I'd already experienced and not after what Rob, Alexis, and Duncan had told me earlier. I half expected the first learning module to be something like *How to Treat a Gunshot Wound* or *Body Disposal 101*. One second I'm getting blown up and Rylee's telling me we have psychopaths on our team, and then next, I'm getting a schedule of events that looks like it was plucked from *The Parent Trap*.

"You look confused," Clakk said. "Is something wrong with the schedule?"

I shook my head. The only thing I *knew* was that Camp Friendship was not what it seemed. Which meant my list of activities was likely not what *it* seemed. Honestly, at that point, my head hurt from trying to keep things straight. Even if I'd wanted something changed on my schedule, it's not like I'd have known what to ask for.

I shook my head. "No. It sounds good."

Clakk raised an eyebrow and then shrugged. "Good, because as I said, it's not like I could change a lot anyway. This year Deltas are required to take Crucible Training. Believe it or not, Ingleton is leading that section."

Rylee gasped. "Robert Ingleton?"

Clakk nodded. "Deltas only, Rylee."

Whatever Crucible Training was, Rylee really wanted to be part of it. Or maybe this Ingleton guy was just young and super good-looking and Rylee really wanted to meet him.

Clakk turned back to me. "You did remarkably well with the preliminary challenge. Just keep up with it and you'll be—" She stopped abruptly and pressed her finger to her ear. A moment later she checked her watch and said, "I'm on my way." She dropped her hands and turned back to us. "I'll finalize these training modules and bring you all your schedules at dinner." She tapped her watch. "Five sharp. Don't be late. Oh, and remember, Matt, Crucible Training modules can start anytime, so be prepared." She bit her lip. "*Always* be prepared."

"I think she had one of those ear-bud communication thingies the secret service uses," I said after Clakk left the cabin.

Everyone looked at me like I'd just pointed at the floor and said, "Lookie, a floor."

I wiped my palms on my jeans and cleared my throat. "So, anyone done this CT/SERE stuff before? I can't remember what those letters even mean."

Rylee narrowed her eyes and stared skeptically at me. "They stand for Crucible Training/Survival, Evasion, Resistance, Escape."

She waited for me to say something, and when I didn't, she added, "Since Robert Ingleton is leading your training, you can be sure it will be brief but focused. It's not like he has time to hang out at a camp for three weeks."

I had no idea what she was talking about, and I didn't want to sound dumber than I already had. So rather than ask another question I said, "Well, at least Ms. Clakk seemed nice. I've had friends go to camp and they've had evil counselors who made their lives miserable." That wasn't true, but I felt I had to say something, and that lie just sort of fell out of my mouth. The truth was, Ms. Clakk wasn't at all what I expected. Every friend I've ever had who went to a camp always came back with stories about how their camp counselor was the lamest person they'd ever met. That's how it was with regular camps. I mean, just imagine what kind of person has to sign up to be a camp counselor.

"I've heard of her," Amara said. "She ran a few operations in Turkey. *Nice* is not a term I'd use to describe her."

"Turkey?" Juno said. "Was she working for the Agency, or are you saying she's—"

"I'm not saying anything other than what I said," Amara cut in.

Juno nodded and looked thoughtfully at the ceiling.

"When did she join the Agency?" Rylee asked.

Amara shook his head. Rylee turned to Angie, and she shrugged. Then Rylee craned her neck and looked at Yaakov.

"Yak?"

He huffed and plopped back onto his bed and began tapping at his computer. "You know, Rylee, you can't just expect me to have every answer to every question your little mind comes up with."

Rylee looked at me and rolled her eyes. "He'll find it."

I nodded, even though I didn't have a clue what Yaakov was looking for or what they were getting so worked up about. She ran *operations* in Turkey? That sounded military. And the way everyone said *the Agency this* and *the Agency that* was weird. It felt like a poke from a stick every time someone said it. There was something about that term I recognized, but I didn't know what it meant.

CHAPTER 14

The mess hall was about the size of an elementary school gym. Large, rectangular tables were positioned end-to-end, forming five long rows that ran the length of the room. At the front of each row sat a circular table with six seats and above each of those five tables hung a banner with a shadowed figure of the animal associated with each team.

Most of the other Deltas were settled at their tables. Alexander Bratersky, looking as mean as ever, sat with his entire group. Chase was seated with the rest of Team Squirrel, and everyone at the table glared across the mess hall at me as I approached the table beneath the bear silhouette.

"She's not here," Rylee said breezily after I'd taken my seat.

"Who?" I asked.

"Becca, of course," she said. She craned her neck around a few other students. "Nope, she's gone. Good."

I glanced down the row of Delta tables to the one beneath the hyena silhouette. Three of Becca's teammates were seated at the table, and all three of them looked like they'd just seen a puppy get hit by a car.

Angie leaned across the table toward Rylee. "Maybe if you hadn't made Yaakov spend the last few hours searching for information on Clakk, he could've hacked the footage for Becca's challenge and we'd know what happened."

Rylee grumbled something she probably didn't care for anyone to understand.

I considered asking Rylee why she hated Becca so much, but her foul expression made me think twice. It was probably something stupid like Becca had kissed the boy Rylee liked or something. Girls were always fighting about that kind of stuff.

"We all had the same challenge," I said. "So, I mean, if she didn't get out of the way of those land mines, she could be really hurt." I glanced around the table. "You guys saw it. I could've been ..."

"Killed," Juno deadpanned.

"Yes," Angie said, "we know. It was all very traumatic for you. I mean, you did get a scratch from it all. How terrifying."

I felt my cheeks flush.

"Yeah, man," Juno said, "we all saw the footage; it wasn't that bad. I've seen worse. Besides, I bet that even if you had been blasted by those final mines, you'd be just fine. Bruised, sure, but *generally* fine. Certainly alive."

"Oh, well, that's fantastic," I said.

Juno opened his mouth to say something else, probably to disagree, but before he could make a sound, Becca Plain was pushed into the mess hall in a wheelchair. Thick bandages covered her head and parts of her face. Her right forearm was encased in a green cast, and her left arm, while bare, bore long red scratches and purple welts. She looked, well, like she'd just been blown up by a land mine.

I turned back to Juno. "What were you saying?"

"Fine," he said, wincing. "Maybe you could've been killed."

"Thank you!" I said. I smiled at that small victory, and then stopped abruptly when I realized it meant I'd been right. I considered that as more campers filed in. I considered, too, the fact that no one seemed concerned that Becca, a fellow camper, had been so badly injured. She wasn't surrounded by teammates or friends fawning over her and asking her if they could do anything for her. In fact, the way her teammates shook their heads as she rolled past, and the way the rest of her Delta team avoided looking at her altogether when she was pushed to the head table, it looked an awful lot like they were annoyed that she'd been so injured. Nice group.

"Welcome, campers." Dalson's voice carried throughout the mess hall, and I turned to the front of the room where he stood in yet another open-collared dress shirt and dress pants. "I hope you've all settled into your cabins and into your teams. I just have a couple of quick announcements before dinner begins. First, the results of the preliminary challenge are posted on the bulletin board outside the main office. Congratulations to all the Deltas. You all performed admirably.

"Second, we've said this before, but it really can't be stressed enough: it's imperative you remember this camp is undergoing the final stages of accreditation this summer. All of you must conduct yourselves in such a way that you appear to be typical campers. When you're out of your cabins or wandering between activities, I'd like you all to keep shoptalk to a minimum."

"Shoptalk?" I muttered.

"Don't forget our motto."

Suddenly everyone in the gymnasium yelled, "*Quisquam. Usquam.*"

They yelled it in unison, and with such force I nearly fell out of my seat. *Quisquam. Usquam.* I didn't know what it meant, but I committed it to memory. Clearly, it was something everyone at camp knew, and knew well.

Doors at either end of the hall opened, and serving staff, wearing aprons and hairnets, pushed long rolling carts filled with food down either side of the mess hall. There was chicken and ribs, potatoes, and rice. There were curried dishes and pots of soups. There were burgers and tacos and several dishes I'd never seen, and I wondered if the diversity of the menu was in part because of the diversity of campers. One minute they were blowing you up, the next they were catering such an array of food that everyone would be happy.

My mouth watered as the delicious aromas wafted around the room, and briefly, very briefly, I wondered if nearly getting blown up had been all that bad. I hadn't really been hurt, after all. Maybe I was overreacting.

Then my mind switched focus to the faint ringing that still echoed in my ears, and I caught sight of Becca across the room, twisted in a mess of casts, bandages, and bruises, and I shook my head.

Of course I wasn't overreacting.

This place was beyond messed up.

CHAPTER 15

I stabbed at the half-eaten pork chop with my fork. It was delicious, but my appetite came in waves. One minute I'd be famished, and the next my stomach would be in knots.

I was vaguely aware of the conversations around me, but I didn't pay any real attention to them. I just kept my head down and tried to consider my next few moves. When at last I looked up, I found myself staring down at a long line of empty tables and chairs. Only Rylee and Juno remained at the Delta table. There were a few other campers scattered around the room who were still eating, or chatting, or just sitting there daydreaming, but for the most part, the room had emptied.

"When you zone out, you really zone out," Juno said. "You look worried."

"I'm not," I lied.

"You sure?" Rylee asked.

"I told you guys I'm not really into this place. If I didn't have to be here, I wouldn't be here."

"Your scores would seem to indicate something else," Juno said.

I shook my head and muttered, "Those scores are a joke."

"As in, not real?" Juno asked. "As in, someone faked your scores?"

My stomach sank. That was exactly right, but hearing Juno say it made me wonder if I hadn't just revealed something that could hurt me or, more importantly, my dad. Why had he put me in this position?

He'd thrown me in a place where *he* had the most to lose? What was he thinking?

"I'm impressed," Juno said. He sounded genuine. "We saw the roster, remember? We saw the scores. Those were scans of actual documents. That means if they were faked, someone would have had to get close enough to where they were being kept to actually make physical adjustments." He nodded again. "Not easy to do."

Unless you're a janitor.

Rylee looked at Juno and then leaned across the table to me. "I haven't figured you out yet, Matt Cambridge, but you seem like you're being straight with us. I'm willing to give you the benefit of the doubt ... for now. But the fact that you don't want to be at the camp doesn't exactly make you unique. There are a lot of campers who don't want to be here. You're not the only one with parents who forced you here."

Juno raised his hand. "I can vouch for that. My dad says this life is in my blood and sees the training we get here as key to my future success." He shrugged. "I think I could learn most of this stuff on the job, you know what I mean?" I didn't have a clue but nodded anyway and he continued. "But honestly, I'm not even sure I want to work in this business."

Rylee rolled her eyes. "Please. I know you, Juno. I know you're a fighter, and you've probably been trained to be a weapon since you were in diapers. What would you do if not this?"

"Movies," Juno said without hesitation. He leaned forward. "Action movies. I could totally do all that Bruce Lee, Jackie Chan, Jet Li stuff. Plus," he gestured around the room, "it's not like we don't get some experience acting when we come to these places."

Rylee laughed. "You know, Juno, I could actually see you doing that."

This was good. I needed to get the others to open up too. The more I learned about their backgrounds, the more I might pick up about this place. It was a start.

Juno flicked a fork into the air, caught it with his other hand, and pointed the prongs at me. "I will say this, though. You might be the only one who got sent here as a punishment for *not* killing a gymful of kids."

"Yeah, well," I said, "I guess I'm just special."

CHAPTER 16

I wasn't anxious to get back to the cabin, so I spent a few hours wandering the pretty extensive grounds of Camp Friendship. First, I walked along the path that ran parallel to the perimeter, which I quickly realized was in the shape of a pentagon, each section dominated by a different Delta team. The Delta cabin for my team and the one for Team Octopus, Dexter Miller's team, were the only two that actually backed up to the forest. The others backed up to open sections of the camp. The Delta cabin for Team Squirrel, Chase's team, looked out over the soccer field. Hyena's Delta cabin backed up to the archery range, and I wondered if Becca would at least be able to do that sport from her wheelchair. Alexander Bratersky's team, Arctic Fox, had their Delta cabin backing up to the BMX track.

The more I wandered, the more this place looked like a typical camp. It was certainly nicer-looking than the ones I'd heard my friends talk about, and it was obviously not a military camp. Still, it was so *normal* that it seemed entirely abnormal. It freaked me out, but it held some strange kind of appeal for me at the same time. This camp was dangerous, and I kind of liked that. I wondered what kinds of things they taught campers here. I wondered what kind of organization *the Agency* was. I also wondered why I was the only one who seemed lost.

"You lost, Grizzly?"

I spun around and found myself staring back at Chase's smirking face.

92

"Shut up, Chase," I said.

He laughed, and as he did, a dozen other campers, each wearing a T-shirt with the shadowy image of a squirrel on it, wandered out from the surrounding cabins and lined up beside Chase. I would have been nervous, scared even, if it hadn't been for Mr. Smith's reprimand on the bus and his warning about unauthorized violence. I straightened and sneered at Chase. Then I shook my head and turned to leave. Another line of campers had formed behind me, and they, too, wore Squirrel team shirts.

"You're in my section," Chase began, "and what reason would you have to be here? To spy?"

I forced a laugh. "Spy?" More and more Squirrel members joined the group. I cleared my throat and turned back to Chase. "On you? Why would I want to spy on you?"

"I don't know," Chase said. "Maybe you just like to peep in windows." Everyone laughed, and then Chase added, "Perv." And they all laughed more.

"Hilarious," I said. "You should go on tour." I turned again and tried to walk around the group of campers blocking my path, but they moved like a human wall. I tried to shove my way through, and they shoved back, hard, almost knocking me to the ground.

Fear twisted my gut into knots.

I turned back to Chase, who was now only half a dozen steps away from me, and asked him, "What do you want?"

"What do I want?" Chase repeated. "You're the one who wandered into my section. I don't think you're stupid enough to just step off the camp path accidentally. So that means you did it on purpose, and if you're not a peeping pervert"—he pointed mockingly at me—"and I still think you might be." He gave his campers time to laugh. "But if you're not," he continued, "then you must be here to finish what we started on the bus." He rubbed his hands together. "And if that's the case, my birthday came early this year."

Mr. Smith had been very clear on the bus, and I distinctly remembered the look on Chase's face when the threat of getting kicked from the program had been levied. He wasn't going to hit me. No way. He clenched his fist and started toward me. I stood my ground and smiled.

"Are you forgetting something?" I asked as he drew back his fist. "No unauthorized vi—"

He swung, and it wasn't until his fist was a few inches from my face that I realized he wasn't going to follow the rules. By then it was too late to move.

Pain exploded in the side of my face. I hit the ground with a thud, and the now-familiar taste of blood filled my mouth. I stared up at a blurry image of Chase.

"Unauthorized violence?" Chase asked. "Is that what you were going to say?"

I rubbed the side of my face and propped myself up on my elbow and waited for my vision to clear.

Chase and everyone around me laughed. "You need to work on your English. The key word was *unauthorized*. We're *authorized* to defend our section from hostiles." He pointed at me. "You look hostile. Plus, you're the one who wandered off the path."

"W-what are you talking about?" I asked.

He flashed an evil grin, shuffled his feet, and then booted me in the stomach. I rolled at least twice, and my dinner surged and blasted out my mouth in a stream that must've sprayed ten feet. I don't know exactly how many people I hit, but the members of Team Squirrel who had had me surrounded scattered. I pushed myself to my knees and forced my focus away from the pain in my face and ribs and took off at a sprint.

Someone clamped hold of my shoulder after only a dozen steps, and I spun around with a raised arm. My elbow smashed into the kid's face, and he dropped to the ground. I let momentum spin me the rest of the way around and kept running.

There were shouts behind me, but none so clear that I could make out the words. I was reasonably certain their shouts had something to do with killing me or tying me to a tree or something along those lines. I dodged around cabins and through shrubs. My heart pounded, and the muscles in my legs burned. I paused behind another cabin. I wasn't there ten seconds before someone charged up behind me and tackled me. We rolled across the grass, and when we stopped, they were on top of me, smashing a fist into my face.

"I got 'im! Over here!"

It was only then I realized a girl had me pinned. "Are you kidding me?" I said. I bucked, but she drove her fist into my face again, and I thought I heard my nose crack.

Panic took hold at that point, and I bucked again. This time she tumbled off. I scrambled to my feet and was mid-sprint when the girl grabbed my foot and screamed again for help. I shook my leg, and I must have hit her pretty hard because she toppled backward, but not before she yanked my shoe off.

I heard other campers coming and cursed. I rushed back to where the girl was lying and pulled my shoe out of her hand. She was dazed, and there was blood on her lip. I spun to start running away, and the crazy girl grabbed my other foot!

I was just going to swing around and pull my foot free. That's all I wanted to do. She'd been on her back when I'd pulled my shoe out of her hand, and I assumed she was still mostly on the ground but had managed to grab my foot. But when I spun around, she was on her knees. I'd whirled so hard that my arms had gone out like the blades of a helicopter, which wouldn't have been so bad since I was a couple feet away from her. But I was still holding my shoe, the one she'd pulled off already, the one I'd retrieved but hadn't put back on yet. I was holding it by the laces, and in my hand, it added an extra foot to my arm, just enough so that when I came around the shoe smashed into the girl's face. Her nose was like a smooshed cherry, and blood oozed over her face.

That's when more of her teammates came around the corner. They hesitated, and I realized it must've looked like I'd just taken my shoe off and beaten the girl with it. Before I could utter an apology, the girl screamed and grabbed her face, and her teammates charged.

I sprinted across the camp, not looking where I was going, and suddenly, I heard more shouts and saw other campers, these ones wearing Fox T-shirts. I must've crossed into Bratersky's area.

I slowed down long enough to see several of Team Fox attacking Team Squirrel, but I also saw several Team Fox members point at me.

I don't know how far I ran, but I must've crossed each section twice. I couldn't keep track of who was fighting who. I was pretty sure I'd seen every animal T-shirt, even Grizzlies, but my adrenaline was pumping so hard I didn't stop even then, just in case I was wrong.

Finally I found myself alone. I sprinted across the archery range and dived for cover behind some trees. I lay there for a few seconds, too tired to run farther but terrified I hadn't been fast enough and someone had spotted me sprinting into the woods and they'd be scrambling after me any second.

No one came.

A few more seconds passed, then angry shouts filtered through the branches, and I peeked out across the range. Five Squirrel team members were backing slowly away from at least a dozen campers wearing Team Hyena colors. The shouts between the two groups intensified, and then all at once, the Hyena members charged, and Chase's teammates turned and scampered away.

This place is insane. I lay there catching my breath while I considered what kind of camp would let their campers protect their sections with that kind of violence. I also thought about that girl I'd hit with my shoe. I felt terrible about that. If my dad found out I'd hit a girl, he'd be furious. "Respect women," he'd always said. "If you hit a girl, you're not a man." But I hadn't meant to hit her. She'd attacked me first. I hadn't done anything to her. I'd just wanted to get away.

The forest stretched out behind me, and I knew that just a few short miles away there was a road leading to the highway. I could hitch a ride. I could just flag down a trucker and have him take me as far away from this place as possible.

If I ran away it would serve my dad right. What had he been thinking, putting me in a camp like this? It was Day One, and I'd been beaten up twice and very nearly been *blown* up. I rubbed the side of my chest, wincing at the pain. Now I was hiding in the woods contemplating ditching this place. On the one hand, I felt like such a baby, but on the other, no one in their right mind would stay at a camp like this. It was crazy!

Even as I contemplated my escape, I knew I couldn't do it. Not because I was afraid of getting caught, or afraid of my father's disappointment when I got home. No, after watching the violent mayhem that had just swept across the grounds, I simply had to know what was going on. I had to.

I'm not sure how long I stayed there, huddled among the trees, but I didn't leave until it was dark. I stopped at the showers in my section of the camp and cleaned myself up. A thin line of black was forming under my right eye, and I cursed the fact that Chase would see it in the morning and have another reason to laugh at me. The only good thing was that my nose wasn't broken. I'd thought for sure that girl had cracked it, but it was still straight and wasn't really that tender to the touch. Also, there was a good chance several other campers would be as beat up as I was.

I snuck back to the cabin and eased my way through the door. Some moonlight trickled in through the windows, but not enough to see much more than a few feet in front of me. The springs of several beds creaked when I closed the door, and I knew my teammates were awake.

"Where were you?" Rylee whispered through the darkness.

I groaned. "I don't want to talk about it."

There was a click, and a flashlight beam blinded me. "Get that out of my face," I snapped.

The beam dropped to my feet, and Juno whispered, "We thought one of the other teams had you."

"Well, thanks for coming after me," I said. Juno kept the beam of light just in front of my feet, making it very easy to find my bed.

"We looked for you," Rylee said, no longer whispering. "After questioning a few campers from other teams, we realized you were probably just biding your time."

"Is it true you beat a girl with your shoe?" Yaakov asked.

"That's harsh by even my standards," Angie said. I could hear the smile in her voice.

I groaned again. "No, it's not true." I rummaged for another clean shirt from my bin and changed into it. "It was an accident."

"Well, everyone thinks you're bat crazy," Angie said. "And that's a quality I like in a team captain. To think I had you pegged as a real novice." She laughed. "Then you go and pull that genius move. I think you must be one of the best actors in this place."

"Yeah, yeah," I said, "Real—" I stopped. Had she just given me a compliment?

"It was risky," Rylee said. "I mean, if they'd caught you, you could've been really hurt."

"I *was* really hurt," I said.

"Why didn't you bring us along?" Juno asked.

"Along where?" I asked. "What exactly do you guys think I did?"

"It's all over camp, Captain," Angie said. "You caused one of the biggest fights of any camp in recent history. You put at least a dozen members of each team out of commission. Team Squirrel got the worst of it. Apparently fifteen of their campers got beat up."

I dropped into bed and put my hands behind my head. "Good. They deserved it." They had, and I didn't mind saying so. For a moment, my injuries hurt just a little less.

"You're inspiring confidence," Amara said. "It's only the first day, and you have the respect of all the campers in Team Grizzly. You probably have the respect of most of the other teams too."

I doubted that. Not once word got out about how I'd used puke to escape Chase's team. "I'm tired," I said after a brief pause. *And confused*, I thought, but didn't say that. "I just want to sleep."

I lay awake in bed for a long time thinking about things, trying to work things out. Clearly the path that circled the camp was a kind of safe zone. I'd have to remember that. The last thought I had before I finally fell asleep was that Chase would be out to get me even more if he thought I'd actually gotten one up on him.

That idea made my stomach and the side of my face hurt even more.

CHAPTER 17

My schedule for Day Two started with Archery. I didn't feel hungry after the night I'd had and decided to skip breakfast. I made my way to the range only to find it deserted. That suited me just fine. Ten target boards were set up on stacks of straw, behind which was the forest. Waist-high wooden poles, each with a bow and quiver of arrows, were set up about forty feet in front of the targets.

I glanced behind me. A dozen or so campers hustled along the path around the camp perimeter. I remembered what had happened the night before and reminded myself, again, not to step off the path unless I was in Grizzly territory.

I wandered along the row and stopped at the pole farthest to the right. I ran my finger along the bowstring and then the feathers of one of the arrows. I'd always wanted to shoot an arrow, but if you don't go to summer camp, it's not exactly something you do on your own at the park or in the backyard.

I waited another few minutes and then lifted the bow off the wooden pole. I raised it the way I'd seen a million times on TV. Then I pulled an arrow out of the quiver. I glanced back one more time at the walkway. It was clear.

One shot, I decided. I could take just one shot before the instructor came and gave us the lame rules that no one needed. Shooting these things wasn't exactly rocket science. I slid the notch of the arrow on to the string, then pulled it back. Drawing it back was actually a lot more difficult than I'd expected, and the string bit into my fingers. But I heaved harder, and then all of a sudden my hand was by the side of my face and it didn't seem so hard anymore.

I imagined I was in the final event of the Olympics, about to compete for the gold medal. When I was certain I had the arrow aimed properly, I released the string ... and screamed.

It felt like a whip had struck my forearm. The bow dropped from my hand, and I hopped around like a crazy person, cursing and rubbing my arm over and over.

"It's called string-slap."

I turned at the familiar voice and rubbed my arm some more, but stopped jumping around. "What are you doing here?"

Juno reached down and plucked the bow from the ground. "Same thing as you." He pulled an arrow from the quiver and notched it in the string. "Archery." He drew the string back and closed one eye. "The trick," he began, "is to make sure you have a bow with the proper draw length—which you had—and also to have proper form." He shifted his eyes at me. "Which you did not have." He kept his gaze on me and released the arrow. The twang that resonated from the bowstring sounded like it had been made by a guitar, and the arrow rocketed toward the target, but when it hit, it splintered into a dozen pieces.

I tilted my head, not entirely sure what I'd just seen.

Juno looked up at the sky and shook his head. "The other thing to remember is that no one actually learns archery at these camps, so the targets are probably not meant to be used."

"W-what?" I asked.

He sighed and put the bow back on the wooden post. "Of course it's a prop. I can't believe I thought this was a real target range." He gestured to the target. "C'mon, help me clean that arrow up before the instructor gets here and I get demerits or something."

"Props?" I muttered as I followed him on to the range. I picked up a shard or two of broken arrow and then walked up and touched the target. "It's made of concrete," I said, mostly to myself. Juno didn't seem surprised, and I figured that must've been what he was talking about when he said "props." I slid my hand along the cool surface. It was painted to look just like a target, and the details were remarkable. There were even a couple spots on the bull's-eye where someone must've drilled out arrow-sized holes, presumably to make it look like it had been used.

I slid my hand along the edge of the target, and my fingers brushed a section of indentation. I pushed some of the straw away and craned my neck. Chiseled on the board's edge were four letters.

"PCIA."

Juno laughed. "Is that carved on there?" I nodded, and he said, "It never gets old seeing that."

I bit my lip, and Juno's smile vanished. "Don't tell me you don't even know what PCIA means."

I waved my hand and did my best to appear as though I did. Juno didn't buy it.

"Property of the Central Intelligence Agency?" he said, as if he were reminding me of something obvious, like my name.

"The CIA?" I craned my neck around the target again. "Why would it say that?"

"Because that's where all this stuff comes from," Juno said. "Well, most of it anyway. There's some from CSIS, Mossad, DID ..." He shrugged and picked up a remaining piece of arrow. "Mostly CIA. Campers etch stuff like that in places as plain-sight hints that this isn't a normal summer camp. Just don't get caught doing it."

I wasn't sure about CSIS or Mossad or DID, but I darn well knew what the CIA was. "CIA." When I said the acronym again, a slow realization spread over me. CIA. I felt a smile start at the corners of my mouth. The Agency. Of course. This was a CIA camp. A secret camp for really young CIA operatives. I'd seen enough movies to know what that meant: the coolest training on the planet! The bombs on the soccer field suddenly made sense ... kind of. It still seemed harsh, but the CIA wasn't going to let any of us die.

It also made sense that Dalson wanted everyone to look like regular campers. These kids had been doing this a lot longer than I had, and their training made them look like soldiers, not kids. How could they blend in to stop national threats if they didn't look like real kids? I scratched my head and wondered if stopping national threats was even what the CIA did. It didn't matter.

Somehow Dad had signed me up on this roster. I bet he had no idea where he was sending me. But then again, he had been nervous at the parking lot. He had mentioned that I'd learn a thing or two about discipline ... hadn't he? CIA. I shook my head. The more I said the acronym, the more it did—and didn't—make sense. Maybe I still didn't have it quite right. Perhaps those other acronyms were intelligence agencies from around the world. Could it be that Camp Friendship was a place where kid spies from all over came to work together?

I was getting ahead of myself. And in case I had it wrong, I decided not to celebrate just yet. If this was a CIA camp and people found out I didn't belong here, they'd kick me out. In fact, there was a pretty good chance I'd get discovered sooner or later anyway. But if I was careful, maybe I'd learn some cool spy stuff before that happened.

Any thoughts I'd had about ditching this place and running away faded. If this was a CIA training camp, it was a dream come true. I wondered if winning the competitions meant becoming a CIA operative, or if being in the camp simply meant I was already one. I dug my fingernails into my palm.

Get it together, Matt. You're jumping to conclusions.

It might mean something totally different. It might be a joke. Juno might just be messing with me ... but if he wasn't ...

I cursed myself again for breaking my phone. Jason would go nuts if there was even a possibility I was in a camp for kid spies.

I rubbed my hands together and turned to Juno. He stared back, his eyebrows very near his hairline.

"You look like someone who just found a treasure map," he said.

I slapped him on the shoulder and headed over to the wooden posts. "In a way," I said, "it's possible I just did."

We hid the arrow shards in the bushes and then waited.

"Listen," Juno said, hesitantly, "last night I said some things that might have made you think I didn't value this place or that I wasn't really into the family business."

I shrugged. "So you want to be an action star. So what?" If this was a CIA camp for kids and we all had a shot at being real CIA operatives, the fact that Juno wanted to be an action star was weird. The CIA was way cooler than that.

He rubbed the back of his neck. "That was just talk. I'd never do anything to dishonor my family, and I don't want it getting out that I would."

How would being a movie star dishonor anyone? It was probably a sore spot between him and his dad. I had a couple of my own and quickly decided Juno's family issues were none of my business. "I'm not going to tell anyone what you said, if that's what you're worried about." I forced a quick breath through my nose. "You know stuff about me too, Juno. How 'bout we just agree to never repeat things that might get the other into trouble."

Juno nodded. "Deal."

I motioned at the bow. "Where'd you learn to shoot?"

"Arrows?" He shrugged. "Don't remember, but I do remember string-slap." He winced and rubbed his arm. "That's a lesson you don't have to learn more than once."

I was about to ask him what other weapons he could have used to "shoot" when more campers started to trickle in. A couple minutes after that, our instructor wandered up to the range.

He was a balding rail of a man, easily over six feet tall, with the posture of a tree. He reminded me of a yardstick my old teachers used to use as pointers. In fact, the more I looked at the skinny instructor, the more I wondered if I outweighed him. He drifted over to the wooden post and picked up the bow. He reached for an arrow but stopped with his hand just over the quiver and glanced over his shoulder at us. His gaze locked on me, and I turned my attention to my feet.

"My name is Byron Fargas," he began. "I am the range master." His voice was as solemn as a graveyard. "I'll tell you when the range is safe and when you're qualified to use the equipment. You do not use anything without my consent." He pulled one of the arrows from the quiver. "That includes the archery equipment."

That *includes* the archery equipment? An excited chill crawled up my spine, and I glanced up at the instructor. C'mon, be something more than archery. If this was a CIA camp, everything would make so much more sense. Please, please ...

He touched his index finger to his ear and said, "Fargas here. I'm ready to begin archery instruction. Do I have the all-clear?" A moment passed, and he took his finger away from his ear and notched the arrow in the bowstring. He drew back and took careful aim at the concrete target.

I glanced at Juno. He looked back at me and shrugged, no doubt as confused as I was that our range master was taking aim at something an arrow couldn't possibly penetrate.

The twang was followed almost instantly by a *thwump*, and when I looked at the target, the arrow stuck out of the top edge. I felt my jaw drop. There'd been a hole drilled in that section of the target, I remembered. I was sure about that, but the idea that this guy's aim was so perfect he'd managed to sink an arrow in a hole the same diameter as its tip seemed impossible. Yet there it was.

I'd barely had time to register how bizarre it was when a distinctive click sounded from the target, and the entire thing, mountain of straw included, slid back several feet to reveal a gaping hole. The range master strolled to the edge of the pit and gestured down. "C'mon. Move it."

I let the other campers go first, and one by one, they disappeared below ground. When I got to the edge, just behind Juno, I hesitated and smiled as he headed down the concrete steps. It looked like the entrance to a crypt. This camp was so much more than it seemed. Life-threatening competitions? Secret passages? There was only one explanation. Juno wasn't kidding. This was the CIA.

"Well," the range master said, "are you coming or not?"

My smile widened as I took the first step. "You bet I am!"

107

CHAPTER 18

A narrow hall stretched out from the base of the steps and continued a dozen yards before it opened up into a room at least three times the size of the largest classroom at Marksville Middle. Bright fluorescent lights illuminated the concrete walls and made the area seem incredibly sterile. Each wall had a wooden door, painted gray so at first I didn't notice them. In the center of the room was a large rectangular table, neatly ordered with safety goggles and ear protectors. The campers grabbed a pair of each as they filed into the room, so I did the same.

The sound of the archery target rolling back into place above us filtered down the steps as Range Master Fargas entered the room.

I probably should have been really nervous, but mostly I was psyched. I was in a freaking spy camp! I didn't understand how it had happened and what role my dad really had in all this, but I was here, and I was actually getting spy training. Now I really did have to fly under the radar. If I got discovered, I'd be kicked out, and I would never get this opportunity again.

"Good," Fargas said, presumably because we all had ear and eye protectors. He ushered us toward the door to his right, and we filed across the room and through the door. The second room was about the size of a basketball court, divided along its width by a sheet of Plexiglas about twenty feet from the door. On the other side of the Plexiglas were sixteen booths that looked down at paper targets. It looked like the shooting ranges in police shows on TV. As I looked some more, I realized that was exactly what it was.

"Impressive, hey?" Juno whispered over my shoulder. "I knew they'd slated this camp to be one of the top training sites, but this is at least triple the size of any range I've seen in other camps."

"Yeah," I said, not sure how to respond. "Me too." If they had this room, I wondered how many other sections of the camp had secret underground rooms. This place was getting cooler and cooler by the second.

"Guns will stay in the range," Fargas began. "Try to smuggle one out, and you're gone. Understand?"

The campers nodded.

"There'll be no warnings," Fargas continued. "No second chances. Steal one of my guns and you'll never set foot in another camp again."

Guns?

He'd said the word twice, but it only really registered with me the second time. Of course there'd be guns. I practically laughed, I was so excited. My dad thought he'd sent me to a camp that would make me a better kid, and here I was about to play with guns. He'd flip out if he realized what he'd done.

"Ammunition too," he added. "It all stays in the range. Sneak a single bullet out and you're cut." His eyes narrowed, and he scrutinized each of us. "It's a rule I won't repeat. You're taught proper firearms handling as a precautionary skill. We prefer if our *campers* are more creative. We hope you'll be more creative when you're out in the real world. But it is fairly obvious that, in our line of work, the chances of coming across firearms are quite high."

He sauntered to the wall behind us and punched a series of numbers into a keypad on a cabinet that stretched at least half the length of the room. Then he slid the door six feet to the left. It collapsed in on itself, accordion style, and revealed columns and rows of meticulously organized guns. Each column was arranged by size. If the rows continued the way it appeared, I figured the guns at the far right of the cabinet were the kind you put on your shoulder to blow up tanks or topple buildings.

Range Master Fargas stood, hands on hips, scrutinizing us carefully. "All right, then, no time like the present to see how well you campers know your firearms." He gestured to the wall of weapons behind him. "Go on, pick the one you're most comfortable with, and head into the range. This is assessment day."

Everyone approached the wall of weapons as if they were browsing a rack of books or DVDs. I assumed my position at the back of the group and watched as the others reached up and lifted one gun after another off the wall. I got more excited with each step forward. In the back of my mind, I half thought maybe the guns wouldn't be real, but the closer I got, the more real they looked. By the time it was my turn to pick a weapon, the nervous excitement building in my stomach was making it incredibly difficult not to smile.

I reached up to grab a gun about the size of my forearm. It was black and silver and had a piece on top that looked like a laser. Totally James Bond. My fingers were an inch away when I stopped.

Assessment day. The range master's words felt like a shotgun blast.

This was a test.

I almost slapped myself for what would have been a stupid mistake. One of the only things I knew about this camp was that I did not belong. If they realized that, I'd be out. The only thing I knew about guns was which end the bullet came out of. If I chose one with all kinds of bells and whistles on it, I'd be lucky if I knew how to hold it.

I shuffled to the other end of the cabinet, trying to be smart about my choice. I scanned the smaller weapons and finally plucked one of the smallest guns on the rack. It was a lot heavier than it looked, but it was the only one I actually recognized, kind of. I was pretty sure it was the kind of gun a police officer carried, and I figured it might be one of the most straightforward. I looked up. Juno stared back at me with a single raised brow. His expression seemed to say, "You're a Delta, and you're picking a small gun like that? What's wrong with you?" The gun he held was huge and looked like it belonged in a movie about killing aliens. I did my best to ignore his expression. It would be a lot worse if I picked a bigger gun and shot myself.

I ducked around Juno and followed the others into the shooting range, and took a spot in one of the empty stalls. I placed the gun and ear protectors on the small ledge atop the waist-high wall in front of me and took a step back.

Juno claimed the stall beside me and stepped close as the others campers filed in. "Check it out." He flipped his gun over and held it close to my face. Carefully scratched in the base of the grip were the letters *PCIA*. He laughed. "See? I told you. People scratch it in everything."

Property of the CIA. I smiled despite my nerves.

"One shot," Range Master Fargas said as he shuffled behind us. He stopped behind me, reached over, and grabbed my gun. I tried to watch what he did, but he moved so fast. The clip slid out of the bottom of the grip, and Fargas shoved a bullet inside and then slapped the clip back into the gun before he returned it to its spot on the ledge. "You each get one shot to impress me. I shouldn't have to say this, but keep your fingers off the bang switch until you're ready to fire." He moved down the line, stopping at each camper's stall for a fraction of a second to load a single round into their guns. "When I say so, you may begin."

There were three more distinctive clicks from down the row, and then the range master took a position midway between the booths, his back against the Plexiglas divider, and said, "Begin."

Juno was on my left, and his arm snapped up like a whip. I don't even think he had time to aim, but an explosion erupted from the end of his gun that made my head spin. It was a reminder that I hadn't put on my ear protectors yet, and I quickly did so. There was another bang from farther down the row, then another, but my ear protectors dulled those shots. Or maybe they just sounded dull because Juno's shot had destroyed my eardrums and I wouldn't hear anything either way.

I picked up my pistol and pointed it down the range. I tried holding it with one hand, then two. Two felt better. I took careful aim and felt someone tap me on my shoulder. I glanced over, and Juno was looking at me with raised brows.

He nodded to my gun and said something I couldn't hear, but I was pretty sure one of the words he said was *bite*.

Another two or three bangs reminded me that soon I'd be the last shot, and then everyone would see how bad I was at this. I shook my head at Juno and turned back to the target. I'd learned to aim a gun on my video games, so I knew to look down the top of the gun. I closed one eye and focused.

Juno tapped me on the shoulder again. I sighed and looked at him. He pointed at my gun and said, "Clock." He nodded to the gun.

I didn't know what he was talking about. I could only assume he was reminding me that my time was running out, but why would he? Several more guns fired down the line. I jerked my head back around, aimed, said a silent prayer that I'd at least hit the target, and then squeezed the trigger.

The gun bucked in my hand, and as it did, it felt like a snake had leaped out of nowhere and sunk its fangs into my thumb. The pistol clattered to the ground, and I half hopped, half hobbled backward, clutching my hand against my chest until my back hit the Plexiglas wall behind me. My eyes were partially closed, and my head hit the glass and knocked my ear protectors off my head.

"Jeez, Cambridge," Juno said. "I told you that you were shooting a Glock. You hold it like that and the slide is going to slide-bite every time."

His words barely registered. I looked down at my hand. Two parallel slices cut across my thumb and the back of my hand.

The range master walked over to me and gave my bloody hand a puzzled stare.

"Slide-bite," Juno said.

The range master nodded thoughtfully. Then he lifted his eyes to mine. "Why did you hold your gun like that?"

I scrambled to keep my emotions checked. "I—I was distracted. It was a stupid mistake." I struggled to find an excuse that made sense, and then, despite my pain, I remembered a scene from a movie where a guy had fired his gun accidentally. I borrowed his excuse. "The trigger was more sensitive than I'm used to." The pain intensified with each passing second, and I held my hand away from my chest so that the counselor could see it.

"If you recall, Cambridge, I told everyone to keep their fingers off the bang switch until you were ready to shoot." He huffed and gestured to my hand. "Well, don't bleed all over the place," Fargas said in an exasperated tone. "You'll get no sympathy from me for not knowing how to hold a Glock."

I pulled my hand back against my chest, shocked that the sliced-up hand bloodying my shirt—and the ground around me—was getting zero attention. I willed myself not to focus on the pain.

Fargas nudged Juno. "Get him to the medic before he gets blood on everything."

Juno looked down at his gun and sighed as if it were a toy he'd just been told he couldn't play with anymore.

"Why didn't you listen to me?" Juno said once we were out of the pit and making our way across the campgrounds. "I told you twice you had the wrong grip." He shook his head and muttered, "What kind of Delta doesn't know how to hold a gun, anyway?"

I did my best to ignore the rest of Juno's grumblings while we walked, and took another look at my hand. It wasn't bleeding as badly as it had been, and I wondered if that was because the blood was clotting or because I'd already lost most of my blood.

Day One: beat up and nearly blown up.

Day Two: almost shot my own hand off.

I really had to get it together. At the rate I was going, I'd be dead before the end of the week.

CHAPTER 19

"You'll be dead by the end of the week if you don't smarten up," Dr. Lester said to me.

He was a short, bald man with a large stomach and a dark mustache. He'd injected something into my hand almost as soon as we walked in, and it had stopped hurting within seconds.

The camp medic's office looked a lot like a miniature version of a hospital ER. Six beds lined the back wall in a room about the size of a school classroom. Drugs and bandages and tongue depressors filled several glass cabinets on the other side of the room, and a large desk sat angled against the adjacent corner. The freshly waxed linoleum reflected back the harsh track lighting overhead.

It struck me right away that Dr. Lester was a real doctor. I'd never heard of a camp staffed with a physician. A nurse maybe, but not its own physician. It was a thought that made me smile. Just one more confirmation that this place was legit. Of course they'd have medical facilities with a real doctor. We're dodging land mines on the soccer field and shooting guns underground, for Pete's sake.

"The drug has obviously kicked in," the doctor said.

I smiled and nodded. "Yeah, thanks."

"How are you finding the rest of camp? Adjusting well?" He sat on a backless stool and started to stitch the two track marks. "Sometimes it can be overwhelming for campers. There've been a few who have made *mistakes* so that they'd get hurt and be allowed to miss events." He stopped stitching and eyed me carefully.

"It was really just a mistake. I was distracted. I'm actually really happy to be here." I thought about the secret shooting range and smiled in spite of my hand. It was such a relief to finally have a hold on what kind of place I was in. I looked back at the doctor as he started stitching again. "I mean the CIA has—"

The doctor jerked his head and held up his hand. "Whoa, kid." His voice was a harsh whisper. "You know the rules. This is just a *regular* camp." He said the word again as if it were a foreign expression I wasn't familiar with. "*Regular.* Keep those kinds of references to yourself." He finished stitching and wrapped my hand in a bandage and then whispered, "The number of agencies that would like to get their hands on one of you guys is staggering. They could be listening right now. Just waiting in the woods for the right cue to let them know you kids aren't really what you seem. Get in the habit of thinking of this camp as an ordinary one."

"*They* could be listening?" I asked.

"There are ears out there," he said. "In the forest." He pointed at the ceiling. "Or from above. Who knows? Maybe one of your fellow campers is a double agent. *You never know.*"

"Double agent?" I echoed. It took a couple seconds to make sense of what he'd said, but then it hit me. I'd seen enough movies to know that where there are spies, there are double agents. It seemed incredible that there might be spy camps for kids in other countries, but then no more incredible than that there was a spy camp for kids in my own country, and here I was. Of course another agency would want to know what was being taught to the next generation of the enemy.

The doctor led me to the door and nudged me out. "Keep it clean and dry. Come back if the stitches open; otherwise, we'll see you next week to take them out. And remember what I told you."

"Thank y—" The door closed before I could finish.

As we made our way back to the cabin, I told Juno what the doctor had said.

"Urban legend," Juno said with a smirk. "Every camp I've ever been to has the same stories." He cleared his throat. "In Dubai, it was the MSS. Everyone swore up and down they had agents in the desert just waiting for an unsuspecting camper to wander away so they could snag them and interrogate them. By the end of the camp, everyone was accusing everyone else of being a double agent. It got pretty dicey. I don't plan on going back there anytime soon."

"MSS?" I said under my breath.

"I know," Juno added, "as if the Chinese are going to set up a snatch-and-grab around a kids' camp in Dubai." He laughed again. "I think the Agency spreads those rumors just to keep the younger kids from wandering too far away from camp."

I bit my lip as we climbed up the steps to the cabin. "Dr. Lester didn't look like he was joking."

Juno shrugged. "Maybe the reason Dr. Lester works at a camp for kids is because he's not all there." He tapped the side of his head. "Trust me. There's no one in the woods waiting to whisk you off to be waterboarded. They're not smart enough to see this camp for what it is." He shoved open the door. Yaakov was on his bed, tapping away at his keyboard.

"What are you doing here?" Juno asked.

Yaakov didn't look up. "They put me in Computer Basics for the morning activity." He shook his head. "Idiots." He gave his keyboard a final tap and then looked up. "I hacked into the instructor's console and destroyed the—" He pointed to me. "What the heck happened to you?"

I shook my head and was about to say "nothing" when Juno opened his mouth.

"His gun bit him," he said with a laugh. "I don't know who taught you about guns, Matt, but they should've told you that the slide on a Glock sits lower than a lot of other guns."

Yaakov grimaced. "Slide-bite? Ouch. That happened to a kid at my first camp. The slide cut his hand right to the bone."

"It wasn't that bad," I snapped. "I'm fine." I held up my hand and wiggled my fingers. Pain bolted through my hand and up my arm.

"Yeah," Yaakov said, "you look fine. Hopefully you have an easier activity for the afternoon."

I walked over to my bed and looked at my clipboard. "Basic Self-Defense." I'd actually been looking forward to this activity even before I realized the camp was part of the CIA. I blew out a breath. *The CIA.* It seemed so obvious now. I mean, every spy needs to know how to fight. Plus, girls love guys who know how to handle themselves. But there wasn't a lot they'd be teaching me with a mangled hand.

"I guess we're together all day," Juno said. "That's what I have this afternoon too."

"*You?*" my voice squeaked. I remembered what Rylee had told me about Juno, and how he'd been training as a fighter since he could crawl. "You're in *Basic* Self-Defense?"

Juno eyed me suspiciously. "Yeah. Why? Has someone been talking about me?"

"I just heard you were already a pretty good fighter."

Juno jutted out his chin. "I do all right. Not that the camp would know anything about it. This is the first time I can fight without having to worry about repercussions."

"Repercussions?"

Juno laughed. "Don't pretend you don't know what I'm talking about. Point is I'm actually looking forward to this activity."

"I'm not," Yaakov said. "I have Self-Defense tomorrow, and I'm going to get pummeled." He waved his palms at me. "These hands were not meant for fighting."

Juno turned and stared at Yaakov. "That's true. They look like they were made for playing with a Barbie."

I laughed, but Yaakov just smiled and then lowered his eyes back to his computer screen.

"Look, Yak," Juno continued, "here's a bit of advice. When you're in a fight, at some point you're going to be in very close contact. If you can, grab the guy's finger and break it."

I winced.

"The biggest guy you'll fight will have a pinky that a ten-year-old could snap. Just don't hesitate." Juno grabbed his own finger and pretended to snap it. "Works every time."

"Great advice," Yaakov said. "Except that once I break a guy's finger, he'll still be able to use his other hand to break my face."

Juno shrugged. "That's true. In that case, do your best to disable his strong hand."

Yaakov groaned.

"Why don't you just hack the system and get yourself out of Self-Defense?" I asked.

"You think I haven't thought of that?" Yaakov said. "I've done that in pretty much every other camp. But I can't do it here, because everyone on a Delta team takes Self-Defense. Everyone. They'll notice if I haven't done it. Then they'll look into why and see that my name is off the roster. Then they'll know I hacked their systems, and I'll be kicked out of the program."

Juno nodded. "That leaves only one option."

Yaakov nearly came out of his seat. "What's that?"

Juno took a step closer to the stick-thin nerd. "Learn how to fight."

"Sure," Yaakov said, "I'll get right on it."

CHAPTER 20

After lunch, Juno and I headed for the self-defense building. At least two dozen campers were already in the room taking instruction from a large bald man with tattoos on his forearms. Most of the kids looked smaller than me, so I was grateful for that. Plus, Chase wasn't among them, so I didn't have to worry about dealing with him. I took another look and realized that none of the other Deltas or their teammates were there.

That was weird.

I was about to ask Juno about it when he nudged me toward a door on the adjacent wall. He opened it and shoved me back outside and into the woods behind the building. I stumbled and nearly tripped over a root.

"What are you doing?" I asked.

Juno cocked an eyebrow. "I was going to ask you the same thing. You know we're supposed to move quickly when we're going to auxiliary locations. You were just standing there waiting for an invitation to step through the door."

I wondered if an auxiliary location was like the underground shooting range. I straightened and dusted myself off. Juno passed me and started walking down a path that became narrower and narrower until it was so narrow it looked like it might have been created by rabbits.

The path twisted to the left, to the right, and then, all at once, we stepped through a wall of foliage and found ourselves in a section of the forest that had been cleared. The canopy blocked out the sky. The clearing was large and circular, about three times the size of my bedroom back home. It was the perfect spot for a picnic.

At least two dozen other campers were already there, including, to my supreme disappointment, Chase. The only good thing was he sported a black eye. I smiled, knowing someone had gotten a good shot the previous night. I wished it had been me.

"Dibs fighting the Grizzly," Chase said with a snicker. "We have some unfinished business that needs sorting."

Other campers laughed, but only those wearing squirrels on their chests. The rest remained mostly silent and stern-faced. I glanced up at Juno. His grin couldn't have been wider.

"Who? Me?" Juno asked, looking almost hopeful. "I would be very happy to oblige, Chase. You know what? It's a date. I can't wait."

Chase's smile evaporated. He took a step closer to Juno, poked him in the chest, and opened his mouth to say something.

"Sit down and shut up." The female voice came from over my shoulder and cut Chase short before he could say anything to Juno.

I spun around. The woman stood with her fists on her hips. Her strawberry-blonde hair was pulled back in a high ponytail, and she wore a dark tracksuit, the jacket of which was open to reveal a tight tank top. She was probably in her mid-thirties, but wasn't much taller than me.

Juno sighed dreamily beside me and whispered, "Beautiful."

"Form a circle," the woman continued, "and sit down."

We spread out enough that the circle was nearly as large as the clearing.

"My name is Lyra Davis. Since we're such a friendly little family here at Camp Friendship, just call me Lyra."

She sneered, and I got the distinct impression that being on a first-name basis with any of the campers was not something she was comfortable with.

"You." She snapped her hand out at a beefy kid with a shaved head and an octopus graphic on his shirt. "And ..." She turned slowly, her finger gliding around the circle. She stopped at me and gave me a stare that felt like a snowball to the side of my head. Then she swung her hand back and stopped abruptly. "You."

The girl she pointed at wore a Team Hyena T-shirt. She jumped to her feet and jogged into the middle of the clearing.

Lyra raised her voice again. "I need to see what I'm working with here." She paused a beat to give the two campers a once-over and then said, "Fight."

I nearly laughed. The girl looked like she might be able to fit in the pocket of the guy. There was no way this Lyra woman was serious about having them fight. That would be—

Before I could finish my thought, the girl lunged out and kicked her opponent in the leg. The blow dropped him to one knee. She spun like a tornado toward him and smashed her elbow against the side of his face. A burst of scarlet shot from his mouth, and he dropped face down into the dirt. The girl tucked a strand of hair behind her ear and sighed, as if the whole thing had been a minor inconvenience.

"I'm in love," Juno whispered to me.

I like a good fight as much as the next guy, and sure, it was cool to see a girl take down a guy four times her size, but the way she did it left me entirely unsettled. I mean, he could have a broken jaw from that hit he took from her elbow.

The instructor pointed at two other students with octopuses on their shirts. "Take your teammate to the first-aid station." She pointed at the ground a few feet away. "I think that's his tooth. Take it with you." One of the campers pulled their teammate to his unsteady feet, while the other snatched up the tooth and put it in his pocket before grabbing the other side of his comrade and heading out of the clearing.

"Who's next?" the instructor muttered to herself.

I tried to make myself invisible while the other campers straightened and seemed eager with anticipation. Two by two, they were called up to the middle to fight. And they did. I felt like I was watching an underground cage brawl.

"You there." Lyra jabbed her finger at Juno. "Is something funny?"

I glanced at him just in time to see his smirk fall off his face.

"No, ma'am," Juno said.

She snapped her finger and pointed to the center of the circle. Juno's grin flashed again when he pushed himself to his feet, and she noticed. "Overconfidence is dangerous," she said. "There's always someone better."

"Not here there's not," Juno whispered.

She pointed at two other campers—older boys with at least six inches on Juno and probably thirty pounds between them. They jumped to their feet and positioned themselves opposite Juno.

"And if they're not better, they're bigger," Lyra added, "or maybe there's just more of them." A smile flicked at the corner of her mouth. "This will help you learn your limitations."

"I appreciate the lesson, ma'am," Juno said.

Lyra raised her hand and then brought it down in a quick swipe. "Fight."

I am not entirely sure what happened after that. One second the two older boys were charging Juno, and the next they were on their backs, moaning and cursing.

Lyra didn't seem upset. She made a notation on a clipboard that I hadn't noticed until that moment and then ordered a couple other campers to pull the injured out of the circle.

"Well, that was interesting," I whispered when Juno sat down beside me. "Aren't you ninja types supposed to be less cocky? In the movies, you're all reserved and opposed to violence."

He snorted. "My family wouldn't have sent me here if they were opposed to violence."

"I wish I could say the same," I said. "I think my dad expected this place to make me a more upstanding citizen."

"That's unlikely," Juno whispered back.

"Deltas," Lyra called out.

The instructor's words only half registered, and it wasn't until Juno nudged me that I realized Chase was already in the center of the circle, and that he and Lyra were waiting on me. Chase rubbed his hands together and looked like he might start salivating at any second.

I cleared my throat. "Oh, I'm sorry, Ms. Davis." I held up my bandaged hand. "I had an accident in the shooting range and—"

"Archery," she snapped, glancing over her shoulder into the woods.

"Er, right," I said. "Sorry. Anyway, what I meant was, I had an accident in *archery*, and the doctor said to keep my hand injury-free for the next few days."

She tilted her head at me and narrowed her eyes. "Then I suggest you not injure your hand or allow it to be injured." She pointed at the ground beside her. "Get up here, Delta. I won't ask you again."

Juno nudged me and I reluctantly stepped into the circle.

"Let's see how our two Deltas fare, shall we?"

"But, ma'am ..." I held up my hand again.

She stepped toward me until her face was only a few inches from mine. "Do you think you won't be out in the field one day, hurt, and need to protect yourself?" She crossed her arms over her chest and frowned, and when she spoke next, it was as if she were talking to a baby. "Do you really think a widdle owie on your hand is going to stop someone from trying to get you?" She shook her head in apparent disgust at me.

I swallowed. She was right. This was CIA spy camp. I needed to be tougher. I turned to face Chase just as she yelled out, "Fight."

Chase's fist came straight for my face, and purely by instinct, I dropped my chin to my chest. His fist struck me on the top of my head, and I heard a crunch. Here's something you might not have known: the top of your head is actually really hard. It doesn't feel nice to get punched there, but it hurts the person punching a lot worse than it hurts the person getting punched.

Chase recoiled, holding his fist, and I smiled. He swung again, this time with his other hand. I didn't react nearly as fast. His hand hammered against my face, and the entire globe seemed to shift on its axis. I didn't even see him kick me, but my leg suddenly buckled under me, and I dropped to my knee. Images of what the girl had done to the first guy filled my mind, and I brought my arms up on either side of my head. Chase grinned and then lunged out to kick again.

I remember seeing the tread on his shoe and thinking he couldn't possibly be about to kick me in the face.

That's about the time everything went black.

CHAPTER 21

When I woke up, I was staring up at the plump face of Dr. Lester. Again.

"W-what happened?" I stammered.

"Really?" Juno's voice came from over the doctor's shoulder. "You got KO'd by Chase." He tsked and then added, "You broke his finger, though."

"On what, my face?" I asked. "I might have had more of a chance if it wasn't for my hand."

Juno and the doctor gave me looks of disbelief. I sighed. Okay, not even I believed that.

"How long have I been out?"

Juno took a slow breath and shook his head. "Days, man. We have a Delta event tomorrow. It's going to be rough."

I felt my mouth drop and jerked my head toward the doctor.

"Okay, take it easy," Dr. Lester said. "You've been out for about three minutes. He's just messing with you. Now stop moving around." The doctor sponged more blood off my face and pressed on the bridge of my nose with his thumb. "Nothing's broken, but you're going to look like a raccoon for a few days."

I groaned.

"And you've opened the stitches in your hand, so I'll have to redo those, as well." He blew out a breath that smelled like onions and coffee grounds. "When's your next self-defense activity?"

I looked at Juno, and he answered. "We have one tomorrow and then again on Thursday. Before the next Delta event."

Labored breathing filtered through the paper-thin curtain that was pulled around the farthest bed in the row. I imagined the breathing belonged to the guy whose face had been smashed by that ninja chick.

The doctor pursed his lips. "Then I suggest," he said, while he set to work on my hand, "that you spend the next couple of days learning how to fight one-handed."

"Thanks for the advice," I said. Although, learning to fight with one hand was probably something best done *after* learning to fight with two. As if anyone could learn to fight in just a couple days.

"I'll teach you," Juno said. "We'll have to do it in the mornings, but Yaakov already asked me, so you should come too."

"Really?" I asked. "You'd be up for that?"

"Better than having two teammates that get beat up every time things get rough."

I nodded. "Sign me up."

Another camper limped into the room, and the doctor put him on one of the other beds and pulled the curtain around it. He went back and forth among the three of us, and by the time I was done, it was getting close to dinner.

When we rejoined the team, Angie laughed when she saw my hand and face, but Rylee and Amara appeared worried. No one made fun of me, though, not even Angie—well, except for her original snicker. But if I had been in their shoes, there were a dozen things I would've said to make fun of me.

We ran into Chase and his crew along the path to the dining hall.

"I owe you a broken finger," Chase spat out at me as he and his people blocked our way. His middle finger had a metal splint, and he flashed it at me. "And I always pay my debts."

I laughed. "Well, people who lend you money will be grateful to hear that."

Chase took a step toward me, and instantly, the rest of my team stepped up and blocked his advance. Even Yaakov stepped up, though he was a few inches behind the rest of them.

Chase stopped and took a step back, sneering. "What a bunch of rejects." His team laughed behind him. "There's a reason none of you have ever been on a Delta team before. You all suck. And now you get an even bigger loser as your Delta." He laughed again. "Pathetic."

Yaakov cleared his throat. "You know, Chase, I caught a glimpse of the admission scores for this year."

Chase crossed his arms. "So? Big deal. My hacker pulled them up too."

"No, he didn't." Yaakov spoke with such absolute certainty it was clear he knew precisely what had and had not been hacked and by whom. Everyone on the path heard it in his tone, and not even Chase tried to insist otherwise. "If he had," Yaakov continued, "you wouldn't be so smug. Matt's not even the only one who had better scores than you."

Chase laughed. "Him? Yeah, right."

"He does," Yaakov said. "But Miller had better scores than both of you."

Chase's team murmured behind him. He jerked around. "Shut up." They did as they were told. "Miller? And that little twerp?" He pointed at me. "No. Possible. Way."

Yaakov shrugged. "If you had hackers on your team worth anything, they'd have been able to tell you that already."

Chase turned again and glared at his teammates.

One of them shook her head. "He's lying," she said. "He couldn't have hacked the system. It isn't possible."

Yaakov laughed, and so did I.

Chase turned around, drew a slow, deliberate breath, and swung at my head. His fist was deflected by Juno's hand. Time seemed to slow down and stretch out at that moment. Rage flashed in Chase's eyes. My gaze drifted over his shoulder where his teammates were each shifting their weight on to the balls of their feet.

Then time snapped back to regular speed, and I swore as team Squirrel—the entire team—attacked at the exact same time, as if they'd choreographed each movement. Juno moved like a cobra and kept deflecting attacks against me. Angie had one of the Squirrels in a headlock and was feeding him punches, street-fighter style. Yaakov was on his back, getting kicked by the girl who'd insisted hacking the camp was impossible. She gave at least three kicks before Rylee came out of nowhere and tackled her. The two of them rolled off the path, grunting and trading blows.

Amara squared off with two others. He was holding his own, but his opponents landed several strikes. I charged over to help him, only to get decked by the guy I was about to tackle. I stumbled back a couple steps as my vision blurred, but not enough that I didn't spot the dark figure rushing toward me. I clenched my fist and swung.

I connected with a satisfying *whap*, and the figure grunted and then swore. The voice was easy to recognize, and I froze. Behind me, the battle came to an immediate stop, and as my vision returned to normal, I found myself staring up at the expressionless face of Mr. Smith.

I swallowed. "S-sir," I said, "I'm so—"

He held up his hand and straightened. "Fighting?" It was a question he clearly didn't expect us to answer. He snapped his fingers, and Chase moved to my right. Smith's voice became a whisper. "The path around the camp is completely, entirely, and without exception off limits for fighting." His eyes flicked over my shoulder toward the forest and then over his own shoulder as two other counselors jogged over. One of them was Ms. Clakk, and she looked positively murderous. Smith shook his head at them, and they stopped a few feet behind him, their arms crossed. "If any of you violates another rule at this camp," Smith said, "you're history. Got it?"

Grizzlies and Squirrels nodded together.

"Laps," he said finally. "Twenty of them." He pointed to the campers behind me who disentangled themselves from one another. "That goes for every last one of the lot."

"Laps of the, er, field ... sir?" I asked.

He rubbed his hand under his nose, then checked his finger as if he expected blood. I suppose I had hit him pretty hard. But in my defense, I'd thought he was Chase, and I wanted to get at least one solid shot before he had the chance to do anything to me.

Mr. Smith drew a breath, rolled his head, and let it out slowly. "The camp, Mr. Cambridge." He gestured to the path. "If you're going to learn there's no fighting on the path, you should become very, very familiar with every part of it."

He turned and stormed away, and Ms. Clakk stepped up and grabbed me by the arm and hauled me a few paces away from Chase. The other counselor went to Chase, and I figured he must've been Team Squirrel's counselor.

"What are you doing?" Clakk asked. She spoke through clenched teeth, half whispering. "Do you want to get kicked out?"

I shook my head.

"When you mess up, it makes me look bad. I decided to give you some slack, Matt. You did well in the preliminary rankings. You had decent scores from past camps. But if you pull another stunt like this, I'll either hold your hand through each event and make you look incompetent, or I'll just tell the directors you're a lost cause and you and your pathetic group deserve to be cut from the program." She sneered at my teammates and then turned back to me. "If you have any shot at winning, you'd better learn diplomacy. Learn to fight smarter. If someone pisses you off, beat them by making them look bad. Don't risk your future with the Agency by showing you can't follow the simplest rules."

Winning was the furthest thing from my mind. Not getting discovered as an impostor on the other hand ...

Clakk rolled her head and then pointed to the path. "No. Fighting. On. The. Path." She eyed me for a second and added, "Got it?"

"Got it," I said.

She turned to my teammates. "Got it?"

"Yes, ma'am," they answered together.

She clapped her hands. "Get moving. It's getting late."

CHAPTER 22

No one spoke for several laps—not until Yaakov and Angie begged everyone to let them walk a bit. Chase's team had started running while Clakk was ripping a strip off us, and they'd long disappeared into the distance. The whole time we'd been running, I had been cursing myself for my stupidity. Why did I always have to draw attention to myself? Here I was, in a bona fide spy camp, with an opportunity to learn how to shoot guns and fight and ... well, I wasn't sure what else, but other cool stuff, without a doubt—and I go and deck one of the head people here. I cursed myself for not listening to my dad. He told me to fly under the radar, and from the moment I entered this place, I couldn't have been a bigger blip on their screen if I'd been hitting it with a baseball bat.

If they hadn't wondered about my history before, they did now. I bet they were having a big meeting about it. I wondered if I'd make it the full twenty laps before Mr. Smith, or perhaps one of the other counselors, showed up and led me away. Deceiving the CIA had to be one of those crimes that landed you in a prison far away in a country no one's ever heard of where they can torture you without violating any laws.

"I can't believe you punched Mr. Smith in the face," Juno said.

Angie laughed.

"I didn't know it was him," I snapped.

"Whoa," Angie said, still laughing, "take it easy. We got laps, and we'll probably miss dinner. No biggie."

"I'm sure they're just waiting until we're done before they drop the news that they're kicking me out," I said gruffly.

"I thought you didn't care," Amara said. "You didn't seem that concerned about getting kicked out of the program before."

"Yeah, well," I started, "*now* I care."

"Good," Rylee said, "it's about time you took this seriously. If we don't win, we'll want to do well enough to be invited back for the fall session. To be sure of a spot, we have to place in the top three." She stuck out her chin. "But I expect us to win the whole competition."

"Yeah, sure," Angie said. "We have about as much chance of winning overall as Yaakov has of getting a girlfriend."

"You're hilarious," Yaakov said, huffing.

Fall sessions? So these camps weren't just a summer thing? I wondered what you got if you won. I made a mental note to broach that subject carefully the next time an opportunity presented itself.

My stomach grumbled, and I suddenly wanted to get this over with. I'd done track in school, and running wasn't something that bothered me much. Missing meals, on the other hand—that bothered me a great deal. I sighed and started jogging again.

"Oh, c'mon," Yaakov said. "We have to run again? We've barely had time to rest."

I turned around and walked backward. "Don't run if you don't want to," I said. "I couldn't care less."

"Then we don't need to run together?" Juno asked.

"Why the heck would I care?"

Juno flashed a smile. "Anyone wanna race? Maybe we'll catch up to the Squirrels and taunt them a bit."

"Don't," I said. "Please. You heard Clakk. I think she's just looking for an excuse to kick us all out."

"Not so easy to do," Amara said. "No matter what she says."

I eyed him carefully. "What do you mean?"

He shrugged. "My father sent me here to be taught the things he can't teach me. If I were to get kicked out of the program for something like fighting, he'd have an issue with that."

Things he can't teach me. Did that mean Amara's dad was a spy? Is that how this camp worked? Were all these kids related to spies? I rubbed my forehead. That didn't seem right. Maybe Amara was a special case. Like how some kids get accepted to universities just because their parents and grandparents graduated from that university too.

I decided not to push with the questions.

"Well ... good," I managed. "That's good to hear." I nodded at the path. "Now if you'll excuse me, I'd like to get these laps over with." I turned and started jogging again. Everyone kept up for a while, almost a whole lap actually, but then Yaakov dropped back, and Angie did too. Juno decided I was going a bit slower than he liked, and he bolted forward. Amara tried to keep up with him, and when the two of them disappeared around a corner, it looked like he was doing a pretty good job of it.

Then it was just Rylee and me. I knew she was beside me, but neither of us spoke, and I welcomed the silence. The *thump thump thump* of my shoes on the paved pathway relaxed me, and soon I was in a rhythm that forced my mind out of the panic associated with having decked Mr. Smith.

I started wondering about how I'd ended up in this camp. My dad had somehow put my name onto a roster that was supposed to be for a company camp. Did that mean Sledge Industries was a CIA front? Was my dad part of the CIA? Had he known the kind of camp he was sending me to? The more I thought about it, the more I decided that Dad didn't have a clue. He couldn't have. He was legitimately worried that someone would find out what he'd done. He'd dropped me off in an alley and warned me that he could lose his job if I was discovered. He wouldn't have done that if he'd known.

Get it together, Matt. Focus. This is a dream come true. Every kid wants to be a spy. But it's not like any kids really get to become one.

"Hey."

Rylee's voice startled me so much that I jerked my head around and tripped over my feet. I'd been so lost in my thoughts I'd almost forgotten she was beside me.

"Don't do that!" I blew out a breath and tried to find my pace again. Rylee kept up.

Rylee cleared her throat as if to offer a warning she was about to speak. "Do you really not know anything about this camp? One minute you seem oblivious, and the next you seem like you know exactly what's going on." Her breath was labored, and I got the feeling that, if I wanted to, I could pour on the speed a bit and leave her behind. If her questions got too intense, I'd do just that.

"I know what's going on," I said. "It's a training camp. We'll all be very dangerous after we finish here." I couldn't help but smile at that thought. I'd always wanted to be dangerous. I was suddenly very anxious for tomorrow's events.

"It is all about training," Rylee agreed. "But all the camps are about training. I was mostly wondering if, maybe ... it's just that you don't seem to be too concerned about the competitions, or you're not really sure about what's expected of you. Because that would be bad, you know, if you weren't."

"It's all part of our training, Rylee." I tried to sound stern and confident, but I wasn't sure I pulled off either. I increased my speed just a bit, hoping it would convey the message that I didn't want to talk about this anymore, but as I did, I pulled a muscle in my leg and had to drop back to a walk to try to loosen it up. So much for that. Rylee probably thought I wanted to talk now, and she might as well have had me in a headlock. I wasn't going anywhere.

"Why are you being like this?" she asked. "I told you I read people. It's what I'm good at. I know you're hiding something."

"Right, you and your sixth sense," I said mockingly. "I nearly forgot."

My jibe didn't seem to faze her. "I'll figure it out, Matt. Eventually I will. I'll admit that you're tough to read. On the one hand, you come across as a total newbie. But then you pull that gutsy move on the soccer field and put us in the lead in the preliminary challenges."

Gutsy. I liked that.

"Of course, the very next day you go and mess up something as simple as holding a gun properly and get an injury I wouldn't expect an eight-year-old to get."

"I was distracted," I said, practically shouting.

She shrugged. "I don't really care if you're trying to quell expectations, Matt. Maybe it's a strategy that has worked for you in the past, and maybe it'll work here. I just don't get why you're not being up-front about it to the rest of us. At the very least, I don't get why you're not just admitting it to me. Where were your other camps? What did they do there? Why haven't I ever heard of you?"

"You ask a lot of questions, Rylee."

"I'm just trying to help, Matt."

"Well, I don't remember asking for help."

I tried to jog again, but my leg tightened. I swore under my breath and walked, trying to stretch the muscle a bit as I moved.

"It's just ... this is our shot," she said. "We really can win this thing. We can be free of these stupid camps and get real missions." She sighed. "I just want to know that you want this as badly as the rest of us."

So that was it, then. Finally some information I could use. If we won the camp competitions, we'd be full-fledged CIA. We'd get real missions. I could actually call myself a spy.

Easy, Matt. Don't let her see you excited.

"Rest assured, Rylee, I want to win way more than any of you guys want to win." That had to be true. If I could pull off a win before Smith or Dalson figured out I wasn't supposed to be here, I'd probably be able to convince them to let me be a real CIA operative. At the very least, maybe they'd let me come to other camps to get more training. Maybe they'd even let me bring Jason.

Okay, that might be pushing it.

"Good," she said, "that's all I wanted to know. That's what I needed to hear. I know you think our team sucks, but—"

"I don't think that," I said quickly. "Have you seen Juno fight? It's insane. And Yaakov, that kid clearly knows his way around a computer better than anyone else. Amara recognized the bombs I'd nearly been killed by on the soccer field just by looking at my injuries and sniffing my shirt." I wiped sweat from my forehead and added, "I'm not sure about Angie. She's clearly nuts, but I'm not sure how that helps."

"It'll help," Rylee said.

"If you say so." The muscle in my leg finally felt all right, and we started jogging again. "You put this team together, Rylee, so I know you know what you're talking about. I value your opinion." She smiled. Flattery seemed to have some effect on her. I decided to try humor again. "Plus, there is that supernatural sixth sense of yours. Never know when that'll come in handy."

Her smile widened. "That's true. Plus, I can read palms and tea leaves."

"Awesome," I said. "We'll have some tea when we're done with our little jog, and you can tell me how sore I'll be in the morning."

"This is a better side of you, Matt. You seem *real* right now. I like you better when you're unguarded."

"And I like you better when you're not doing so much prying," I countered.

She smiled. "Point taken. I'll ease up. And I'll be sure to tell the rest of the team that you're going for the win this session."

"Do that," I said.

We settled into a good pace after that, and before long, I felt the comfortable rhythm of the jog. I'll admit, also, that once Rylee stopped hassling me for answers, and we were just running beside each other, it was kind of nice.

CHAPTER 23

It was nearly eight o'clock when Rylee and I finished our last lap. We both grabbed fresh clothes from the cabin, ignored the jeers from Juno about how slow we'd been, and headed to the showers. I don't know how long I was in there. My muscles started aching as soon as I stopped walking, and I wanted to let the hot water loosen me up. When I finally came out, it was really dark, and I ran straight into Alexis, Duncan, and Rob.

"Jeez, guys," I said to the young campers, "do you just hover around showers, waiting for me to come out? You can come to the cabin, you know."

Alexis and Duncan remained stone-faced and kept their eyes trained on the area around us. Rob, on the other hand, smiled, thrust his hand out, and pressed something against my chest.

The phone was black, with a large screen. Not as nice as the one Jason had given me, but still sleek and modern. I dropped my voice to a whisper. "Is this—?"

Rob nodded. "It's Chase's. We got it while he was running laps."

Alexis pointed at the phone. "I hope that shows how serious we are."

I laughed and shoved it into my pocket. "I can't believe you got his cell phone." It was the tiniest of victories, and I knew that, but for some reason, it felt like something more. I sighed. Having a working phone also meant I could call Jason and tell him what was going on. Maybe he could swing by my place and see if he could get some information out of my dad. "This is really great, guys. Well done."

I turned to leave but stopped when Rob grabbed my arm. I spun back around.

"Sir," he said, "I mean, Matt. We did like you asked, right?"

I nodded. "You did."

We stared at each other for several awkward seconds.

"We just want to know if you're going to use us for real stuff now," Alexis whispered. "Did we pass your test? Can we be used for actual events?"

I nodded. "Yeah, sure." I scratched the back of my head. "How about you go and find out what the first team event is going to be?"

"Um, sir," Alexis began, "it's a paintball version of Capture the Flag, sir. It's always Capture the Flag."

"Right, sorry," I said. "Of course it is." That actually put my mind at ease a bit. I used to play Capture the Flag with my friends. "And we're having the first team event pretty soon, right? I mean it's just ... um ..."

"At the end of the week," Rob said. He spoke slowly like he wasn't sure if he was saying what I wanted to hear. "They're all at the end of the week. Three-week camp, three events. So, you'll use us this Friday?'

"You bet," I said.

Rob and Alexis nodded to each other. If I hadn't been there, I bet they'd be tossing up high fives.

"Anything you need," Rob began, "just let us—"

Duncan held up his hand, cutting Rob's words short. Voices drew nearer from down the path, and a moment later, Angie and Yaakov came into view. I turned back to Rob and his teammates, but they were gone.

I'm really not going to get used to all this cloak-and-dagger stuff, I thought as I shoved my new phone into my pocket.

"Hey, Captain," Angie said as they neared me. She sounded remarkably happy, considering she'd just walked a dozen miles. Yaakov, on the other hand, ambled along with a limp and grunted with each step.

"I have a blister the size of a fist," Yaakov said.

I winced. "Gross."

Angie asked, "Why are you just standing outside the showers?"

I sighed. "I was talking to some campers from our team. They want me to include them in the challenge this week."

Angie cringed. "Really? They *want* to be used? How?"

"I don't know," I said. "I told them I'd think of something."

"They can have my spot," Yaakov said. "I'm not going to be running through the woods with a foot like this."

"You're such a wimp, wire-head." Angie gave him a shove, and he stumbled against the door to the guys' shower. "We're all tired and hungry." She suddenly smiled. "But you can't say that fight wasn't fun." She looked off, I assume into the memory of her pounding on that Team Squirrel kid. "We should do that again sometime."

"Yeah," I muttered, "I'll be sure to schedule it for next week." I glanced at Yaakov, and he gave me a pained *please don't* look.

Angie's smile widened as she headed to the girls' shower. Yaakov blew out a breath and shook his head, and then he pushed through the doors to the showers, and once again, I was alone. The only silver lining to all this was that none of the counselors had come to get me. Maybe in the world of the CIA, hitting a camp counselor wasn't really that bad.

Yeah, right.

Despite my exhaustion, the closer I got to the cabin, the more I wanted to use the phone and call Jason. He'd go nuts when I told him what was going on. I waited until the coast was clear and then ducked into the woods about a hundred yards from my Delta cabin. I crept through the blackness until I was sure my voice wouldn't carry far enough for anyone to overhear me.

Jason picked up on the fourth ring.

"Yeah?"

"Jason, it's me."

"Cambridge? Are you back? Whose number is this?"

"I'm not back," I whispered. "I'm still at camp."

"Too bad, bro," Jason said. "Daren and Mark and I are headed to the quarry tomorrow to shoot off some fireworks. You're missing out."

"Don't tell me you're still buying stuff from that guy who sold us the smoke for the talent show."

"Um, okay, I won't tell you that if you don't want me to," Jason said with a laugh.

"I can't believe you'd still deal with him," I said.

Jason laughed again. "I still deal with him *because* of that crazy smoke stuff. I mean that stuff worked better than advertised. It worked like a freaking charm."

I blew out a frustrated breath. At least Jason was consistent. "Listen," I said. "This camp is not what I thought it would be."

"Oh, no!" Jason said. "They got to you, didn't they? You actually like it there, don't you? They've turned you into one of those leather-belt-making camp losers, haven't they? Resist the programming, Matt. Resist it!"

"Jason!" I said his name louder than I'd intended, and I knew my voice had carried. I lowered my voice to a whisper and crouched a bit lower, even though I was pretty sure someone could be a few yards away and not spot me. "Shut up. Listen, man, this isn't a joke."

"You sound serious," Jason said.

"I am," I whispered. "You're not going to believe this, but ..." I told Jason all about camp and the campers. I told him about the shooting range and the martial arts. I told him about being a Delta and what that seemed to mean. I even told him about Chase, though I decided not to mention the fact that he'd beaten me up twice. Jason argued at first, called me a liar, and said I was crazy to think he'd believe all that. But eventually he must've heard something in my voice—panic, probably—because he started to believe me.

"Dude," he started after a lengthy pause, "if you're making this stuff up, I'm going to be choked."

"C'mon, man. I told you I'm not. Somehow my dad got me into a CIA training camp for kids, bro. It's crazy."

There was another pause, and then Jason said, "You lucky dog!"

I smiled in spite of myself. I knew he'd be jealous, and hearing that did make me feel better about being there.

"You can't get kicked out, man. Learn everything and then get back here and teach me. Or, if you can recommend someone else for the camp, give them my name! Wait, do you think my dad could pull some strings and get me in there?"

"Don't even try!" I said. "It would be cool to have you in here, man, but if your dad starts asking questions about getting you into the camp, they're going to realize our connection, and then the spotlight's going to be even more on me."

"You're right." Jason took a deep breath and let it out in a single burst. "So what do you need, Matt?"

"I'm totally lost here," I said. "Everyone knows what's going on, and I don't have a clue. I need you to find out as much about this place as you can. There has to be some information out there. Just be smart about it. Okay?"

Trees rustled behind me, and I heard a *snap*. "Someone's coming," I whispered, then quickly ended the call and shoved the phone back in my pocket so that the illuminated screen wouldn't give me away. I flattened myself against the dirt and held my breath.

More rustling, this time on my right. It was probably just a raccoon or something. It would be crazy if the camp had people trolling the woods, searching for stray campers, but then another thought suddenly rolled through my head. The doctor had said there were people out in the woods. People who wanted to get their hands on the kids in this camp. I shook my head.

C'mon, Matt, keep it together. Juno said it was just an urban legend.

Several long seconds passed while my pulse pounded in my neck. Then I heard another *snap*, this time from my left, and it sounded very close. The doctor's urban legend took hold of my mind with an iron grip. He was older and smarter than Juno. He'd been trying to warn me, not scare me. In my head, I swore a dozen times.

I told myself it was dark, and if I could move fast enough, they'd never see my face. I forced my brain to stop freaking out and counted.

One. I carefully moved back into a crouched position, keeping low, and shifting my weight onto the balls of my feet.

Two. I took a breath, held it, and peered through the darkness, mapping, as best I could, my way out.

Three! Trees rustled behind me, and I imagined the sound to be a blast from a starter's pistol.

I charged forward, ducking under branches and leaping over logs. When I burst out of the woods, I ran in the opposite direction from my cabin. If they spotted me, whoever *they* were, I didn't want them to see me run toward Team Grizzly's Delta cabin. Instead, I sprinted back to the parking lot, crisscrossed very carefully through at least three other sections—but not Team Squirrel's section; I wasn't interested in another fight—and then ducked behind a cabin close to the perimeter walkway. I waited there for a solid minute before I drew a breath and forced my pulse to slow to a regular beat. Then I stepped casually out of the shadows, strolled to the main path, and headed back to my cabin. When I passed the archery range, something stepped out of the woods. I froze and stared into the shadows. It took me a moment to realize what I was seeing, but when I did, I laughed.

A deer. It was just wandering between the targets, munching on some of the longer grassy areas, without a care in the world. "It was a deer, you idiot," I said to myself. "Stop being so freaking jumpy."

By the time I got back to the cabin, exhaustion had a pretty good hold of me. I ignored the comments and questions from my teammates about what had taken me so long. I just collapsed face first onto my bed and fell instantly to sleep.

CHAPTER 24

"Wake up."

I groaned and rolled onto my back.

"C'mon," Juno said, shaking me again, "let's go."

"W-what?" I propped myself up on an elbow. The cabin was still mostly dark, except for some dull light seeping in through the partially opened windows. I spotted Amara, Rylee, and Angie still sleeping. Yaakov sat on the edge of his bed, tying the laces of his shoes. I fell back and groaned again. "Go where?"

Juno held up his fists and jabbed out a couple punches, then gestured to the door again.

I'd totally forgotten he'd offered to teach me how to fight. I sucked in a lungful of air and swung my legs over the bed. That's when I realized just how sore I was. My legs felt like they'd been trampled by sumo wrestlers riding elephants. I sat there for a minute while he rolled his eyes at me and tapped his wrist. I shifted my weight, pushed myself to my feet, and sighed, relieved I'd had the good sense to fall asleep wearing jeans. There was no way I would've been able to get a pair of pants on otherwise. I slipped into my shoes and headed, mostly stumbling, outside.

"How are you guys walking?" I asked when I'd caught up a dozen yards from the cabin. "My legs feel like they're going to fall off."

"Just my feet hurt," Yaakov said. "My legs don't."

A bandage poked up from the back of his shoe, which must've helped since he wasn't limping half as badly as he had been the previous night.

Juno led us into the woods behind the cabin. We clambered over fallen trees and pushed through patches of thick undergrowth; fortunately, the little walk helped loosen the muscles in my legs somewhat. We finally stepped out into a small clearing about the size of my bedroom back home.

Juno looked around and nodded. "This'll work."

"Here?" Yaakov asked. "This is where you're teaching us?" He kicked at roots that jutted up through the earth and then wandered around the perimeter, seemingly disappointed.

"Where did you think I was going to teach you?" Juno asked. "Out in the open?" He pointed back the way we'd come. "We can go back if you want. Maybe practice in Team Squirrel's section of the camp. At least you'd get lots of experience in getting your face punched."

I winced and turned to Yaakov, who was now just a couple feet to my right.

"Yeah," Juno said, "that's what I thought." He drew in a breath, let it out slowly, and then strolled up until he was right in front of me and Yaakov. Then he lunged out and slapped us both in the faces. Hard.

"Hey!" My face stung, and it had happened so fast I wasn't even sure which of us had been hit first. I rubbed my cheek. "What was that for?"

"If you're fighting someone," Juno began, "you're not going to block anything if you don't have your hands up. So that's lesson one."

He stepped up again and swung at my face. This time I raised my hand, and he hit my arm. Yaakov gave a frightened yelp and stepped back when Juno went for him next. He avoided the smack but tripped over a root and landed with a thud.

"Keep your hands up," Juno said, "but keep your eyes open too. Look around. Falling down during a fight isn't going to do you any favors." He tapped his chin. "We can call that lesson two."

Yaakov groaned as he pushed himself to his feet and cursed. "I didn't come all the way out here just to be—"

Slap!

Yaakov staggered to the side, his hand pressed against his reddening cheek. I laughed.

Slap!

I stumbled back, clutching my face.

Juno's strikes happened so quickly I could hardly track them, and they were starting to feel a lot like punches. He tilted his head and raised his arms again. My hands shot up to protect my head, and Yaakov did the same.

"Better," Juno said.

Yaakov rubbed the side of his face and whimpered.

"When are you gonna teach us how to hit back?" I asked.

Juno raised an eyebrow and looked both of us up and down. "I've seen you both fight. Let's focus on blocking for now."

For over an hour we did nothing but block Juno's punches. He showed us inside blocks and outside blocks. He showed us high blocks and low blocks. But most of the time, our blocks were as simple as putting our hands up to cover our faces. I tried to count how many times he slapped us and gave up when I got to forty-seven.

When our lesson ended, I had a bloody lip, and Yaakov had the start of a black eye. My face was so numb a dentist could have probably done a root canal and I wouldn't have felt anything. The only plus was I felt a bit more confident about my ability to block a punch, and all the ducking and dodging had really loosened me up, so my legs weren't sore at all anymore.

We got breakfast, and I checked my schedule. I couldn't help but laugh.

Arts and Crafts.

CHAPTER 25

Arts and Crafts was in the main building near the parking lot. I entered and made my way toward the room hesitantly. If I'd learned anything from "Archery" and "Basic Self-Defense," it was that "Arts and Crafts" was going to be anything but artsy and craftsy.

I turned the handle and stepped inside. Campers sat across from each other along rectangular tables, chattering away while they made leather key chains and bookmarks. They had stampers that pressed shapes into the leather and little tools to cut designs. I smiled, instantly reminded of how Jason had called me a belt-making camp loser. Here I was looking at a room full of them.

Alexander Bratersky shoved past, glaring at me over his shoulder as he walked across the room. A second later Becca Plain did the same. She was on crutches now, which I guess was better than a wheelchair, though she still looked like she'd been attacked by a pack of hyenas— which would have been pretty ironic. Delta for Team Hyena attacked by a pack of hyenas. I nearly smiled at that thought. Nearly.

"What are you looking at?" she snapped.

"Nothing," I said, drawing back a step. "Just glad to see you're healing."

"Sure you are," she said with a sneer. "Make one more comment like that, and I'll beat you with this." She held up her crutch.

I felt my eyes widen. "You'll beat me for saying I'm glad you're healing?"

Her eyes became slits. "Yeah. I will." She turned back and crutched her way across the room and through a door at the far side. While I stood there wondering who was crazier, Becca or Angie, a dozen other campers trickled past me and disappeared through the same door. *Becca*, I thought as I crossed the room; *Becca's clearly the craziest.*

The door led to a small staircase that descended into a cool basement with exposed pipes and a concrete floor. On one of the conduits I spotted a careful etching of the letters *PCIA*, and it made me smile. It felt like a reminder about what we were doing here, and I wondered if that had been the reason campers did it in the first place.

I followed the other campers down a corridor that probably stretched the length of the main building, then up a set of stairs, and then through another door. When I stepped through, I was looking at basically the same room as before, only the campers sitting across from each other in this room appeared deadly serious, and the woman at the front of the room stuck me with an evil stare that felt like a warning to sit down.

I plunked myself into the first free seat I spotted, and only realized after the fact that I was sitting across from Becca. I cursed, and she glared at me like she was trying to develop heat-vision to cook the skin off my face. Before I could change tables, the counselor marched over to the door and set the lock.

"Getting out of a tough situation can be as simple as having the right identity," the woman said. "Today the focus is on creating authentic birth certificates."

"What?" I said under my breath.

The counselor glared at me and then continued, indicating the list on the blackboard behind her. "Gather your supplies, and let's get started."

* * *

Three hours later, I was officially a fourteen-year-old Swedish boy named Gunnar Konstantan. At least, that's what my birth certificate said. I smiled at the document. I wasn't entirely sure if I'd ever have a need to pretend to be Swedish, but the possibility of missions that might require it was intoxicating. I imagined being on some super-secret spy assignment in Europe and the only way I could get out of a country was to convince officials I was from Sweden. It was right out of a movie, and here I was getting trained.

"That's it," the counselor said. "Shred the documents before you leave."

I clutched the certificate to my chest. Shred it?

As the campers got up and headed for the industrial shredder at the end of the room, Becca leaned across the table and grabbed my wrist.

"If you sit at this table or anywhere near me ever again—"

"Yeah, yeah, you'll beat me with your crutches," I said, twisting my hand out of her grip. "Cool." I pushed myself up and added, "Can't wait."

I gathered up the scraps from my work and headed across the room, leaving Becca muttering curses and hurling imaginary ice picks at me through her eyes. It felt good to stand toe-to-toe with another Delta, even if that other Delta was a crippled little girl who couldn't really stand right now. It made me feel like I belonged at the camp.

While I waited in line for the shredder, I carefully folded the birth certificate and stuffed it in my pocket. I wasn't going to shred my first attempt at a fake ID. Next lesson, if I did better, I'd shred the old one, but until then, I was keeping it. Jason would totally be jealous when he saw it, and maybe by the end of the summer I'd have a full set of fake IDs for Gunnar Konstantan. I wasn't sure what I'd do with it yet. But having an alter ego sounded fun.

* * *

Archery was after lunch, but after nearly having sliced my thumb off in the previous lesson, I didn't hold much hope that Range Master Fargas would welcome me back.

I was right.

"Cambridge!" Fargas barked as the other campers collected their weapons. The man stalked forward and stopped just a few paces away and glared down at me.

"Sir?"

"Got a surprise for you, Cambridge," Fargas continued. The other campers hesitated on their way to the range and faced me. "Do you like surprises?"

"Um, I suppose, sir." I had a feeling I wasn't going to like this one.

He reached behind his back and pulled out a water gun. It was pink and had yellow daisies painted on the grip. The campers burst out laughing. Even Juno didn't hold back. I guess I would've laughed too if it hadn't been me getting the gun.

"This is your new weapon, son." He shot a blast of water that hit me in the side of the face and then thrust the plastic weapon toward me. "You'll be using this until I see that you know proper holding and handling techniques." He indicated the door to the shooting range. "Get going."

I made it a few steps before Fargas called after me, "And remember, Cambridge, it's loaded."

It probably wouldn't have been so bad except the rest of the campers in the shooting range kept calling me *Squirt*—a nickname I'm pretty sure Juno started.

I was learning, I told myself. And if being a spy meant getting teased for a few weeks, I could take it. As dorky as I felt holding a water gun designed for three-year-old girls, I did exactly as Fargas told me, and by the end of the lesson, after being yelled at only a half dozen times, Fargas seemed to notice.

"Not bad, Cambridge," he said. "That's the proper way to hold a gun. Next lesson, maybe I'll bring you one of those guns that shoots marshmallows."

Goody.

* * *

That evening I went for another "walk" and, as soon as it was dark enough, ducked into the woods near the archery range. I found the same spot I'd used before and quickly dialed Jason's number.

"Dude," Jason said, "you don't tell a guy that 'someone's coming' and then hang up and not call back for a full twenty-four hours. I thought you were dead, bro."

"Sorry," I said, recalling how I'd ended the last conversation I had with Jason. "It was a deer."

"What was?"

"The person I thought was coming. Last night when I hung up on you."

"The deer was a person? What are you talking about, Cambridge?" I groaned. "It doesn't matter. What did you find out?"

"Nothing, man. I even went to see your dad and asked him if I could see the brochure on the camp. I told him my dad was thinking of sending me there next year. He told me he didn't have one, and that it probably wasn't the best fit for me anyway." He laughed. "I don't think your dad likes me very much."

"Well, you *are* a terrible influence."

"That's true," Jason said, "but listen, I have another idea. A CIA camp isn't going to advertise itself. But there might be some information on the people running it. That might be helpful for you, right?"

"Yeah," I said. "Of course it would."

"Thought so," Jason said. "So I was thinking, you know how there's that program online where you click on a picture and it finds the same face anywhere else online?"

"Um, I remember you showing that to me last summer. But I also remember that you tried to find pictures of yourself and ended up getting a dozen pictures of Harry Styles back."

"Can I help it if I'm a heartthrob?" Jason laughed and then stopped abruptly. "Seriously, though, it's gotten a lot better."

"So you want me to ... what?"

"Send me pictures," Jason said. "Send me pictures of the leaders, of the campers, of anyone you can get a picture of, and I'll check it out on the web. Maybe I'll find something."

"Yeah, right." I said, "I'm not supposed to have a phone at all. If I start walking around snapping pictures, someone's probably going to notice, and I'll just get kicked out."

"So do it at night or something. If you want me to figure anything out, we need to start somewhere."

"I'll think about it."

Jason asked a dozen other questions about the camp and laughed at me for almost slicing my finger off. "Who doesn't know how to hold a gun?" he'd asked, as if he knew exactly how to hold and shoot one. I could hear the jealousy in his voice though, so I didn't bother calling him on that comment. When I hung up, I sat down on a log and just listened to the forest. With the exception of the wind whipping through a few of the branches, there wasn't a single noise.

As much as I'd love to see what Jason could dig up about some of my fellow campers, I didn't want to risk getting kicked out.

A bit longer, I decided. I'd just keep going the way I was going and see if I could figure it out on my own. That, or figure out another way to get Jason some images.

CHAPTER 26

Between self-defense, making fake IDs, and the shooting range (where I had worked my way up to a BB gun), the days came and went at a crazy pace. I didn't realize it was Friday until I woke up to Juno talking about how fun it was going to be to destroy everyone in Capture the Flag.

"That's today?" I asked.

"As if you could forget," Juno said.

I rubbed my eyes. "Of course not."

"You better not have forgotten," Rylee piped up. "We need to go over strategy."

"Strategy ... right. Um, yeah ..."

"I have some thoughts, if you want," Rylee said. She turned to Yaakov. "Can you get an image of where we're playing?"

Yaakov tsked. "Of course." His fingers blurred across his keyboard.

"Have you done this before?" I asked. "Played Capture the Flag at one of these camps, I mean."

"I have," Amara said.

"So have I," Rylee added.

Yaakov shook his head. "Never at one of the camps. If you're not on the Delta team, it's all about luck to get picked up as an extra."

"Do you have anyone in mind for the extras?" Juno asked. "Because I've seen a couple kids on our team who look like they can probably handle themselves."

158

I remembered Rob, Alexis, and Duncan. I owed them for nabbing Chase's phone for me. Besides, the way they always snuck up on me and disappeared whenever anyone wandered by probably meant they were pretty good at sneaking around. "I have an idea for three of them," I said. "How many extras do we get?"

The door to the cabin swung open and Counselor Clakk entered. She hadn't bothered with us much since we'd fought Chase's team on the path, except once or twice when she warned me to stay clear of Mr. Smith. I got the impression she had gone to bat for us, to make it so that one incident didn't result in any expulsions. Occasionally, during meals mostly, she'd catch my gaze and toss out a warning look, but for the most part, she hadn't been around. That was probably the reason most of us jumped when she marched in.

"You'll get an additional twenty teammates." She spoke as if she'd been part of the conversation from the start, and I immediately wondered if the room was bugged or if she'd been lurking outside listening in to the conversation through the door. Either way, I made a mental note to be careful about what I said from then on and to ask Yaakov to do another search of the room for listening devices.

Ms. Clakk strolled around the room, looking at each of us with an expectant expression. "Well?" Her gaze locked on me like a missile. "What's the plan? Have you worked out a strategy?"

Sure, I wanted to say, we get the flags off everyone else before they get ours. But being snarky would probably get me in trouble, and besides, there was something about Ms. Clakk that made me squirm.

I cleared my throat. "We were just finalizing that." I looked around the room, pleased to see the rest of the team nodding. If nothing else, the CIA picked kids who are excellent liars.

Ms. Clakk folded her arms across her chest. "Do I need to remind you that the events at this camp are elimination events?"

"No, ma'am," I said, even though I had no idea what she was talking about.

"Good." She drew in a breath and let it out slowly. "Listen, I know this isn't a camp for novices. In the incredibly unlikely event that you make it to the end and win, you will actually be in the field doing *real* missions." She shook her head and muttered, "Lord help us." She blew out a quick breath and continued. "Because of that, I'm not interested in holding your hands. You can either do it, or you can't. Though I have to admit, after that scene on the path a few days ago, I have reservations about your judgment." She slowly swept her gaze over each of us. "All of your judgments."

"We're taking it seriously," I said. "We want to win."

"We *plan* to win," Rylee added.

"I'll be sure to hold my breath," Ms. Clakk said, rolling her eyes. "More to the point, I want to stress the importance of being *aware* during the Delta events. Things are not always as they seem." She pointed at me. "Obviously, as you experienced, there was more to the soccer ball challenge than just kicking it into a net. You'd be wise to remember that." She did an about-face and paced across the cabin, only to turn again and pace back. "But Capture the Flag is pretty straightforward: go get the other team's flag, bring it back to your base, and protect your flag at all costs." She pursed her lips and raised an eyebrow. "You know that, right?"

I wanted to say, "Capture the Flag? Isn't that the game with horseshoes?" Did she think I was a complete moron? Every kid over the age of eight was familiar with Capture the Flag.

"Yes, ma'am," I said instead. "I do."

She nodded. "Good. Just pick your team carefully." She looked at her watch and tapped the digital face. "Noon," she said. "Have your team gathered at the soccer field at noon. Understood?"

I nodded. Without another word, Ms. Clakk marched out of the cabin and disappeared down the path.

"She hates us," I said. "And she must think we're a bunch of idiots."

"She's just trying to prepare us," Rylee said.

"I agree," Amara added. "It's like she said, if we can't handle a couple of simple competitions, we're just not ready for real missions."

"No," Angie said, "I think there's more to it than that. I think she genuinely hates Matt. But I'm pretty sure she likes me."

"Well, who wouldn't?" Juno said in a matter-of-fact tone. "You're incredibly friendly. You and Clakk are like kindred spirits."

"Careful," Angie said. "I don't like sarcastic people, and I haven't stabbed anyone in a really long time."

I glanced at Rylee. She mouthed the word "psychopath" and rolled her eyes.

"See what I mean?" Juno said, glancing around at the rest of us. "You can't buy that kind of friendship."

"All right," I said, "no one's stabbing anyone today. At least not anyone on our own team." I thought it was obvious I wasn't being serious, but saw Angie give a resigned nod, as if I might have just given her the okay to stab someone on another team, so I added, "Let's just not stab anyone at all. Got it?"

She plopped down on her bed and folded her arms.

"Okay, I'm open to suggestions. Who has an idea for strategy for today's event?"

Rylee stepped up. "I do."

"Of course you do," Angie muttered.

Rylee ignored her and began to lay out her plan. It was like listening to a football coach explain the most complicated play in history. There was lots of talk about flanking and something about a hammer and anvil.

When she was done, I shook my head. "I don't think so, Rylee."

Her face sank. "It'll work, Matt. I know it will."

"Don't you think it's a little too complicated?" Amara asked.

"I don't think it's complicated at all," Rylee grumbled.

"I do," Angie said. "Can't we just rush in and take the flag and rush out?"

"Oh, that'll be smart," Juno said, sarcastically. He turned to me. "If we go in without a plan, we're screwed. They'll pick us off like college students near a bell tower."

Amara offered a suggestion that Juno insisted was suicide. Then Rylee tried to re-suggest her plan with some modifications, only to be shot down by Angie, who called it "stupid" rather than complicated. In seconds, the cabin had erupted into a frenzy, and every one of my teammates was shouting and looked ready to start swinging. Even Yaakov, who I didn't think would be interested in this kind of thing at all, was making wild hand gestures and shouting along with everyone else.

While they fought I thought about what an idiot I was going to look like. When I played Capture the Flag back home, it was way less intense. For one thing, we didn't do it with paintball guns, and for another, we mostly used the strategy Angie had suggested: rush in, steal the flag, and rush back before the other team made it back to their base. There was only one thing that would come from me directing my teammates during this challenge: I'd show everyone how much of an amateur I really was.

"Enough!" I hollered. "What is wrong with you guys? It's just a game of Capture the Flag."

Rylee humphed. "Yeah, it's an *elimination* game." She said the word like it was a curse. "So pardon me for wanting to make sure we don't do something stupid and come in last."

"We wouldn't have had a shot with your plan," Angie said.

Rylee spun around, her finger pointed and her face twisted into an angry sneer.

"Stop!" I said before she could speak. "Just stop." I shook my head. "You guys are nuts. Now listen, I have a plan." Which probably surprised them as much as it had surprised me moments before when I'd come up with it. "I've been thinking about it for days," I lied.

"You have?" Rylee asked. "A minute ago I thought you were confused about what Capture the Flag was."

I dismissed Rylee with a wave of my hand. "Ms. Clakk said we get to add twenty campers to our team, right?" My teammates nodded. "So here's what I suggest. Rylee, you are going to work with Juno and Yaakov. Make a plan; implement it. You get to pick seven other campers to join your team." I turned, not giving Rylee a chance to interject. "Amara, you and Angie are a team. You guys also get to pick seven campers."

"And you?" Rylee asked. "What'll you be doing?"

"I'll choose the remaining six, who will stay back and guard the flag while I go out on my own and try to kill as many of the other players as I can." Or, in other words, I'd find a really cool hiding place and only shoot people when I was sure I could hit them.

"Oh, brother," Angie said, "are you seriously trying to be one of those stupid lone-wolf Deltas who thinks they're hot stuff? Because if you are, it would be a lot more convincing if you didn't have two black eyes and a bandaged hand."

"That's true," Amara added. "It's hard to really trust in your abilities when I'm pretty sure the only fight you won was against that girl you bashed with your shoe."

"Argh," I said, "why do people keep bringing her up? It was an accident."

"And speaking of bandaged hand," Angie added, "what is it they call you in archery again?"

"Squirt," Juno said, laughing.

The others joined in.

"Yeah, yeah," I said, "hilarious. I won't have a squirt gun today, now, will I?"

Angie tsked. "Twenty bucks says Captain Squirt gets shot in the first fifteen minutes."

"I'll take that bet," Juno said.

Really? I wouldn't have taken it if I were Juno. It did feel nice that someone believed in me, though. I smiled. "Thank you, Juno."

"Don't mention it." He shook hands with Angie, sealing the bet, and added, "I think he'll make it twenty minutes. But just barely."

CHAPTER 27

We met at the soccer field just before noon and geared up. I had to admit that, dressed in camouflage and holding paintball guns, we looked intimidating. I felt like a commando. The other teams were grouped along the sidelines. They looked pretty intimidating, as well. Most of them, anyway. Team Hyena still looked a bit weak, what with their captain on crutches. It was a bit difficult to be frightened by someone who couldn't walk. But I had to give her points for being tough about it. Most girls at my school would've left in tears if they'd been confronted by a mosquito, let alone a land mine.

Our extra campers were also there dressed in camouflage and already divided up into groups. Rob, Alexis, and Duncan were front and center. They had been thrilled when I approached them and said they'd be guarding the flag.

"We won't let you down," Rob said. "No one will get the flag."

Alexis placed her small fist into her other palm and grinned. "Yeah, if anyone gets near our flag, we'll crush their faces into the dirt and stomp 'em."

I laughed, and then stopped when I noticed that none of them were laughing. "You *are* joking, right?"

The trio looked at one another like they hadn't understood what I said. I was about to remind them that I didn't want them to do anything crazy. We were just supposed to protect the flag. If they ended up crushing some poor camper's face into the dirt, it would be because things went very wrong. But before I could speak, Mr. Dalson stood on the raised platform and addressed the teams.

"Welcome to the first group Delta event." He wore khaki pants and a polo shirt and looked like he was ready to go to a church picnic—just as soon as he sent us paintballing kid spies out to the woods to blast one another. "You've been given the rules," he continued, "so let's not waste time. When you get to your bases, you'll wait until you hear this horn." He held up a can that looked like it might hold spray cheese and pressed the top, splitting the air with a blast that sounded like a ship's horn. "At that time," Mr. Dalson continued, "you can begin. Understood?"

The kids in each group nodded.

He pointed across the field into the woods. "Off you go, then."

Our base was a circular clearing about the size of a classroom. In the center was a chest-high wooden pole bearing a flag embroidered with a grizzly bear.

"Cambridge," Juno said, "give me your gun."

"Why?"

"Just hand it over." Juno smiled as he took it and dropped to his knees. He pulled out a small knife, opened up one of the side panels, and started messing with it.

"What are you doing?"

Rylee and Amara leaned over him and nodded.

"You're making it automatic," Amara said. "Resourceful."

"Pleased to have your stamp of approval," Juno said. He took out a piece of the gun, reassembled it, and then handed it back to me. "You'll use more paint, and you might go through your Co2 pretty fast, but one squeeze will fire half a dozen balls."

"Thanks," I said, though I wasn't sure an automatic paint gun was really what I needed.

Rylee grabbed a stick from the ground and called everyone over. "Yak and I looked up the locations of the other bases on satellite this morning." I wished I'd thought of that. She drew a circle in the dirt. "This is us," she said. She drew four other circles, one by one, glancing over her shoulder into the trees, presumably to get her bearings before each one. "Octopus," she said, pointing at the one farthest away, "and this is Squirrel ... and Hyena ... and this is Arctic Fox." She looked at me. "Which flag do you think we should go for first?"

I shrugged. "The plan was for you to come up with your own plans. Go for whichever flag you want."

Rylee tsked at me. "You're really just going to leave us to it while you go commando through the woods?"

Juno burst out laughing. "Go commando?" He laughed again, and I couldn't help but laugh as well.

Angie wrinkled her nose. "Our captain goes commando? That's gross and TMI."

"Ha ha," Rylee said, without a hint of humor. "You know what I meant." She glanced down at the circles she'd drawn in the dirt. "We're going for Squirrel."

"We're going for Arctic Fox," Amara said.

Rylee winced. "Can you go for Octopus instead?"

"Why?" Amara asked.

Rylee huffed. "I have a temporary alliance with Arctic Fox. Just for this game."

Juno swore and shook his head. "You can't trust Bratersky. He's not going to honor that alliance. He doesn't even try to hide his background. Why'd you even bother?"

"What do you mean?" I asked. "What background?"

"His tattoos," Juno said. "He's ROC, it's as clear as the scowl on his face."

ROC? What in the world did that mean? I decided to just nod and figure it out later.

"He'll honor it," Rylee said. "It's just for this one game."

I nodded. "Great! It sounds like we all have solid plans."

"Where are you going?" Rylee asked.

"Hyena," I said.

"Hyena?" Rylee asked. "Everyone's going to go for that flag. It's going to be a shooting gallery down there."

It didn't matter. I wasn't going to Hyena. I was going to find a large tree, climb it, and sit there and shoot people who wandered by. "Well, you're not going," I said. "Maybe others had the same thought."

She considered that for a moment and then nodded.

The horn blast echoed, and birds scattered from the trees.

I imagined all the sports movies I'd seen over the years, ones where the coach gives the team a big pep talk and the players get all worked up and run out onto the field full of energy. I tried to remember one, or part of one. Nothing seemed to quite fit for a game of paintball with a bunch of kid spies. So I just forced a smile and said, "Good luck, everyone." I spun on my heel and took off into the woods.

When we played Capture the Flag back home, it was mostly in the neighborhood. Sometimes it would spread out into a park, but never a forest. The trees were really dense in here, and under some of the sections of canopy, it actually felt like dusk. I tried to keep my bearings, but not five minutes later, I was turned around and unsure which way was out. I stopped in a section of sparse woods that had some sunlight streaming in through the breaks in the canopy and turned around, hoping one of the directions would jump out at me as the right one.

Should've brought a compass, you idiot.

Twigs snapped to my right, and I dropped into a crouch, ducked behind a bush, and held my breath. A full minute later two campers crept into view, their guns held like they were ready to use them. They scanned the woods, back and forth, as they walked.

I adjusted my grip and brought my gun up to my shoulder. This was going to be great!

The campers moved carefully a few paces past where I was hiding. I considered taking them hostage, but then decided they might turn around and get a lucky shot before I managed to shoot them. I'd only played paintball once, but it was enough to remember the sting of getting shot. I wasn't keen to feel that again.

I held my position. I'd let them get three more steps, and then I'd pop up and blast them.

One.

Two. They paused and then ...

Three—

Just as I was about to stand, someone cleared their throat behind me, and I froze.

"You can stand up now," the voice said.

I turned and faced the wide smile of Chase Erickson and two other campers beside him.

"Hey, Bryce?" Chase said.

"Yeah?" said one of the campers I'd been planning on shooting a second before.

"Is it Christmas? Because it feels like Christmas."

"Then it must be Christmas," Bryce said.

The five of them laughed, and then Chase's expression dropped.

"Take his gun," Chase said.

Someone from behind me snatched my weapon out of my hand. I raised my hands. "Okay, okay, you got me. Congratulations."

Chase shook his head. "You're our prisoner."

One of the campers behind me grabbed my arms and pulled them behind my back, hard.

"Hey!"

They jerked me backward against a tree. Chase removed a roll of industrial tape from one of the pockets on his cargo pants and threw it to another camper. They quickly moved over to me, mask still down so I couldn't see their faces, and started taping me to the tree.

"Okay," I said, "really funny." I struggled to get away, and the camper wrapping me in tape paused and punched me in the stomach hard enough to knock the wind out of me. By the time I stopped coughing, I was secured to the trunk by three thick bands of tape—one across my chest and upper arms, one across my waist that also pinned my arms to my side, and one over my knees.

I cursed and struggled against the restraints and then cursed some more. "You can't do this," I said. "This is a total violation of the rules. No physical violence."

"Are you in pain?" Chase asked.

I nodded to the camper who'd just punched me in the stomach. "He hit me, so obviously I am."

"I slipped, sir," the camper said. He tossed the mostly empty roll of tape into the air and deftly caught it. "I certainly wasn't *trying* to hit him."

"There," Chase said, "you see? It was all a misunderstanding." He walked over and patted my face. "So we're not using violence to hurt you. We are simply restraining a POW." He looked over at one of his teammates. "Is that against the rules?"

"No, sir," the camper said. He glanced over his shoulder and then up at the sky. He took a couple paces to his right until he was standing beneath the leafy branches of a huge tree. Then he reached into his pocket and pulled out a cell phone, or a camera, or maybe a cell phone with a camera, and held it up to record what they were about to do.

Chase nodded at his teammate and then moved half a dozen paces away and held up his gun. "We can shoot you too, and that's not considered too violent."

"Once," I said. "You can shoot me once." Every muscle in my body tensed. "So get on with it already."

"Once?" He turned back to his teammate. "Is that the rule?"

The camper smiled and shook his head. "In the event that the paintball does not break," he recited from memory, "the camper will not be presumed hit and will be entitled to stay in the game."

"Wha ..." I felt my mouth drop as Chase unscrewed his paintball feeder from the top of his gun and took another one out from a bag at his feet. Steam wafted from the new tube, and frost covered at least three quarters of it.

Chase screwed it onto the top of his gun and then turned to me and fired. The round hit me in the shoulder, and I yelped as pain ricocheted down my arm.

"There," I growled through clenched teeth, "I'm hit. It's over. I'm out."

No one moved. I glanced around the clearing. Why hadn't I started shooting right away the instant I'd seen them?

"You're not hit," Chase said. He pointed at my shoulder. "It didn't break."

I glanced down. Sure enough, my shoulder was paint free, and a few feet away, the yellow paintball that had come from Chase's gun sat unexploded on the ground.

Chase fired again. This time it hit my thigh and felt like someone had punched me with an incredibly tiny fist. I forced myself not to cry out, but when I looked down and saw that once again the paintball hadn't broken, I let out a string of curses that only stopped when Chase fired another round, hitting me in my other leg.

"Oh, no," Chase said. "Somehow the paintballs I have must've been frozen before the game. None of them seem to be breaking." He glanced toward his teammates.

With the exception of the one recording it all, the other Squirrel members unscrewed their paintball feeder tubes and replaced them with ones from the same backpack where Chase had retrieved his. Each was just as frost-covered as the next.

"Help!" I yelled. "He—" One of the campers pressed their palm over my mouth, silencing my shouts for help, while another pulled out the tape again and, this time, pressed a piece over my mouth.

Chase held a finger to his lips. "Quiet now," he said. "Don't want the enemy to know where you are." He gave me an evil grin, the kind of grin you get from the big kid at school who's about to steal your money and shove you into a trash can. "Oh wait. We are the enemy."

The paintballs came in quick succession, sometimes in spurts of two or three, sometimes in bursts that felt like at least a dozen. Each time it was like being pelted with rocks.

I wasn't counting, but the number of times I was hit had to be over a hundred. It felt like I'd stepped on a wasp's nest and now they were taking their revenge.

The shots ended abruptly, but I kept my eyes closed for a few more seconds.

"Well, this is ... unexpected," Juno said.

My eyes opened, and sure enough, there was Juno, standing behind Chase and his four goons as if he had every reason in the world to be there. The five members of Team Squirrel spun and leveled their weapons at Juno and seemed at a loss as to whether they should shoot him or wait to find out why he didn't seem the slightest bit worried.

I fought again against my restraints and tried to tell him to get out of there or to start shooting or something ... anything. But all I managed was a stream of frantic mumbles that even I didn't understand.

Chase looked at his four teammates, then back to Juno, and smirked.

Juno didn't even look at me. Instead, he raised an eyebrow at Chase, and Chase responded by squeezing his trigger.

The paintball hit Juno square in the chest and bounced off. Juno didn't even flinch. Chase's mouth became a thin line.

"Hmm," Juno said, without taking his eyes off Chase. "It didn't break. I guess this is my lucky day." The barrel of Juno's gun snapped up, and a steady stream of paintballs flew out. I could only imagine he'd made the same adjustments to his gun as he had to mine. In a blink, five members of Team Squirrel were splattered with paint.

Then Juno dropped to his knee beside Chase's backpack and, in a single movement, snatched out a frosted tube of paintballs and somehow swapped it on to his gun as he spun back into a standing position. His gun sent the frozen paintballs out like water from a hose.

The paintballs pelted Chase and his team and sent them scampering back into the trees, hurling curses and warnings of revenge at Juno.

When they were gone, Juno strolled up to me, his gun resting on his shoulder. He eyed me carefully and then pulled the tape off my mouth.

I gasped. "Thanks, Juno." I nodded at the tape securing me to the tree. "A little help?"

He pulled out his pocketknife and cut me loose.

I dropped to my knees and pulled the tape off my chest and legs. "What a bunch of psychos!" I grabbed my gun from the ground, pointed it into the trees where Chase had run, and squeezed the trigger. I swept it back and forth until every last paintball was gone.

Juno grabbed my arm and pulled me up. "Feel better?"

"No."

"Well, you're going to feel worse if you don't start moving around." He took a breath. "Get hit as much as you just did, and the adrenaline ripping through your body is the only reason you're not in a world of pain right now." He nudged me forward. "C'mon, let's go."

My body did hurt, but Juno was right. I wasn't in nearly enough pain for what had just happened. Plus, my hand was bleeding again.

Juno nudged me forward. "Well, as crappy as it is you got lit up like that, you did distract Chase long enough that Rylee snagged his flag."

"Rylee snagged his flag?"

Juno nodded. "She got Octopus's too."

I smiled. "So we didn't lose yet?

"Lose?" Juno said with a genuine laugh. "We might have won."

It would have felt better to win if pain weren't slowly taking over my senses. I nodded toward the edge of the clearing, and Juno led me through the trees as easily as if he were following a path. A few minutes later, we stepped into the Team Grizzly clearing. My teammates were all there, celebrating. Only seven of the twenty extras we used were still there, but our flag, as well as two others, hung on the pole.

"Found him," Juno said. He gave me a look and added, "He was taking care of Chase and four of his punk buddies."

Angie ran over and slapped me on the back. "Guess you knew what you were doing after all, Captain." She drew herself back. "You don't look so good."

I forced a smile. "If Juno hadn't come along when he did, I'd be a lot worse."

Rylee strolled up, looking like she'd just gotten the blue ribbon at a science fair. She gestured to the flags on the pole. "Whaddaya think?"

"Way to go, Rylee," I managed. "I don't know how you did it. Especially Chase's base. I thought his was going to be impossible to get through."

"It was a team effort," she said.

"And these three," Amara said, pointing at Alexis, Duncan, and Rob, "defended this flag like animals. I bet they took out forty campers from opposing teams on their own."

The three young campers kept their mouths shut, but their chins were raised just a bit. They were pleased with themselves.

"So is it over, then?" I asked. "Are we done? Because I think I need to see the doctor again." I held up my hand. Blood oozed out the edges of the bandage. I glanced around the clearing. "Where's Yaakov?"

Juno shook his head. "He may be good on the computer, but that kid does not know how to keep his head down. He was shot and out of the game almost before we started."

"He was probably relieved," Angie said.

"So, then, it is over?" I asked again. "We can go?"

Rylee checked her watch. "Any minute now. I think the score is going to be three flags for us and two flags for Arctic Fox." She smiled. "It feels so good to beat Becca. I hate that chick."

A yellow blast exploded on Rylee's chest. I blinked, not really putting together what had just happened, and in that moment of confusion, dozens of other shots streaked through the edge of the clearing and burst on the rest of the team. I spun around and caught a paintball to the forehead. Juno dove and rolled along the dirt, firing his weapon into the trees, but then three yellow blasts exploded across his back and leg. Whoever it was, they'd just taken out our entire team.

"You hate me?" Becca's voice carried through the trees a moment before she crutched her way into the clearing, her weapon slung over her shoulder and her face mask lifted so we could see her evil smile. "I'm just crushed. Here I thought we were besties." She gasped dramatically and then narrowed her eyes and snapped her fingers. Six other Hyena campers popped out of the trees, weapons ready.

"What's the matter, Rylee?" Becca asked with a sneer. "You look like someone just forced you to eat dirt." She laughed and crutched to the wooden pole, tore all three flags off, and handed them back to one of her teammates. Then she turned and headed back into the woods. She paused at the tree line and looked over her shoulder. "Don't worry, Grizzlies. Third place isn't so bad. At least you're going to get the privilege of being beat by me again in the next event."

No one moved for several long seconds after Becca left.

"So ..." I began, "we didn't come in last? We're still in the games?"

Juno nodded. "Yep. Dexter and his team, Octopus, were wiped out early. They'll be eliminated. But unless Chase's team was decimated, which I highly doubt, we're second to last."

I turned to Rylee. Her hands were tight fists at her side. Her lips were pulled back a bit, her teeth clenched so tight you could see her jaw muscles.

"You, um, okay, Rylee?" I asked.

She drew in a huge breath and opened her mouth. I think a string of curses poured out, but I didn't hear them because, at that precise moment, the horn signaling the end of the game echoed through the trees and drowned her out.

CHAPTER 28

Becca and Team Hyena had bragging rights after the Capture the Flag win, and they weren't afraid to let the rest of the camp know it. Two days after the event, they were still whooping and hollering about it every chance they got. It didn't help that Smith and Dalson played the footage from the event on a projector during dinner for two nights straight. Nothing like a little shame to motivate us.

Team Octopus and Dexter Miller were eliminated as we expected. There wasn't any fanfare about the dismissal; they just were no longer a team. Their flag was removed from the grounds, and the campers were dispersed among the other teams. We received about twelve of them; other teams got more. Dexter ended up on Becca's team, and at dinner, he sat at the opposite end of the dining room. He couldn't have gotten any farther away from the Delta table if he'd tried. He kept his chin permanently against his chest. His reaction to losing was a bit babyish. I mean, it was just a game, after all. I shook my head, because that might not be quite true. Was any of this *really* a game?

A few nights later, after dinner, I collapsed on my bed and stared at the ceiling. Angie and Amara argued about the proper techniques for throwing a knife, and both, with expert precision, threw one after the other at the back wall of the cabin, each time using a very different technique and each time getting the same results as the other. Rylee and Yaakov sat together on a bed, looking at something on the computer.

Juno was across the room from me, eyeing me suspiciously.

"Yes, Juno?" I asked.

"We're a few days away from the end of Week Two. You don't look the least bit worried."

I sat up. "Why would I be worried?"

"Well, they're bound to start your Crucible Training any day."

"Crucible ... right." I vaguely remembered Ms. Clakk mentioning something about Deltas being required to participate in Crucible Training this year, but I hadn't given it any thought. My days were so full with other activities that I couldn't imagine adding another one. "Wait, why should I be worried about it?"

"Why should you be worried about it?" Yaakov asked. "Because of who Clakk said would be teaching you."

"Right," I said. "I forget his name."

"Robert Ingleton." Yaakov said it in a whisper, as if the name itself were a password to some super-secret place. "He's worked for the CIA for twenty years. He *still* works for the CIA as their top counter-terrorism interrogator. Can you imagine working in Langley *and* here?"

"Yeah," I said, not really knowing what all the fuss was about. Was it hard to squeeze a few lessons to campers between terrorist interrogations? Ingleton was clearly someone to be respected at this camp, so I added, "That's ... um ... pretty impressive. He must be pretty good at time management."

Yaakov balked. He glanced around the room before settling back on me. "You, my friend, are either very brave or very stupid."

"Mostly stupid," I said.

"That's what I figured," he said.

It was doubtful that Crucible Training was anything I could really prepare for. It would be yet another class in which I would embarrass myself by not knowing as much as anyone else, and because of that, it wasn't worth stressing about.

I pointed at the computer in front of Yaakov and Rylee and tried to change the topic. "What are you guys doing, anyway?"

"Rylee wanted to watch the Capture the Flag event one more time." Yaakov sighed and rolled his eyes. "Well, one more time—five times ago."

"You have access to that?" Angie asked.

Yaakov nodded. "Sure, I have access to that. I have access to the entire network. Everything on the main database is accessible through this console."

"Isn't that dangerous?" Amara asked. "For all of us, I mean?" He looked at me with a single cocked brow. "We get caught with a teammate who hacked into the system, and we'll get kicked out of the program."

"Give me a break," Yaakov said. "There is absolutely zero chance that I'll get caught. Zero. I'm way better than the best techie they have on their staff. I'm not saying it wasn't a challenge. It was. They have a better setup than I thought. But I don't make mistakes. And I don't get caught. Ever."

"It's still us you're putting at risk," Angie said. She glanced up at me. "Is there a reason you're not putting an end to it?"

I'd decided several days before that the reason people didn't want to be kicked from the program was because it might mean you couldn't be eligible for full spy status. Despite everything I'd been through, I didn't want to be kicked either. Still, Yaakov's confidence was refreshing. He reminded me of my friends back home. Especially Jason, only a really nerdy version. Also, I believed him. I bet he was as good as he said he was.

I shrugged. "I trust him. Yaakov's the best in this place."

Yaakov beamed.

"But I still want to know why you're studying that video."

Rylee hadn't taken her eyes off the screen until I'd spoken to her. She touched the keyboard and looked up. "The way Chase played the game didn't make sense."

"Maybe he just didn't have a good strategy," Amara said.

Rylee shook her head. "As soon as the horn sounds, he takes almost his entire team to Dexter's camp, blows every last one of them away, and steals their flag. He brings it back, takes four of his teammates, and leaves the entire rest of his team behind to guard that one flag. He knows he's not going to be in last place unless one of Dexter's teammates managed not to get shot and somehow gets through to Chase's teammates. And that's just not possible since he leaves fifteen to guard it." She looked up at me. "Then he comes and hassles you."

"Hassles me?" I scoffed. "You make it sound like he stole my lunch money."

Rylee shook her head. "I'm sure it would have been very bad for you if Juno hadn't come along."

"*Would have* been bad?" I choked on the words. "Are you kidding?" I turned to Juno and then back to Rylee. "*Would have?*"

"That's not the point," Rylee said. "Chase wasn't trying to win. He was trying not to lose."

My teammates nodded thoughtfully.

"And?" I asked. "What does that mean?"

"I've been to three camps with Chase," Rylee said. "He never tries to do anything but win."

Juno nodded. "I've been to a couple with him too. I agree."

"So he had a plan," Amara said. "That's not exactly a big deal."

"Actually it is," Rylee said. "He's come in second place at the last several camps. I think his goal is all about eliminating the people who might stop him from winning. Capture the Flag was his eliminate-the-competition round. And he picked Matt and Dexter as his first targets. He succeeded with Dexter, and now Matt will be next. He'll be gunning for you, for us, during the next competition."

I glared at Yaakov. "This is your fault," I spat out at him.

"What? Me?"

"Yes, you," I snapped back. "You told him that Dexter and I had better scores than him. He wouldn't have taped me to that tree if it weren't for you."

Yaakov opened and closed his mouth like a fish. I don't think he would've gotten much out anyway, but Rylee stepped in pretty quick.

"No," she said, "he wouldn't rely on Yaakov's comments. He must've seen your file."

"So his hacker got through," Amara said. He looked disappointedly at Yaakov. "I thought you said no one else could get into the system."

"I did say that," Yaakov said, suddenly finding his voice. "I'm telling you. No one at this camp could get past my blocks. No one. At least not without me knowing."

"Yes, Yaakov," Rylee said, "I know. It's *impossible*. Unless by some unbelievable odds, there was someone out there in the vast world of hackers who was actually better than you."

Yaakov's mouth snapped shut like Rylee had just slapped it.

"Or," she continued, "maybe he broke in and found the hard copy. Or maybe he's got some leverage on one of the counselors and they told him."

"Or any other one of the hundreds of possibilities," Juno said.

Rylee nodded. "We just need to be ready. Chase is planning something, and we need to figure out what it is. Right now, he thinks he's playing us."

"He *is* playing us," Angie said.

Rylee nodded. "Fine. Yes. He *is* playing us. He has a plan. We need to have one too."

"Agreed," Amara said.

Juno and Angie nodded, while Yaakov looked as though someone had just cooked his favorite toy in a Crock-Pot.

"Fine," Yaakov said. "But I've given it some more thought, and I'm going on the record that it's unlikely anyone would be able to hack past the extra blocks I put up to keep other team hackers out of the system." He shook his head and lifted a finger. "No, not just unlikely. Improbable. If I weren't such a believer in the fact that *nothing* is impossible, I'd say it was impossible."

A long pause followed Yaakov's comments, and then Angie said, "Well, that settles it; our little techie here is officially a megalomaniac."

CHAPTER 29

"**A**re we part of the next event?" Rob stared up at me and bit his lip. He, Alexis, and Duncan had caught up to me while I walked back to the cabin from dinner the next night.

"I'm not sure yet," I said.

"Didn't we do a good job in Capture the Flag?" Alexis asked.

"You did fine," I said. I felt myself getting annoyed. I wasn't in the mood to coddle a bunch of kids. "I'll let you know later."

"When?" Rob asked.

I rolled my eyes. "I just don't know what the next event is, so how can I decide if I want to use you for it?"

"We'd be good at anything," Alexis said.

I shoved past them. "I'll let you know."

"Let us prove ourselves again," Rob said, keeping pace. "We can get revenge on those guys who taped you to that tree."

Rage flashed, and I spun around and shoved him, hard. He hit the edge of the path, rolled onto the grass, and then quickly righted himself back up to his feet. I took a swift step toward him, fist raised, fully prepared to smash the little twerp's nose for even mentioning the tree.

He didn't flinch.

If I had actually swung at his face, I don't think he would have even tried to block or dodge it. "How'd you know about that?" As soon as I asked, I remembered that one of Chase's teammates had filmed the whole thing. I'd hoped that film wouldn't surface. I half expected Chase to keep it secret since cell phones were supposed to be banned. Clearly, he was showing it around, and word was spreading.

I heard Jason's voice in my head. "Suck it up, Cambridge. Chase is a punk. Get revenge." I took a deep breath and let it out slowly. There was too much I didn't understand about this place. Not knowing the rules here made it very difficult to keep them ... and to break them. I needed more information. I needed Jason to come through and find out some useful stuff for me.

An idea struck me like a brick, and I whirled around, planning to call out to Alexis, Duncan, and Rob, but I stopped short when I realized they'd stayed with me.

"You want to prove you're really worthy of a spot on a Delta team?" They nodded.

I reached into my pocket and handed them Chase's phone.

Rob took it from me and stared at it as though he wasn't sure what it was. "You want us to take it back now?"

"Pictures," I said. "I want you to take pictures of campers, counselors, Mr. Dalson, and Mr. Smith. I want as many pictures as you can get."

"Why?" Rob asked.

"Because," I said, "that's the price."

"It's a test." Alexis sounded like she was talking to herself. Then her head snapped up, and she smiled. "At least it's more challenging than stealing Chase's phone." She turned to her teammates. "He's upping the stakes."

Rob shook his head. "We get caught taking pictures with this, and we're out. Not just kicked from the program. Kicked from any part of any program."

If that happened, I thought, I'd have done all three of them a favor. This spy camp wasn't at all like the movies, and there was always going to be a camper like Chase who would torment someone they thought was weaker. Or maybe these three would grow up and become punks like Chase, in which case I'd be doing some future camper a service. Either way, I wasn't going to lose any sleep if they got kicked out.

"I want a picture of Chase too," I said, without even acknowledging their concern. Jason could look him up and maybe find some dirt I could use against him. Something embarrassing. I almost smiled at the possibilities. "And I want the footage of what happened during Capture the Flag."

Rob hesitated, and his lips pursed for a second, but Alexis snatched the phone out of his hand and shoved it in her pocket. "Not a problem," she said. "When do you want them by?"

"Just get them to me as soon as possible. If I'm going to use you in the next event, I want those pictures back ASAP so we have lots of time to add you to our plan." Mentioning the word *plan* out loud hammered home the fact that we didn't have one, and the reason my teammates hadn't suggested one was probably because of how angry I'd been.

Rob nodded. "Okay. Then we'll get to be part of the challenge?"

"We don't know what it is yet," I said, "but if I need extra players, you three will be my first choices."

Rob glanced over at Alexis and Duncan, and then the three of them looked at me and nodded. Without another word, they jogged away.

I did one complete loop of the walking path before heading for the cabin, and as soon as I stepped inside, I said, "We need a plan."

"Well, welcome back," Angie said. "We were wondering when you'd snap out of your little slump."

"A plan for what?" Amara asked.

"The next event," I said. "It's only a couple days away. We need to be ready for it. More ready than we were for the last event."

"We placed third," Juno said. "That's not bad."

"We placed third, ahead of Chase," I said. "And as Rylee already pointed out, that was Chase's plan all along."

Rylee nodded, and Juno scoffed at her from across the room.

"Well, we can't very well make a plan if we don't know the event," Amara said.

"And remember what Clakk said," Rylee added. "She said the events would be different this year."

I saw an opening to get more information, and I took it. I pointed at Rylee. "Good point. So let's brainstorm. What are some of the events from previous camps that you guys remember?"

"I was in a camp in Dubai a couple years ago," Amara said. "The Delta teams were sent on a scavenger hunt for one of the challenges."

"Doesn't sound so bad," I said.

Amara shrugged. "They had to get items like prosthetic limbs and the sidearm from an on-duty police officer."

I blinked.

"I've seen the scavenger hunt before too," Angie said. "The list is always difficult stuff, but it's not something you can really prepare for."

Difficult? That sounded impossible.

"But the scavenger hunt's a pretty common one," Angie added. "So if Clakk says it'll be different this year, I bet that's not one we need to worry about."

Good.

"There was one challenge," Yaakov said, "about a year ago, in Singapore. The teams were told to identify the one person in the group who was not like the others." He looked up at the ceiling. "They called it Find the Spy or Find the Infiltrator or something like that."

I didn't get it, and I was just about to ask Yaakov what he meant when Juno spoke. "Yeah, I've seen that too," he said. "They'd give you a group of ten Japanese people, for example, and tell you that one of them is a Korean spy and you have ten minutes to identify them."

I rubbed my head. "What question could you ask a group in ten minutes that would reveal a spy?"

Yaakov shook his head and said, "You don't ask a question. You come up with a shibboleth. It's really the only way if you're just looking for quick identification."

I nodded. "Yeah, a shibboleth, sure. That makes sense." I was going to have to do some research to figure out what in heck a shibboleth was.

"This isn't helping us prepare," Angie said, obviously frustrated. "If it's different from other years, we're not going to get anywhere by hashing out previous challenges. They're never exactly the same anyway."

"I'm not willing to wait around," I said. "I'm not going to let Chase beat me again." Angie snickered. My hand snapped out, and I pointed at her. "He is *not* going to beat us. I need everyone to take it seriously. If you can't do that, fine, no problem. But I'll go ahead and exercise that right I have to kick you out of the program so you don't bring the rest of us down. I don't want us to lose because we're unprepared."

Angie's smile vanished. And a glance around the room revealed that none of my teammates were amused.

Good. Take it seriously. I was tired of getting shoved around. I wanted to shove back. And the next Delta event was exactly where I'd do my pushing. I needed my team to be ready for that.

"We'll be ready," Rylee said.

"Darn right we will," I said under my breath.

CHAPTER 30

My outburst, or maybe my threat of flexing my muscle as team leader, jolted the group into overdrive. The morning martial arts session with Juno turned into a team-building exercise. Everyone turned out for it. Everyone, that is, but Angie. She insisted that no amount of training would protect us if we messed with her sleep. Rylee suggested we not take the threat lightly, and so as a group we decided it was just fine for Angie to stay in bed.

My actual fighting skills had improved considerably. Blocking was second nature now, and Juno had conditioned us to block and strike in almost the same movement. It hadn't seemed possible to build a skill in just a few days, but he was an excellent teacher. He insisted we still fought like a couple of clumsy, one-legged baboons, but he said that was a step forward.

In the evening, despite Angie's insistence that we were wasting our time, we brainstormed every possible event that might be thrown at us in the next competition. We considered a Capture the Flag rematch. An obstacle course. A skills test. Rylee said that in one of the previous camps she'd been to, the Delta teams had been deprived of sleep and then made to get something from a locked building downtown. At first the idea of breaking and entering seemed, well, illegal. Then again, this was a CIA training camp, so it wasn't really illegal. Spies had licenses for breaking the law, and besides, in all likelihood, the building had been owned by the CIA in the first place. When I suggested that, the group laughed.

"You're probably right," Juno said. "That would be hilarious."

I didn't think it was all *that* funny, but people in high-stress situations sometimes laughed at things that weren't funny just as a way to relieve stress. We'd been eating and breathing the training, so I figured it was pretty normal to be a little tightly wound.

We trained and planned and strategized, and then the next day we did it again. So when Friday rolled around, we were ready—as ready as any team at the camp could be.

Which was why it was such a shock to our system when Counselor Clakk did not stroll into our cabin at the crack of dawn, and an even bigger shock when, right in the middle of breakfast, Mr. Dalson delivered a bit of news:

"Campers," Mr. Dalson said from the front of the hall, "as you may have guessed, this week's Delta challenge has been canceled." His expression hardened. "We will let you know if anything changes."

And that was it.

Had such an announcement been made in any other mess hall in any other camp across the nation, it would have been met with a chorus of moans and sobbing twelve-year-olds. This camp being what it was, I seemed to be the only one disappointed. Everyone else simply turned back to their breakfast.

I kept my mouth shut until we got outside, and then I kicked a rock in frustration and sent it skittering a few feet down the path.

"So we get it in a few days, or at the very latest, next week," Juno said. "No big deal."

Amara nodded. "Juno's right. Plus, it wouldn't surprise me at all if this were all some kind of ploy. A trick to make us drop our guard to see how we'd react to a surprise challenge. But at the very least, we have more time to prepare. This is a good thing."

Somewhere in some dark corner of my mind I knew they were right, yet I still wanted to scream and punch someone—no, not *someone*, Chase. I wanted to pound that kid into the dirt. I shoved my hands into my pockets and clenched my teeth to keep from saying something I'd regret. We walked in silence a ways before we came up behind two campers walking right down the middle of the path, totally blocking anyone behind them. Like us.

I opened my mouth to tell them to get out of the way but stopped just short when I heard what one of them was saying.

"We already know why." The boy talking had toffee-colored skin and short dark hair. "There's been a rumor about it since the first week."

The kid he was talking to was at least a head shorter than he was. The smaller one shook his head as we came up behind. "Don't be stupid. You know how many times we've heard these stories of camper abductions? It's ludicrous."

"Abductions?" The word fell out of my mouth before I knew it was there, and the doctor's warning about people watching the camp rolled back into my mind. "No way."

The boys spun around, disdainful, and mouths partially opened like they were ready to sling a few well-aimed insults, but both of them hesitated when they saw us. No doubt an entire Delta team would be a bit much to take on, even for the gutsiest camper. Instead of speaking, they stared at us for a long second, and then both turned and jogged away.

"That's right," Angie called after them, "you better run." She turned back to me. "It's because you beat that girl with your shoe."

I groaned. Would I ever live that down? I tried to ignore her and said, "Abductions? Do you guys think that's why they canceled the event?"

Juno shook his head. "C'mon, don't be gullible like the rest of these idiots. No one is getting abducted. Even if someone knew there was a camp somewhere training a bunch of kids to be dangerous operatives, they'd have no chance at figuring out where that camp was."

We started walking again, but the conversation continued.

"That's why they're getting accredited," Rylee added. "Remember that lady from the first day?"

I nodded.

"It's another layer of protection. If you were going to try to narrow the number of camps you wanted to investigate, you'd probably assume a camp like this wouldn't be an accredited one." She shook her head. "I'm with Juno; no one's getting abducted."

I considered that for a moment. "But the doctor—"

"It's a scare tactic," Juno said. "That's all. They want us to leave here and think every shadow is hiding someone we need to beware of. No one is getting abducted, because we're not really on anyone's radar."

Angie scrunched up her face. "I don't agree with that. I was in a camp two years ago, and three campers disappeared."

"Disappeared?" Juno asked. "Or left the camp?"

"Or were kicked out?" Rylee added.

Angie shook her head. "I think I've been around long enough to know the difference between disappearing and leaving the camp on their own."

Juno rolled his eyes. "Well, I didn't know the Agency had camps for aspiring magicians. I'll have to sign up for one of those next time. I've always wanted to learn that rabbit-out-of-a-hat trick."

Angie glared at Juno but didn't speak.

"What about you two?" I asked, looking at Amara and Yaakov. "Do you believe it?"

"Darn right I believe it," Yaakov said without hesitation. "I'm not going near those woods."

"Yaakov also believes in the Yeti," Rylee said with an exasperated sigh.

"I said I didn't *not* believe in the Yeti," Yaakov snapped back. "There's a difference. I believe in the possibility. Same goes for the abductions. I could list a dozen agencies who would love to get their hands on one of the campers here." He shivered. "Especially me. It's not good, all the things I know."

"Oh brother," Angie said. "Here we go again."

"Amara?" I asked.

Amara slowed his pace a bit and stroked his chin like a wise, old sage. "It is unlikely, but like Yaakov, I believe in the possibility."

Juno threw his hands up. "Great, we have a team of idiots. Maybe Matt was right to threaten to kick some of us out."

No one laughed. In fact, the entire group became utterly silent, and it was as though we were on our way to a funeral, rather than the start of another day.

"Oh, for Pete's sake," I said, "I'm sorry I threatened to kick people out of the program. I didn't mean it. I have no intention of kicking anyone out." I turned back to my group. "Now can you all please stop being so weird?"

No one responded, and I was about to say something else when Angie pointed off the path. "Aren't those your little minions over there?"

I spun around, and sure enough, Rob, Alexis, and Duncan were huddled against one of the cabins trying, it seemed, to be discreet about wanting to talk to me.

"I'll meet you guys back at the cabin." I stepped off the trail and made it a few steps before I realized someone was behind me. Rylee stopped when I turned around. "What?" I asked.

"I'm coming with you."

I shook my head. "I said I'll meet you back at the cabin."

She nodded to Alexis, Rob, and Duncan. "How do you know them?"

"We used them for Capture the Flag, remember?"

"Of course I do," Rylee said, "but *why* did we use them?"

"I will meet you back at the cabin, Rylee." Each word was punctuated with my irritation to the point that she finally understood. I shoved past her and crossed the rest of the distance to the trio. I glanced at the trail when I got to them. Rylee and the rest of my team were just disappearing around a bend.

Rob handed me the cell phone, and I shoved it into my pocket. "You got them?"

He nodded. "Piece of cake."

"Really? Even the video of what happened during Capture the Flag?"

"The video was tough," Rob said, "but we got it. What are you going to do with them?"

I'd prepared for this question. "I'll delete them as soon as I check that you actually took them."

"So this *was* a test?" Alexis asked.

I nodded.

"So we're still good? If the Delta event happens, you'll use us?"

"I said I would, didn't I? But you heard Dalson; it's canceled."

195

Rob snickered. "I doubt it. Those rumors of abductions are stupid. No one gets abducted. If you believe that, you're a—"

Alexis elbowed her teammate as a group of campers headed toward us.

"Okay," Alexis said, looking at me. "We'll wait, then. If the challenge happens, you'll tell us how we can help, right?"

"Sure." I patted the phone in my pocket. "Good job, guys."

I ducked into the bathroom on my way back to the Delta cabin and locked myself into a stall. When I checked the pictures, I had to smile.

These kids were smarter than I'd thought. The pictures were clear as day, and each one looked like the counselors had posed individually for them. Which, clearly, they hadn't. The last picture in the series was of the Camp Friendship accreditation brochure. Somehow Rob, Alexis, and Duncan had gotten hold of the material used to make it and uploaded it to the phone.

Smart.

They also had a dozen pictures of Chase, each appearing to have been taken from bushes or behind buildings. Some of them were pretty bad, but there were a couple that were pretty good. And to cap it off, there were quite a few pictures of my team. I felt a bit silly for not having seen them when the pictures were taken.

I texted Jason with the pictures attached and told him I'd be in touch and that he should not, under any circumstances, text me back.

He instantly texted back, **Okay**.

Then, **Oops**.

And finally, **Sorry**.

Only Jason could read a message that said **Do not text me back** and promptly send me three messages. I had the phone on silent mode, but it wasn't worth the risk. I took the battery out and stuffed both pieces into my pocket.

If they think they're going to catch us off guard, they're underestimating how badly I want to be here.

It was time to get training.

CHAPTER 31

I hit the ground hard. My breath came out in a single gush, and I lay there, looking up at the trees while I tried to will precious air back into my lungs.

"You're letting your emotions get the best of you," Juno said.

I rolled and pushed myself up but stayed hunched over, hands on knees, while I caught my breath. "Th-this sucks," I said. "They really did cancel it. The camp's almost over." It had been six days since the last Delta event had been canceled, and every day since, my team and I had expected news that it was back on.

Yaakov landed in a heap at my feet and groaned. Rylee walked over and pulled him up and helped dust him off. Then she looked at me. "Why are you still mad? Tomorrow's Friday. There's only a couple days left. They're not going to cancel two events in a row. They do that, and there's no time to have a clear winning team. I think we have a great shot at winning."

"Or at least not losing," Yaakov said. He picked a couple twigs and dried leaves from his hair. "What we need to know is, are they going to eliminate just one team tomorrow or two? It's usually just one elimination per event, but since they missed last week's ..."

"Let's just not end up in the bottom two," I said.

Juno nodded and then tapped his watch. "C'mon, it's time to get cleaned up. We're already going to be late for breakfast. Angie might clean the kitchen out of all the food before we get there."

We laughed, and then Rylee said, "I'm going to tell her you said that."

Juno's smile dropped dramatically. "Don't. I might be a pretty good fighter, but she's got that crazy streak in her."

Rylee nodded. "It's called psychopathy."

I shook my head and wondered what the chances were that Angie really was a psychopath. Probably wouldn't get past a psychological screening if she was, right?

It didn't matter. What mattered was tomorrow. Another scheduled competition and there had been no word that it would be canceled. I was determined to make it through. At first, all I'd cared about was staying in the camp until the end of the session. Being able to tell my friends that I'd been in a real spy training camp would have been awesome. Having some skills of a spy would've been even better. But now I wanted more. I wanted to actually *be* a spy. If I could just win a couple events and prove myself, when they discovered my true identity they wouldn't kick me out. They might be mad. I might get in trouble. But they'd see my potential and let me continue.

At least, that was what I told myself.

The rain started about mid-morning, and became a full-blown thunderstorm by late afternoon. I ducked into the cabin after getting caught in a downpour on my way back from Arts and Crafts.

"There you are," Juno said, poking his head into the cabin. "You coming?"

"Where?"

"Self-Defense, of course." He shook the rain out of his hair. "Did you forget or something?"

A clap of thunder rattled the windowpanes, and I gestured outside. "We still have the class? In this?"

Juno laughed. "Are you kidding? Hurry up. I don't want to get in trouble for being late."

I grabbed my jacket and jogged after him. It didn't take long to get to the clearing, but I was so wet that it looked like I'd swum there.

"Cambridge," Ms. Davis shouted over the din of the rain. "Get in here."

"Good luck," Juno said.

I shrugged off my coat. It wasn't keeping me dry anyway.

"Pick your opponent, Mr. Cambridge."

I smiled and pointed at Chase. "Him," I said. I glanced back to Juno. His face was scrunched up, and he shook his head.

"I can't believe you picked me," Chase said. I turned back around. He was standing opposite me with a huge grin. "I mean, it's almost as if you enjoy getting your butt kicked."

"Fight!" Ms. Davis said, her word punctuated by a clap of thunder.

Chase swung for my head, and my arm went up, blocking the punch. Just like Juno had taught me, my other hand flew out and caught Chase in the chin. He staggered back a step, eyes wide, as though me connecting a punch was the last thing he'd expected.

Juno whooped.

I seized my chance and lunged forward, aiming for Chase's head. I wanted to make him hurt as badly as he'd hurt me. Finally, I was in a position to do it.

Chase caught my arm and yanked me off balance. Then his foot hit my knee and dropped me to a crouch. I was just standing back up when I realized Chase's foot was on its way to my face. And then I was in the air, looking up through the canopy of trees while droplets of rain pelted my face.

I hit the ground hard, and in a single beat, Chase hammered me in the stomach. I rolled, struggling to catch my breath, and Chase kicked me in the ribs. Coughing, I tried to push myself to my feet, but he kicked out my arm and then stomped me in the stomach. Then he leaned over and brought his face beside mine.

"Two weeks learning basic fighting moves in the woods and you thought you had a chance against me?" He laughed right in my face. "How did you even get in to this camp?"

"That's enough," Ms. Davis said. "Erickson, fall back." Chase did as he was told and returned to the perimeter. I pushed myself to my knees. "Cambridge," she said, "I saw some improvements."

Yeah, I'd stayed conscious this time. I didn't get it. I'd worked so hard with Juno, and even after all that, Chase had pummeled me just as easily as he had before. What was the point of all the lessons if they didn't help me become a better fighter?

"Keep at it," she added.

While I half crawled, half staggered to the edge of the circle, Ms. Davis called out another couple names, and two other campers fell into combat.

"What were you thinking?" Juno asked when I made it beside him.

"What do you think I was thinking?" I snapped. "I thought you'd given me some training that actually worked!"

"You've been at it for a couple weeks, Matt. You don't even know the basics. Maybe if you keep at it for the rest of the year, you'll be ready for next year. But Chase trains too, remember."

I spat out a mouthful of blood and watched as the two other

campers scrapping it out in the center of the clearing pounded each other. "I just wanted some payback."

"Well, you got it," Juno said. "I think he really hurt his foot on your face."

"Shut up."

CHAPTER 32

I was getting really tired of having Chase stomp me every chance he got. As I showered and cleaned myself up, I wished for the Delta challenge we'd be facing in the morning to be something I could really destroy him in ... but off the top of my head, I couldn't think of anything I could do that he couldn't. It made me hate him even more, if that were even possible. My foul mood continued into dinner and made eating impossible. My appetite came in waves; one minute I'd be famished, and then the next, the idea of eating made me want to vomit.

I stabbed the piece of chicken with my fork and twisted the prongs into it.

"I don't think it's going to tell you what you want to know," Rylee whispered across the table.

"Yeah, well," I said, "maybe it just needs more incentive." I took my knife and stabbed the tip into it.

Rylee grimaced. "You and Angie could develop some interrogation protocols."

I looked up and realized she and I were the only two left at the table. The team table to my right was mostly empty, as well. In fact, with the exception of a dozen campers scattered among the tables, the dining hall was deserted.

How long had I been zoned out?

Rylee eyed me suspiciously, and she must've seen my confusion

203

on my face because she answered as if reading my mind, "A while. Are you finally ready to tell me what's going on, Matt Cambridge? We're in the final days now. I think it's about time."

"What are you talking about?"

She leaned across the table. "Look, *Matt*," she said my name like she was saying a made-up word. "I wasn't kidding about how good I am at reading people. I'm really good. Scary good."

I leaned back, putting a bit of distance between us. "Well, I'm starting to believe you about the *scary* part."

"I've been watching you the past few weeks. When you talk about never having been to one of these camps before, you're not lying." She pointed to the empty chairs around our table. "They all think you're just playing it cool, that you're pretending to be inexperienced. You have scores from previous camps, but I don't think those are real. I think you manipulated the system somehow. I'm not sure how or why, but I'm impressed enough to think you probably deserve your spot as a Delta. But most other times, well, you're completely out of your depth."

I forked another piece of chicken into my mouth. I couldn't respond with food in my mouth, right? My mother taught me that was rude.

"And that display on the soccer field," she continued. "I've watched it a dozen times, and you know what I've noticed?" She didn't wait for an answer. "You were utterly terrified." She shook her head. "You did what you did because you had no idea there'd be danger on the field. And you managed what you managed on sheer dumb luck."

I didn't speak. I chewed.

She leaned forward and grabbed my hand. I hadn't had a bandage on it for a few days, but there was a nasty scar. "This injury is from someone who's never held a real gun or someone who hasn't held one enough to develop a habit to do it properly." She shook her head. "How could you be a Delta without practically being an expert in firearms?" I swallowed my food and searched my plate for more.

"Look. We're almost done here. Just a few more days. Tomorrow's probably going to be our last challenge, and then it will all be over. But if there's something I need to know, you need to tell me. If you fail, we all fail, and I'm not about to fail. I can always have Yaakov dig up every scrap of data on you. And he can do it, you know. He can find out who you really are. He's that good."

"Who I really am?" I muttered to myself. That was new. That was something I hadn't considered. I hadn't outright lied about who I was, but as I stared at the girl across from me, I realized it was entirely possible that she had. Maybe everyone had. Maybe that was how it was supposed to work at these camps. Anonymity. At camp, Rylee was "Rylee," but outside of camp, she might be someone else entirely. My whole team might not be who they seemed. The more I thought about that, the more it made sense.

Long seconds passed before I made a decision on how to deal with Rylee. I stood up from the table, wiped my mouth with a napkin, and left without uttering a single word.

CHAPTER 33

As I made my way back to the Delta cabin, I hoped I'd done the right thing by just walking away. I liked Rylee. She had my back. I thought I could trust her. She could've made things very awkward and asked her questions in front of everyone, but she hadn't. Still, the way she'd said that she'd have Yaakov find out who I really was had put my mind into overdrive.

My dad had forced me to watch a documentary once about people who lie. It was all about how their friends and family don't trust them and stuff like that. But there was one part I remembered most. Some professor who specialized in psychology or lies or something said that people who lie see lies where there are none.

Rylee might have been good at reading people, but I wasn't lying, at least not about being Matt Cambridge, and she still thought I was. That made me think she was lying about who she was. It made me think that everyone was lying about who they were.

I stopped a dozen or so meters from the cabin. The lights were on inside, and it sounded like my team was getting amped up for tomorrow's event. I shook my head. I should have just talked to Rylee. She wanted to help me.

A twig snapped behind me, and I smiled. "Rylee," I said, turning around, "I was thinking about what you asked and—"

A gloved hand clamped over my mouth, and an arm, covered by a leather jacket, wrapped around my chest and yanked me back toward the trees. I tried to shout, but as soon as I drew a breath, my nose and throat burned with a toxic scent that made the world around me swirl. I flailed my fists and kicked my feet. But everything around me continued to spin, faster and faster with each second.

As I was dragged into the forest, everything went black.

CHAPTER 34

"**W**ake up!" The words sounded like a bark from an angry dog.

I groaned. My head felt like it was moments away from splitting open and spilling my brains onto the floor. I tried to raise my hand, but my arms wouldn't move. Couldn't move.

Something had happened. I tried to think. I'd been outside the Delta cabin when ... when someone had grabbed me?

There was a *slosh* and then a blast of ice and water hit my chest and face.

Any lingering dullness in my senses vanished in an instant. I had been grabbed and drugged.

It wasn't an urban legend.

Abductions were real, and I was a victim of one.

I gasped and blinked rapid-fire, doing my best to make sense of where I was. The room was well lit and posh, like one of those apartments you see on the covers of magazines. Elegant frames filled with images of happy scenes and content people hung on the walls. Bright, modern light fixtures hung from the ceiling. Along one side of the apartment, large picture windows bordered a sliding glass door, and sunlight poured in. Dark hardwood covered most of the floor except on the square I was on, which had thick white carpet. I was seated in a stiff, high-backed armchair. Rubber cords bound me to the armrests. I tried to move my legs, but realized they were tied down too. The same

- DISRUPTION -

rubber cords were cinched tight around my chest.

Panic coursed through my veins like liquid fire, and I thrashed against the restraints. I tried to twist my arms and kick my legs, taking deep breaths to stretch out the rubber cords. Nothing worked, and each time the bands bit into me farther. Tears blurred my vision as I became more and more desperate. This wasn't a stupid game. This was for real.

I had to hope that someone saw me get snatched. It was a CIA camp, after all. They had access to satellite imagery. They'd realize I was gone, play back the satellite images, and follow the kidnappers. Wasn't that how it worked? Could they rewind and zoom in anytime? Or did they have to be recording it? I was just about to rethink my decision not to scream for help when I heard footsteps behind me. Slow, careful footsteps. I couldn't see directly behind me, but the room went far enough back that the footsteps I heard belonged to someone who had just watched me thrash around in the chair.

"What is your name?" The man stepped into view. He had a stubbly face and dark hair, and he wore a black three-piece suit and a black tie. He looked like he was on his way to an awards ceremony but had stopped by to check on the old kidnapped kid to make sure he was still tied to the chair.

"Sir," I said, "please let me go. I don't know who you think I am, but you have the wrong guy. I promise."

He cocked his head and held up his finger, signaling me to shut up.

That single act was enough to unhinge me. This was a crazy man, and he had me tied to a chair. "Help!" I screamed. I thrashed in the chair again. "Somebody hel—"

He lunged out and slapped me across the face. The sting knocked any words I wanted to scream out of my head and sent shockwaves down my entire body.

"Your name," he said. He slipped off his suit coat and carefully draped it over the back of the couch. "Tell me your name."

You'd think the shock of getting slapped would have made my panic worse. But it had the opposite effect. I suddenly took in the scene carefully. I had been taken at night. I glanced again at the sunlight pouring in through the windows on the far wall. It had been hours. The CIA would have known I was gone. They'd be looking for me. And it didn't matter whether they could get the footage from the satellite. The CIA had all kinds of other gadgets, and they knew the really crazy people. They'd find me. They'd see how I reacted in this situation. I was suddenly determined to prove I had what it took to be a spy.

The man had just finished rolling the sleeve on his left arm. He glanced at me expectantly. He wanted my name. I pursed my lips. He wasn't going to get it.

I didn't even see it coming. His fist hammered into the side of my face. Blood oozed from my nose and trickled into my mouth. I coughed and spat. Ninety percent of my determination and resolve evaporated with that one hit.

"P-p-please," I said, struggling to find words. "W-what do you want?"

The man drew a breath and smiled. "Your name."

"Y-yeah," I said. "Sure." I took a few deep breaths. I searched for a fake name to give him, but the thought of him figuring that out and punching me again made me not want to lie. Then he did something that made it so I didn't have a chance to lie. He picked something up from the end table beside the couch.

A wallet.

My wallet.

Darn it.

"Let me guess," he said. "You're trying to sort out if you want to pretend to be Matt Cambridge of Marksville ..." He pulled out another paper and shook it at me. "Or Gunnar Konstantan from ..." He glanced down. "Sweden." He laughed. "I dated a Swedish girl when I was in college. She used to carry a million pieces of ID in her wallet." He tossed the wallet back onto the table. "Go with Matt. You make a more convincing case for being Matt Cambridge." He shook his head. "Of course, I'm not an idiot. I know you aren't Matt, either."

I sniffed and tried to blink away some of the tears. What was he talking about?

"But I'll play this little game with you if you want." He lowered his face to mine. "But eventually you *will* give me your name." He straightened. "I'll call you Matt. But you really don't look like a Matt ... or a Gunnar for that matter." He pulled an ottoman from behind him and took a seat. "More like a Dennis or a Walden." He shook his head. "But I digress. Tell me about that camp, Matt."

"The camp?"

He leaned forward and sighed. "Do I really have to hit you again?"

"Look ... sir ..." I sniffed again. "This is a mistake. You have the wrong guy. I don't know what's going on here."

"Please," the man said, "call me Butler."

"B-Butler?"

Butler tsked. "Look, kid, I already know what kind of camp it is. I know, and you telling me won't make a bit of difference. I just want to hear you say it."

Juno had said the rumors were that the Chinese had abducted some of the others. This guy looked as Caucasian as they came. I should have had Rylee give me a breakdown of the people who might have wanted to get their hands on one of the campers. There was a hint of an accent in Butler's voice. It wasn't English. It wasn't Australian. It was almost like Amara's accent, only a more professional version of it.

All at once I wasn't scared, or at least, I wasn't *as* scared. Trying to sort out who he was detached me from the situation just enough to calm me down. Plus, I didn't think he wanted to kill me. He wanted information. I could do this. I could hold out until they got here.

"S-sir," I said, forcing my voice to shake. "It's a camp." Jason's words flooded my mind, and they practically fell out of my mouth. "It's just a camp for a bunch of leather-belt-making losers."

One of Butler's eyebrows rose.

"I don't even like it there, sir ... but it's just a camp."

"Uh-huh." Butler drew a breath, nodded, then stood up. "Are you sure that's the way you want to play this, kid?"

I clenched my jaw. I guess that single gesture was enough for Butler to take it as an answer. His foot, shiny leather shoe and all, struck out and drove into my stomach. The chair toppled backward, and I went with it. I caught a glimpse of another man behind me, but before I could really look at him, he dropped to his knees and placed a leather glove over my eyes and pressed my head into the chair. Then something sharp stabbed into my neck. Coolness spread down across my chest and then throughout the rest of my body.

It was over before I had a chance to react, and as the hand came away, my vision clouded with a fog that darkened like a brewing storm until it was black, and I was out.

* * *

When I woke up, my body ached like I'd ... well, it felt pretty much like I'd been tied to a chair for a couple days and beaten senseless. My mouth felt like I'd fallen asleep in the desert.

Who was this guy and what the heck did he want? And why wasn't the CIA busting through the doors yet? Yaakov would've had the images of my abduction pulled up instantly. But maybe he wouldn't want to tell Dalson or Smith about them because he'd have to admit to hacking their system.

"Can I get you something?" the man asked. His tone was as pleasant as if he'd invited me over for tea and was now asking if I'd like some sugar.

I hesitated and then said, "W-water."

He nodded and poured a glass of ice water from a jug on the end table beside him. Then he took a straw from a container beneath the coffee table, put it in the cup, and held it up to my lips. It was the best-tasting water on the planet, and for a moment I thought maybe I'd get out of this mess. And then Butler pulled back a step, threw the water in my face, and slapped me across the cheek. Hard. My whole face stung. That's when I did something very, very unspy-like.

I started to cry.

I tried not to. I didn't want to do it, but the tears just came, and then my nose started running, and I started sobbing even harder.

Butler shook his head, and that mysterious hand gripped my head from behind, jabbed the needle into my neck, and then, again, the world went black.

CHAPTER 35

Four times I woke up, and four times, Butler was there. Sometimes he was smiling and talking to me as though we were old friends. Then he'd suddenly turn into a raging lunatic and pound on me some more. Each time he asked me about the camp.

"Tell me about the camp."

"What do they teach you at the camp?"

"Who runs the camp?"

"What made you join?"

"What is your real name?"

I answered his questions as honestly as any camper would do if they really were a camper and not a CIA operative.

"It's a stupid summer camp."

"They teach us arts and crafts and archery."

"Mr. Smith and Mr. Dalson."

"My dad made me join. My dad put me in this stupid camp."

"My name is Matt. Matt Cambridge."

I cried a lot. I wish I hadn't. I hated looking like such a baby. But I couldn't help it. This guy was nuts, and he was about to use my skin to make a new pair of boots or something. I cursed myself for getting caught. I cursed the camp for not having better security, and I cursed the CIA for not getting their butts in gear and getting me out of here.

If the curtains had been drawn, I wouldn't have had a clue about how long I was in there, but twice when I woke up, it was night, and twice, it was day. Each time, a pit of despair sank deeper into my stomach. The CIA wasn't coming for me. No one was coming for me. It didn't make sense, except maybe they couldn't find me. Or maybe they had that rule of disavowing all knowledge of captured agents, like they did on *Mission Impossible*.

That's just a movie, Matt. Keep it together.

They're coming ... aren't they? If they could find me, they would've by now. My mouth opened as if my mind had split and one half of me, the half that controlled motor skills, wanted to talk. To tell Butler everything he wanted to know. The other half of me, the half that handled speech, refused. Barely. It was a thread of resistance that could be snapped with one more strong word.

I wasn't going to make it.

I swore. And when I did, Butler smiled and injected me with whatever it was that kept knocking me out.

* * *

"Well, kid," Butler said when I groggily woke up for the fifth time, "you've done a good job. Been real convincing. But time's a-wasting. Why don't we just cut to the chase? I don't like hurting kids." He smiled and shook his head. "Okay, I guess I do kind of like it. But it doesn't have to be kids. I like hurting adults, too."

And small animals, I bet. I hadn't noticed at first, but my feet felt cold, and I glanced down. My pant legs had been rolled up to my knees, and my feet were in a very large mixing bowl, like you'd find at a family reunion where your aunt makes enough potato salad for forty people.

"W-what's going on?" I glanced up at the crazy man, and then back down at my bare feet, and then back up. Now I knew what a true psychopath looked like. "What is this?"

Butler stretched out his back and frowned. Then he nodded and walked across the room to a small closet and pulled out a metal trolley, the kind you see at school dances with the plates of brownies. It had a greasy blanket draped over the top, and the grin Butler wore as he pushed it across the floor made me want to puke. He was going to show me severed body parts and then tell me how he was going to add mine to his collection. That didn't explain the bare feet in the mixing bowl, but who knew what kind of crazy stuff this guy could think up?

My breath came in quick, shallow rasps.

"Sure you don't have another name?" he asked. "Absolutely certain you want to stick with Matt Cambridge? And you're sure there's not something else going on at that camp of yours? Something you'd like to tell me?"

"Please, whatever you're about to do, don't. Please. I'll tell you anything, but I can't tell you what I don't know."

"I know you will," he said. Then, with the flourish of a magician, Butler pulled the blanket off the trolley, revealing three very well-worn automobile batteries. Wires ran from the terminals of each battery and disappeared into the end of a fist-sized box with a switch. Three long wires emerged on the other side of the box, each with an alligator clip on the end. Butler looked up at me and smiled.

"This is a real treat for me," he said. "I don't get to do this nearly enough." He attached each clip to the metal bowl and then pulled a large jug from the bottom of the trolley and poured water over my feet, filling the bowl enough to cover my ankles. Then he stood back to examine his work and smiled. "Do you know what it feels like to be electrocuted?" He didn't wait for an answer. "It's like your insides are on fire. It actually cooks you. Did you know that?" He wrinkled his nose. "Burning flesh is one of those smells that takes a long time to get used to. I'd say it's only been in the last year or so that I've started to like the scent, and I've been doing this for years and years."

That did it.

I totally lost it.

I screamed and thrashed against my straps. I threw my head back against the headrest of my chair, hoping to somehow nudge the chair enough to get my feet out of the water. My screams turned to shrieks, the kind you'd hear from a girl at a haunted house, only a hundred times worse. It felt like the screech was coming from deep within my chest. Like my whole body was begging for its life.

Butler's fist struck the side of my face and silenced me completely. The world flickered for a moment.

"Shut. Up," he said. "Got it? Shut. Your. Mouth."

I blinked until my vision cleared and licked at the blood I felt oozing over my lip.

"Tell me your name," he said. "It's the easiest question I can ask. You'll tell me your name, and I'll check it out. If it's true, we'll have a little talk, and I'll let you go." He pressed his hand to his chest. "I am a man of my word."

I spat a mouthful of blood onto the carpet and blinked away the tears that were once again streaming down my cheeks. "Y-you d-don't understand. You have the wr-wrong kid." I sniffed. "I am Matt Cambridge. That's really who I am. I swear."

Butler rubbed his nose and put his hand on the switch.

"One."

"Please," I begged. "Please don't."

"Two."

I couldn't go on. The idea of having this crazy psychopath cook me from the inside out was too much to handle. "Okay, okay!" I said quickly, "I'll tell you what you want to know. I will. I'm a spy. Well, not yet. I will be. I will be a spy. For the CIA. That's what the camp is. It's a training camp for the CIA where they train kids. It's a spy camp."

He raised an eyebrow.

He wanted a name. He didn't think I was Matt, and he certainly didn't believe I was Gunnar. I blurted the first name that came to my mind.

"I'm Chase. Chase Erickson. I'm just some punk wannabe. A real loser. I'm not the kid you want. But that's the truth. Please. I'll tell you everything."

Butler's smile widened. I thought he was going to let me go now that I was telling the truth ... well, except for the name. But instead he looked at me and said, "Two and a half."

"What? No!" I shouted and thrashed in my chair, "Please, Butler, no! I told you, the camp is run by the CIA. Please!"

"Three!"

He flicked the switch.

CHAPTER 36

Sparks burst from the ends of the alligator clips on the metal bowl. I screamed and thrashed, and screamed and thrashed again, and then ... I stopped thrashing and stopped screaming. There was no pain. No massive jolt of electricity coursing through my body. No smell of burning flesh as Butler had suggested. The sparks were shooting to my knees, but I didn't feel anything. I wiggled my toes. There was no electricity at all.

Butler flicked off the switch, and the sparks stopped. "Well done, Cambridge. Well done."

What was going on? I breathed quick heavy breaths and felt my head lighten.

"All right, take it easy," he said. "Breathe slower. Purse your lips. You'll hyperventilate if you keep that up."

This was another trick. Wasn't it?

He took a small remote control and pointed it at the ceiling. A small red light that I hadn't noticed before blinked twice and then stayed off.

My head swam, and I forced myself to take slower breaths until I started feeling more ... present. Butler strolled casually into the kitchen and returned with a wooden chair.

"All right, look ..." He sat down and rubbed his hands together. "I'm supposed to go over the interrogation with you. Now that it's over,

I mean. Crucible Learning Protocols, CLPs, and all that nonsense. You know the drill."

"C-crucible?" That was the training I was supposed to get, wasn't it?

"But honestly, kid," Butler continued, "you did great." He rocked back in his chair. "I gave you my A-game too. I mean, I was all over the place. Happy, angry, nice, mean." He smiled. "You took it on the chin, son. Well done." He rubbed his hands again. "Right up until the end, I thought you'd figured out it was a Delta challenge. Right up to the end. But those were real screams at the end." He nodded. "I know screams, Cambridge, and those were real."

I tried to clear my throat. "Delta challenge?"

"I knew it," he said. "Wow. I'm really impressed, kid." He pulled out a clipboard from behind his chair. "Right, I'm supposed to impart some wisdom, so here it is." He cleared his throat dramatically. "Interrogators are like vintners."

I felt my brow furrow, and Butler must've seen it, because he added, "Vintners. You know, winemakers."

I blew out a breath. "I don't get it. This ... this was a test?"

"Delta event, Cambridge. C'mon, let your mind catch up. Don't fight it." He tapped his pen on his clipboard.

My mouth gaped. This had all been a test? This was the Delta event and this psychopath worked for the camp? He worked for the CIA? No, it's not possible. It can't be that. It's another trick. My heart pounded in my ears, and all I could think about was escape.

"Anyway," he continued, "a vintner is a winemaker, and every winemaker thinks their wine is the best. They say it's because they have better grapes or a better process. Let's be honest: grapes are grapes. But process, that's something that has effect. Same goes for interrogations." He tapped his index finger to his temple. "It's all about the method. As you might have guessed, I employ the keep-'em-guessing method. I give you the opposite of what you expect, and in return, you become mentally fatigued."

He smacked his lips. "Point is, when you're getting interrogated, take your mind off what you're feeling and focus on sorting out the methods of the interrogator. Each one is different, and each one has their own unique method. Their own brands of wine, as it were." He shook a finger at me. "For example, and this is a funny story, my mentor used to start every high-level interrogation by breaking one finger of the suspect." He smiled. "No questions. He just walked into the room, and before a single word, he'd break the finger."

I felt my eyes widen, and I started breathing heavy again.

"I know, it seems harsh," he said, "but when you're talking about high-profile political targets, you need to know who you're dealing with, right?"

The door at the end of the room opened, and Mr. Smith and Mr. Dalson walked in as casually as if they were entering a coffee house to order their daily latte. I wanted to shout out for help, but they appeared entirely at ease and not shocked in the least to see me bound to a chair. I made a quick decision to keep quiet.

"Let him up," Dalson said.

Oh, thank goodness!

Butler put a hand on my shoulder and smiled again. He leaned over and untied my legs, then my arms, and then reached around me. I heard a click, and the straps holding me to the chair fell away. I jumped. The top of my head struck Butler's chin, and he stumbled back. I shoved his cart after him, and it smacked into his legs. He cursed and grabbed his shins. I sprinted for the balcony door, but my feet were wet, and I slipped as soon as I stepped off the rug. I scrambled to my feet again and, this time, managed to stay upright and get to the door. I heaved on it, but it didn't budge. I moved the lock and pulled again.

"It doesn't open," Mr. Dalson said. His voice was as calm as a hypnotist's. "Adrenaline is ripping through you right now, Matt. I need you to get it under control."

I whirled around and pressed my back against the glass and raised my fists. Butler was rubbing his chin and limping, and Mr. Smith was as stone-faced as ever.

Dalson took a step forward. "This was your Crucible Training, Matt. It was also a Delta competition." He gestured to Butler. "Butler is a pro. He's been the head CIA interrogator for fifteen years; we're lucky he agreed to help us out."

Butler dabbed a Kleenex to his bloody lip and nodded at me.

"Butler's done a couple others tonight. You're only the second one not to crack."

My teeth clenched, and my hands shook. "You dragged me to this place and kept me strapped to a chair for ... for ..." My mind raced. How long had I been there? I'd seen the sun come up and go down at least twice. "Days," I said. "You kept me tied to a chair for days just for a stupid ... freaking ... competition?"

"Crucible Training," Dalson said, without a hint of being put off by my tone. "Crucible, by definition, means *occasion of extreme trial.* Besides, I'm sure if you give it some thought, you'll realize you haven't been in a chair for days."

I blinked. "I haven't?"

Dalson smiled. "It's only been ..." He glanced at his watch and muttered, "Let's see, dinner was at five ..." He looked up. "It's been five hours."

"Wh-what? It's only been hours? Not days?" I shook my head and nodded toward Butler. "It was night when he snatched me. Then daylight when I woke up. Then night again, then daylight ..." I shook my head. This was another trick. Another test.

Dalson nodded to Butler, and the interrogator walked over to a switch in the kitchen and flicked it. Instantly the dark windows behind me illuminated. I turned and found myself looking out at a daylight scene. I heard the click of the switch being flicked again, and the scene outside the window changed to night.

"It's ... it's fake?" I asked breathlessly.

Dalson nodded. "It's fake." He extended his hands palms up and walked toward me. I scuttled sideways along the wall. He sighed and said, "The drug you were given messes with your sense of time. Add the false lighting, and it's easy to convince your mind of anything." I flinched again with his next step, but only slightly. "Take it easy. This has been part of the training, Matt. It's why you're here."

"To get beaten up?" My voice cracked, and I felt fresh tears sting my eyes. "What the heck kind of camp lets their campers get strapped to a chair to have the crap kicked out of them? You can't keep me here. You can't. You—you have to let me call my parents."

Dalson raised an eyebrow and looked about ready to say something when Butler started clapping. "Oh, I am impressed," he said, laughing. "This kid is method. He doesn't break character for anything." He pointed to the metal bowl of water. "I bet we really could've fried him, and he still wouldn't have talked." He shook a finger at me. "You wouldn't have talked, would you?" He threw his head back and laughed again. "Where do you find these kids, Dalson? I bet he's better than that crippled girl. I mean, she just sat there and stared daggers at me. She's tough as nails, sure, but anyone interrogating her would know she's hiding something. But this kid ..." He laughed again. "He's so convincing I almost thought you gave me the wrong kid."

Mr. Smith gave Butler a hard look, and as soon as Butler noticed, his smile vanished. Then Mr. Smith turned to me. "Who taught you counter-interrogation techniques?"

Counter-interrogation techniques? Really? That was what we were doing? I drew several long, deep breaths. My heart stopped hammering to get out of my chest. *This was part of it, Matt. Get yourself together.* I realized that, at the end of it all, I really had spilled my guts. I'd told Butler everything. Well, I had at least told him enough that, had the interrogation been real, I would never have had a chance. Still, Butler seemed impressed. Why? Because I lasted five hours?

"Matt!" Smith barked.

I jumped so high I think they might have thought I was trying to fly away. "W-what?" I managed.

Butler grimaced. "My last punch might have been harder than I intended." He hunched and lowered his face so it was level with mine. Blood smeared his lip where my head had connected. "Hope I didn't do any lasting damage." He smiled. "You've got a lot of promise, lad. Real top-shelf material. If you don't win your last competition, I look forward to seeing you at the next camp. I bet I could work with you to make you a real expert."

"N-next camp?" I stammered.

Dalson checked his watch. "Right. Well, it's time for you to rejoin your team, Mr. Cambridge. I suspect they'll be wondering where you are right about now. And you're going to want to be preparing for tomorrow."

"Tomorrow?"

"Final Delta competition."

I clenched my fist when Dalson walked over to put his hand on my shoulder, but I let him guide me toward the exit. I flinched when Butler jabbed me playfully in the shoulder as I walked by. I was led up a metal staircase, and when I stepped out of the door at the top, I found myself in the middle of Camp Friendship. The building I'd emerged from was a shed with red brick walls and a corrugated steel roof. It looked like a place where you'd store a lawnmower and hedge trimmer, which was no doubt exactly what they'd intended it to look like.

"An underground interrogation room," I said under my breath.

"What was that?" Dalson asked from behind me.

I swallowed and shook my head.

"Well, good job, Matt," he said. "I suggest you get some rest." He and Smith turned and headed off together, leaving me alone on an almost deserted campus.

My hands shook as I made my way back to the Delta cabin. I didn't really know how, but clearly I had made it to the final competition. Except, after what I had just gone through, I wasn't entirely sure I wanted to be a spy anymore. My face hurt. My stomach hurt ... in fact, every part of me hurt.

I wasn't sure I had what it took to be a spy.

CHAPTER 37

"So you didn't lose?" Angie asked. "We're still in the competition?"

I shrugged and then flinched from pain and exhaustion. "I dunno the score. Dalson told me to be ready for tomorrow. For the final competition." The idea of having just one more competition was almost a relief. This camp had been great, except when it wasn't, and when it wasn't, I was usually getting my face beaten in.

It was almost over. One more event. That's it. Just one more. I could see the light at the end of the tunnel.

Rylee nodded at me. "Who ran the interrogation? Was it really Ingleton?"

I'd barely managed to tell my team the gist of what had happened. Recounting the whole thing made my head hurt. Rylee's question only half registered. "Huh? Oh, he, um, he said his name was Butler."

"Butler!" Juno blew out a breath and looked up the ceiling. He said something that sounded Japanese, and then said, "So it *was* Robert Ingleton. I didn't think he'd personally be doing the interrogations. I figured he'd be observing. Wow. You learned from the best."

"He is the best," Amara added. The others nodded knowingly.

"I had a cousin in another camp," Angie began, "and Butler broke his nose in the first forty-five seconds of an interrogation." She grabbed my chin and turned my face one way, then another. "You fared pretty well."

I blew out a shuddering breath. "I didn't fare well at all. That guy was certifiable. He was nuts."

"Nuts?" Rylee asked. "I doubt it. Brilliant, maybe. He's the CIA's top interrogator. Imagine all the stuff he could teach us. What he could prepare us for."

"Practical as ever, Rylee," Angie said.

"What's that supposed to mean?" Rylee asked. She stood up and pointed at Angie. "I've had just about enough of your snide little comments, Angie. You might be a psychopath, but that doesn't mean I'm afraid of you."

Angie stood up and took a step toward Rylee. "Oh no? You should be."

I wouldn't have thought Rylee so aggressive, but she stood toe-to-toe with Angie, and the two of them shouted at each other. Their argument quickly gathered steam, and before long, everyone was yelling at each other. Everyone but me. I was entirely fixated on what Rylee had said about Butler. The same thing Dalson had said about him: he worked for the CIA as head interrogator.

Of course, Rylee was right. He could teach us so much. He was crazy, no question, but if I did end up becoming a spy, and I got discovered and interrogated, I needed to know how to handle myself. I placed a cold pack on the side of my face and lay back on my bed.

There was something else too. Something in the back of my mind that scratched at this CIA idea like a rat trying to escape a cage. I couldn't quite get a handle on it, but it wasn't right.

One thing was the fact that my dad had signed me up. How had he done that? I'd been to his building. I'd seen him work. That had to be what was bothering me: how in the world had my dad gotten me in here in the first place? Was the company my dad worked for a front for some clandestine operation, and they just had real janitors working there? No. That wasn't it. There was a piece to this puzzle that I couldn't put my finger on. A piece I wanted to discover.

One more challenge, I told myself. *Just one more.*

"Enough!" Yaakov shouted. The arguments in the room silenced at once, which was good, since it looked as if punches would've been thrown with one more insult.

"Thank you!" Yaakov added in response to the silence. "Whether you're keen to learn from Butler, or hate his guts, it doesn't matter."

I glanced over at our hacker. His forehead was beaded with sweat, and his hands shook like the branches of a shrub.

"The only thing that matters is that tomorrow we're in the final Delta competition, and we need to be ready."

"Fine," Angie said.

Rylee folded her arms across her chest and plopped down on her bed. Juno and Amara went to their respective beds as well, and in a matter of seconds, the room had gone from chaos to silence.

I cleared my throat. I needed to be careful about how I was going to ask my next question. I wanted one more shot at getting information from my teammates, and this might be my last chance. "Okay, let's be smart about this. Let's just talk it out. Let's start with the basics. What can we *know*, based on experience, about the final competition?"

Rylee nodded. "Right. Well, we know it's the *final* competition. We couldn't be sure about that because of the cancellation last week, but now we know it's really the final one."

I nodded. I didn't see how that made any difference at all, but since Rylee felt it was worth mentioning, I pretended her comment was a valid point. "Good," I said. "What else?"

Amara paced across the room. "We know we'll get mission parameters," he said.

"It'll be a location," Angie added, "and probably a goal."

"There's always a goal," Yaakov said.

"You'll have to interpret what the goal means," Rylee added. "Like that competition I mentioned before, about how the teams were supposed to steal something from the building downtown. They were told it had to be something of great importance. That's all. They had to interpret what the term meant."

I rubbed the back of my neck. "Good. So it's fair that we expect the challenge to be off-site, right?"

"Good question," Juno said. "Can anyone remember a camp where final challenges were on-site?"

Everyone shook their heads.

"Anyone have a cell phone?" Juno asked. "We might need it if we're in the city."

I knew Yaakov had seen me toss Jason's broken cell phone into my storage bin on the first day, and it was entirely possible that the others had seen it too, so I said, "I had one, but it broke the first day when I fought Chase on the bus."

"Seems like a million years ago, doesn't it?" Rylee asked.

I nodded. It did. I could hardly believe it had only been three weeks. It really did feel like we'd been together for months.

Yaakov sighed. "I turned mine in when we got here, but it doesn't really matter. If we need phones, we can get burners from pretty much any convenience store."

"Money?" Angie asked. "How much do we have?"

"I don't have much," Rylee said. "A few bucks."

"Me too," Juno added.

"I think we'll need to remember something," Amara added. "This could be totally different from previous years. From the start, Clakk has been saying things might not play out the way they have in previous years."

"Good point, Amara," I said. "So we don't really know what to expect, and either I'll be setting the overall mission, or I won't be." I sighed along with a few of my teammates. "Basically this is one mission that there is absolutely no way for us to prepare for."

"Basically," Juno said, "I think that's exactly right."

"Wouldn't be fun if it were too easy," Angie added.

"I don't know about that," Yaakov said. "I think an easy mission would be great fun."

I had to agree with that. Still, we were one competition away from the end. One event away from my goal of making it to the end of camp with my secret intact. I had thought I'd be okay with not winning, but not anymore. I was too close. I wasn't sure who the last three teams were, but I knew Team Grizzly was one of them.

I could taste victory. It was right there, dangling just out of reach like a carrot on a stick. I could do this. We could do this.

"Let's get some sleep," Rylee suggested. "Tomorrow's going to be here before we know it."

CHAPTER 38

There were rumors circulating around the camp during the morning, but it wasn't clear who had been eliminated in the previous night's competition until we walked into the mess hall for breakfast. The tables and chairs had been arranged into three rows, and Arctic Fox's banner was gone. Squirrel, Grizzly, and Hyena were the only ones that remained.

"And then there were three," Juno said.

"How did Bratersky lose before Becca?" Rylee asked under her breath.

As we walked down the line toward the Delta tables, the campers in Team Grizzly congratulated me.

"Well done, Captain."

"Glad you didn't break, Captain."

What? That comment caught me off guard. I *had* broken. I'd broken badly. I was kind of relieved no one seemed to realize that.

"Way to go, Matt," another camper said. "I knew we were on the winning team."

It continued the entire length of the table and even trickled around us after we'd taken our seats. When we were allowed to get our breakfast, it continued in that line as well. I actually started feeling pretty good about myself. Sure, I hadn't lasted all that long, but maybe that was the point. Maybe everyone has to break. Clearly, I'd lasted longer than Bratersky, and that alone was reason to grin. If nothing else, I'd proven myself to have some worth. I had myself half convinced that if they figured out who I was now, they'd still keep me around, but just before that belief really took hold, a knot formed in my stomach. No. No, they wouldn't. I had to do something really great. Really remarkable. I had to prove myself in this last event. That was the only thing that would work.

Once everyone had eaten, Dalson stood at the front of the room and pointed a remote control toward the ceiling. A large screen unrolled behind him. "Campers," he began, "in a few minutes, we will begin the final event. And three days from now, Camp Friendship will come to a close. Many of you will not be back until next summer. Others will be back in the fall." He straightened. "And of course, some of you will not be back ever again." He glanced down at the remote and then pointed it up at the projector mounted on the ceiling. "Let's take a look at how we got here, shall we?"

"Oh, this is going to be great," Juno whispered.

The video montage played out, complete with soundtrack.

It started with the soccer ball challenge and paid special attention to Becca and her explosion. It turned out she'd stepped on a mine on the sidelines behind the goal. The explosion had thrown her into the goal. She'd ricocheted off the post and then settled in the netting unconscious. You could almost hear her bones crunching. I glanced across the room. Becca was as red as a beet.

Scenes from the paintball game played out next. From a bird's-eye view we got to see how the teams had moved. It was as if they'd received months of military training. The scene cut in a number of times to images that could only have been recorded by cameras in the woods.

It made me wonder just how safe I'd been calling Jason, but then the paintball course was a different part of the camp, and they probably planned on using that section all the time. They either knew about my calls to Jason and didn't care, or didn't know. I decided not to worry about it.

The next series of images was a montage of Butler pounding the stuffing out of us in the interrogation. It was nice to see that I wasn't the only one who'd gotten pummeled. The final scene that played out was one of me:

"Okay, okay," the screen version of me said. "I'll tell you. I'll tell you everything."

The room went silent, and everyone's attention fixated on the screen. I felt my cheeks heat up.

"I'm Chase. Chase Erickson. I'm just some punk wannabe. A real loser. I'm not the kid you want. But that's the truth. Please. I'll tell you everything."

The mess hall erupted with laughter, none louder than Team Grizzly, but even several members of Chase's team chuckled.

"Two and a half," Butler's voice said from the screen above.

"What? No!" I shouted and thrashed in my chair. "Please, Butler, no! I told you, the camp is run by the CIA. Please!"

More laughter from the campers.

"Three!"

The sparks shot up from the bowl at my feet, and the screen went black. Laughter was reignited, as was a smattering of applause.

"Well done, Cambridge," Juno said. "I can't believe they couldn't break you. I heard everyone breaks."

But I *had* broken. What was he talking about? I'd given my real name half a dozen times, and then spilled everything about the CIA involvement in the camp.

"For obvious reasons," Mr. Dalson said from the front of the room, "Team Grizzly took first place in that competition. Well done, Mr. Cambridge." He turned back to the campers and began talking about how the last couple days of camp would work.

His voice faded into the background. I didn't really hear what he was saying. His *Well done, Mr. Cambridge* was all I could think about.

Well done? What part of that interrogation had I done well? The crying? The begging? The spilling of my guts? The only thing I might have done well was giving a false name, but that was only after I'd given my real name a dozen times.

That feeling I'd had days earlier—the gnawing, scratching feeling in my gut about Camp Friendship and the CIA—returned full force. I glanced around the room, and then around my table. It was as if my mind was screaming that the answer was right in front of me, but I just wasn't connecting the dots.

"Good luck!" Dalson's words rocked me out of my daze. "Buses leave in fifteen minutes."

"Buses," I said. "So we were right about it being off-site."

My teammates nodded. The nervous tension at the table was palpable.

"All right," I said. "Let's grab our bags and get going. We have one more competition to win."

Everyone pushed away from their tables and made for the doors, but I hesitated. It seemed every time I thought I had a handle on things, something else swept my feet out from under me and reminded me that I was an uninformed trespasser in this camp. It made absolutely zero sense that I'd won the last event for *not* breaking when clearly I had broken down in a child-like fit. I considered the options. There really were only two. Either "not breaking" meant not breaking *first*, which might have been true since we didn't get to see clips of how Chase or Becca had done. Or what I'd said to Butler wasn't true.

A chill of panic settled over me like a wet blanket, and the thought that everything I thought was true about the camp really wasn't true just about got away from me. Butler was a CIA interrogator, I reminded myself. Rylee had told me that, and Dalson had mentioned it as well, right after the interrogation. If Butler was CIA, this camp was CIA. As if to confirm my thoughts, my gaze fell on the back of one of the chairs at our table and I spotted the familiar *PCIA* etched carefully into the wooden backrest.

Since Juno had pointed out the first *PCIA* at the archery range I'd seen hundreds of the etched letters. They were on doors and handles and plates. Almost anywhere those letters could be etched without being obvious, there they were. *Property of the Central Intelligence Agency.* It was, as Juno had put it, a reminder, and that reminder was exactly what I needed to put my mind at ease. Nerves were getting the better of me, and I had to get it together.

I followed my team to the cabin where we grabbed our things. When we opened the door to head to the buses, Alexis, Rob, and Duncan were standing there, bags in hand.

"Where do these little twerps think they're going?" Angie asked.

I looked at the trio.

Rob stood straight. "You said we'd be part of the team if you were allowed to bring more players."

"You're allowed," Alexis said. "For the final Delta event, you can bring as many more players as you want."

I turned to Rylee. "Is that true?"

She nodded. "Yeah, but you shouldn't. No one does. This is when the Delta teams stand on their own." She nodded in the direction of the parking lot. "No one else is going to bring anyone other than their main team."

"They're especially not going to be bringing a bunch of children," Amara said.

Angie leaned forward and put her hands on her knees, and when she spoke, it was in a voice a mother might use when talking to an infant. "Is this your first camp, little ones?"

The trio didn't respond. They just stared at me with eyes that seemed to frost the air between us.

"Sorry, guys," I said. "Maybe next time."

I took a step, and Rob grabbed my arm roughly and jerked me toward him. Instinctively, I turned and punched him in the chest, knocking the younger camper to the ground.

Alexis and Duncan helped their teammate to his feet and then turned to me. Alexis looked like she'd just been told someone had melted her favorite doll.

"You said ..." Alexis said. "You said if we ... we could come along."

"What did they do for you?" Yaakov asked.

"Nothing." I felt my cheeks flush. "If other teams were bringing extras, then I'd bring you along. But they're not, so we're not."

"You *did* promise," Duncan said. He didn't look upset, but his tone felt like a warning.

Juno must've heard the tone too, because he stepped forward and poked Duncan in the chest. "Stand down, camper."

Duncan glared at Juno for a beat and then fell back in line with Alexis and Rob.

"This is why you never involve such little kids in your events," Rylee said. "They just lack any trace of maturity to know their place." The muscles in Alexis's face flexed, and Rylee rolled her eyes.

I blew out a breath and started walking toward the bus. "Let's go, guys."

Counselor Clakk stood at the door to the bus, tapping a clipboard impatiently against the side of her leg. The other two buses were already being driven away, kicking up dust behind them.

"About time," she said. "Guess you wanted to give the other teams a fighting chance, huh?" She smiled and rested her hand on my shoulder. "Very, very well done with the interrogation, Matt. I'm not convinced you're going to be able to bring 'er home for a win, but you have succeeded in making me think you're not entirely incompetent. That's no small feat."

"Um, thank you, ma'am ... I think."

She shook the clipboard at me and said, "This is the directive for this Delta event." I reached for the board, but she pulled it back behind her. "You have to pick a target. Tell your driver where to take you. You must then execute your plan before three o'clock. Miss that deadline and you will be in last place. Understand?"

I didn't have a clue, but I nodded all the same. She pulled the clipboard from behind her back and handed it over. It held a single piece of white paper with a single word typed in the center of the page: *Disrupt*.

I looked up at Ms. Clakk and felt my eyebrows draw together. "Disrupt what?"

She stared at me stone-faced. "That would be the target you need to come up with."

"So, then," I began, "we're just supposed to ..."

"You are to *disrupt* something, Mr. Cambridge. Or cause a disruption. Or cause something to be disrupted. It is not a difficult concept. Believe it or not, this is not a difficult task. Show the judges that you can execute a mission in broad daylight, without being compromised. This challenge," she continued, "is all about adapting."

"Disrupt and adapt," I said, under my breath.

Counselor Clakk blew out a breath. "Get on the bus. Pick a location before you get into town." She started to walk away and then turned back to us. "Three o'clock." She held up three fingers. "Don't blow it by being late."

I climbed the steps along with the rest of the team and made my way to the back of the bus. I plopped myself into one of the seats and waited for everyone else to get on board. The bus started moving as soon as we were all in our seats.

"Thoughts?" I said.

"Disrupt," Amara said. "*Disrupt* is a term that gives us a lot of leeway. I can think of a dozen ways to implement that directive."

"Can you?" I asked.

"I'm sure we all can," Amara said.

"That's not the point," Rylee said. "The idea is originality. If we don't win, this event will be key to us getting into the fall session. And if we want to win, the disruption has to be original."

"I think scale is more important than originality," Amara said. "Think infrastructure."

I scratched the back of my head. "Infrastructure?" The word sounded familiar, but I couldn't remember the meaning.

"Yeah," Amara said, "infrastructure. You know, transportation, communication, power ..." He looked at me expectantly.

"What if we disable the city's sewage system?" Yaakov asked.

"That would work," Amara said, nodding thoughtfully.

"Eww, no!" Angie said. "I'm not messing with sewage."

"I'm with Angie on that," I said. I wouldn't have had the first clue how to disable a city sewage system anyway.

Rylee nodded. "It has to be something obvious. Something that is a clear disruption. Something that happens between now and three o'clock."

"We could blow up a bridge," Amara suggested. "That wouldn't be so hard, and it would be really disruptive."

I laughed. "Yeah, that would be real great." The rest of the team didn't laugh, and I looked at Amara. He seemed almost offended that I'd dismissed his suggestion so quickly. "No!" I said more forcefully. "We're not blowing up a bridge."

"A building, then?" Juno asked. "Or mess with a transportation hub?" He pointed a finger at me. "Oh, we should go to the airport. It's easy to cause a disturbance there. Everyone's on edge all the time. We could cause a pretty bad panic with some minor effort."

"That's not a bad idea," Rylee said. The rest of the team nodded.

I shook my head. Messing with flights was crossing a line. People were freaked out about flying enough as it was. "We need something more original," I said.

"True," Angie said. The bus bounced over a cattle guard and then pulled onto a paved road.

"What then?" Yaakov asked. "A disruption isn't rocket science."

I leaned forward and pressed my palm into my forehead. A

disruption. A disruption. I could do this. I was the king of disrupting stuff. Heck, the reason I was in this camp in the first place was basically because of a disruption. That's when it hit me. A disruption. "Like a prank." I spoke without meaning to.

"A prank?" Rylee shrugged. "Sure, I guess so. We're not setting whoopee cushions under your teacher's chair or anything. It has to be a significant disruption. As long as it's a particularly disruptive prank, you can think of it however you'd like."

I rubbed my hands together and felt my mouth spread into a grin. All limits were off. This was the CIA. I could pull any prank I wanted and face no risk of jail, since the people who arrested me were probably going to be CIA anyway. And if they weren't, the CIA would swoop in and rescue me.

It suddenly became very obvious what the disruption had to be. "Driver," I called down the aisle.

The man at the front glanced at me through the rearview mirror.

"Central Subway Station," I said.

He nodded, and I turned to the rest of the team. "It's a transportation hub," I said, "and I have just the disruption in mind."

Jason and I had already formulated the plan. We'd discussed it dozens of times. I made a checklist in my head. I'd need to use my phone, and I'd need Jason to make some calls for me, but, yeah, I could do this. My hand went to my pocket, and I felt the cell phone—battery still separate. I was just about to pull the pieces out and call my friend, but I remembered the bus driver and thought better of it. Also, for all I knew, if my teammates heard me call Jason, they might get suspicious and think it was cheating. They hadn't wanted me to bring any extra campers. They probably didn't want me using outside help either.

I'd make the call privately as soon as I had the chance.

I smiled as the bus turned off the side road and onto the highway. This was good. It would work. No one was going to cause a bigger disruption than the mass evacuation of the central train station.

"I like that look," Angie said. "Do you have a plan?"

"I'm formulating one," I said.

The plan Jason and I had hatched for the train station was at least a hundred times larger than anything we'd done before. It was one of those things you never really intended to do; it was just something you talked about. Like kidnapping the principal or stealing a car.

But the plan was good. And what's more, it was something I'd really had a hand in creating. I wasn't going to win by accident. I was going to prove to these superspies that I belonged in this camp.

CHAPTER 39

"Okay," I said, plopping back into my seat, "I'm not going to pretend I'm the best leader here, guys."

"Oh, goody," Juno said, smacking his hands together. "This must be your inspirational speech."

The others laughed.

I ignored the comments. "We're using fireworks to cause a disruption at the central train station."

No one spoke for a moment. Then Rylee said, "Well, the station is certainly a pressure point. It's a good location."

"Thank you."

"What kind of disruption did you have in mind?" Angie asked. "I'm sure it's more than just showing up and setting off a few Roman candles."

"Um ... yeah," I said. "Of course there's a lot more to it than that." A bead of sweat trickled down the side of my face. Firing Roman candles *was* actually part of the plan. However, it sounded juvenile the way Angie said it, and I started second-guessing the entire thing.

Angie made tiny circles with her hands. "And do we get to know what the rest of the plan is?"

I drew a breath and held it. Either I embraced the plan fully, or I told them I had nothing, giving them yet another reason to think I'm a horrible Delta. I blew out a breath and made my decision. "I thought we'd modify some different kinds of fireworks and set them off in strategic locations at strategic times."

Juno scratched the back of his head. "Fireworks?"

"Um, yeah," I said.

Amara folded his arms across his chest. "I don't think it'll work. An explosion might work, but not fireworks. Who's afraid of fireworks?"

"Not everyone was raised in a bomb factory," Rylee said. "Fireworks *might* work to cause a disruption." She looked at me. "But he's right, an explosion would probably be better."

If she hadn't looked so serious, I would have laughed. "An explosion?" I looked around the group, hoping to see at least someone else wearing an expression of disbelief. They weren't. "No. No, absolutely not. We're not blowing up the train station. We could kill someone."

"Or *lots* of someones," Angie said. Sometimes she seemed entirely normal, and then she'd say something like that and her psychotic side really came through.

"Dis-rup-tion." I said the word carefully. "Not de-struc-tion."

"He's got a point," Juno said, cocking his head to the side. "If they wanted casualties, they'd have worded it differently. We might even get docked points for killing people."

He was joking. Juno was always joking.

Wasn't he?

"I still don't think that will be very effective," Amara said again.

"Very effective?" Yaakov said. "How long do fireworks last? A couple seconds? A minute? That's not a sufficient disruption. It might inconvenience a few passengers, but it's not going to disrupt the trains."

"And you could disrupt the trains?" I asked.

"Of course I could." He tapped his computer. "Do you want me to crash a couple into each other?"

"Now that would be a disruption," Angie said, pumping her fist in the air. "Let's add that to the fireworks plan, and then we'll have something. Plus, we could do it slow enough so that it would be unlikely for anyone to die."

"No. We're not having Yaakov crash any trains." I blew out a breath. "What's wrong with you people?"

"He's right," Rylee said. "It's a team exercise. If we're going to crash trains, we'd need to do it in a way that we could all be involved."

"That's not really what I meant," I said, trying to reel in the conversation. If I got to come to another one of these camps, I'd look for a camp activity that would help me manage crazy teammates. *Working with Psychopaths*, or something like that. "Ooookay," I continued, "if we're done talking about mass destruction and killing trainloads of people, how about we get back to the actual plan? Disruption via fireworks."

"I'll need a place to work," Amara said. "Modifying fireworks isn't something you do on the front steps to the station."

I rubbed my hands together. "Great, now we're on the right track. Who has suggestions for where we can do the work?"

Yaakov flipped open his computer and punched a few keys. "There's a public library a couple blocks away from the station. It's closed for renovations. We could work there."

"Nothing closer?" Angie asked. "I'm not a fan of walking great distances."

Yaakov rolled his eyes, turned back to his computer, and muttered, "I said a couple blocks, not a couple miles." He tapped a few more keys. "There's a bakery kitty-corner to the station's east entrance. Its security system is simple. We could work there."

"Great," Rylee said.

"Wait," I said. "You mean ..." I cleared my throat. "We break into it?"

Yaakov looked around the bus. "Well, it's Saturday, so they're probably going to be open—we'll have to give them a reason to close early."

"That'll be easy," Angie said.

"Easy?" I asked. "Really? Even if they closed early, we'd still have to break in."

Yaakov nodded slowly. "Um, yeah. Obviously. Unless you have a key, or a different safe house we could use?"

"What about the police?" I asked.

Yaakov sighed. "I told you; the security system is simple. It'll be off before we break in."

I leaned in and nodded to the front of the bus, indicating the driver, who I was quite sure would report us if we did something wrong. "And the camp won't care if we do that?"

"I don't see why they would," Juno said. "They don't want us getting picked up by the police, which is what would happen if we started modifying explosives out in the open."

"Relax, Captain," Angie said. "I'll personally secure the site for us."

I felt a burst of excitement I hadn't felt in a very long time. Already this was turning into the biggest prank of my life. It seemed there weren't any limits with this camp. Even though they didn't want us to get caught, I bet there was a simple way for them to get us out of trouble if they needed to. We were talking about the CIA, after all.

"What else do we need?" I asked.

"I'll need some time to hack into the station's security," Yaakov said.

"And someone needs to prepare exit routes," Juno added.

"I'll do that," Rylee said.

I nodded.

"Weapons," Angie said. "We're going to need weapons."

"For what?" I asked.

"In case someone tries to stop us."

"They're not going to stop all of us," I said. "We'll get the disruption without hurting anyone."

"Is that your thing?" Angie asked, giving me a disgusted look. "No harm to anyone? That's not—"

"Can we just get past this?" Rylee asked. "He said we're not using weapons on anyone, so let's just move on." She nodded at Yaakov. "Tell Angie where the bakery is, and she can secure the site. Maybe they'll have a guard dog she can wrestle or something."

Angie smiled. "I'll cross my fingers."

"Can we go over the plan in detail?" Juno asked. "I mean, I'd just like to know exactly what we're going to be doing."

Angie put her elbows on her knees. "Yeah, Captain, impress us by giving us just a bit more of your plan."

I rubbed my hands together and leaned back. "Okay, here's what I propose ..."

CHAPTER 40

When I was done, no one spoke. At least not for several minutes. At first I thought it was stunned silence. Like maybe they were so impressed they couldn't find the words to tell me how brilliant I was.

Then Angie spoke and shattered that illusion.

"It's like a plan a kid in middle school would come up with," she said.

Well ... yeah.

"It is really amateurish," Rylee agreed, deflating me even further. Then she added, "But it might work."

Yaakov eyed me suspiciously, then nodded. "He's not telling us everything."

"What?" Angie asked. "How do you know?"

"Because it just doesn't fit. He's not revealing everything."

"Cambridge," Juno pressed, "don't leave us out of the loop. We're a team."

Amara nodded. "It'll be more effective if you let us in on at least a bit more."

"Guys," I said, "this is our last challenge. We will not lose. I will not lose. We are winning this thing."

Juno licked his lips and nodded. "Yaakov's right. He's planning something else."

I groaned. "Can we just do this?"

For the rest of the ride, everyone kept to themselves, lost, it seemed, in their thoughts. They had the same expressionless faces you'd see on professional athletes before an event. Like they were envisioning what they'd be doing when we arrived.

An hour and a half later, the bus rolled to a stop on the curb outside of the Fourth Street subway station. We unloaded, and the driver leaned out of his seat.

He pointed to an alley across the street. "This bus will be parked there until three fifteen." He tapped his wrist. "Three fifteen. Not three sixteen. If you're late, you find your own way back to camp. If you decide to put your disturbance into effect before that time, you will have five minutes after you execute to get to the bus, or I leave, and again, you find your own way back." He turned around, pulled the doors closed, and the bus lurched forward.

"He's a real peach," Angie said as the bus pulled away from the curb. "We're really lucky to have such a sweetie for a driver."

"All right," I said. "So I guess we better not be late for our ride. The sooner we get this done, the better."

Yaakov turned his back on the station and pointed across the street. "There's the bakery."

The building was a bit run-down, but it was open, and I saw at least a couple people through the glass window.

"And you and Angie can get in there even though there are people in there?" I asked. "Are you sure we're not going to come back and find you arrested?"

"It's a bakery," Angie said, "not a bank."

"Yeah," Yaakov added. "We'll cut the power for a few minutes, wait for people to leave, and then secure it. Besides, even if the cops did show up, they'd probably just think we were two kids breaking in to make out."

All eyes turned to Yaakov, and no one spoke for several seconds. Then everyone started laughing at the same time.

"Making out?" Juno asked. "You and Angie?"

Angie cracked up again. "Keep your hands to yourself, techie."

"You know what I meant," Yaakov said.

"Fine, fine," I said. "Go." I turned to Rylee. "You and Juno figure out the escape routes and the best places for a disturbance."

"And me?" Amara asked.

"You and I will go get some fireworks." Part of me wanted to go alone, but I wouldn't know what to get. I'd probably end up with the wrong stuff, and we'd be in real trouble.

I felt like a quarterback who'd just laid out a play to his team. It was exhilarating. I smiled to myself and then realized everyone was looking at me and quickly dropped my grin.

"Right," I said. "Let's do it." I checked my watch. "It's just about ten o'clock. Let's meet at the bakery at noon." I felt like we should all put our hands into the center and give a team cheer. It was a fleeting thought, one that vanished instantly when everyone headed off in different directions.

"You want to call your asset, right?" Amara asked. "There's bound to be a phone over there."

"My asset, yeah. Right. A phone. Sure ... yeah ..." I rubbed my hands together. Okay. Here we go.

"I'm sure there's a phone inside the bakery," Amara said.

We didn't have time to leave the station and double back to the bakery. I checked my watch, and then my hand went to the pieces of my cell phone, except I wasn't sure how Amara would take my having a cell. I didn't want him to see it.

"I'll find one," I said. "You wait here."

"Wait here?" Amara's eyebrows inched together. "Why would I wait here?"

I shook my head. "I just have something to check on. I'll be right back. Wait here."

Amara glanced at his watch. "Okay, but I need time to make modifications, Matt."

"I'll be right back."

I ducked into the station, sprinted down one of the side halls, and squeezed between two blocks of lockers. I dug out the pieces of the phone, quickly put them together, and dialed Jason's number. He picked up on the third ring.

"Hello?"

"Jason, it's me."

"Cambridge?" His voice was a whisper.

"Of course it's me, you dolt."

"Shhh," he said. "Dude, where have you been? I've sent you a dozen messages."

I'd known it was a smart move to break down the phone. Jason clearly didn't understand the concept of "do not text."

"Look, man," Jason continued, his words coming in a rushed whisper, "I uploaded those photos you sent me so I could track down some info for you, and, dude, the freaking FBI showed up at my door."

"What?" I pressed myself flatter between the lockers. "What are you talking about?"

"They wanted to know where I got the pictures."

"What did you tell them?" I asked.

"Dude," Jason said, "it was the FBI. What do you think I told them?"

I swore. "You told them I sent them to you?"

"Not at first," he said. "First I told them I snapped them last summer at that family reunion I had to go to. They hauled my parents in for questioning, Matt. Eventually they figured out that I'd lied, so I told them the pictures were from some random camp websites I thought looked good."

"Good thinking," I said. My heart was pounding.

"No!" Jason said. "Not good thinking. They searched my computer and knew in a second I was lying. More people came to the house, bro. And not just more FBI either."

"Who else?" My stomach sank as he said the three letters I hoped he wouldn't say.

"The CIA, Matt. The freaking FBI and the CIA both came here and accused me of lying."

"They'll figure it out soon," I said. "It's only a matter of time. I bet they already have it narrowed down. I'll be kicked out just for violating the rule against cell phones."

"I haven't given them your name yet, man. I just told them a friend of mine is at a CIA camp."

"What did they say?"

"They said I was lying since there's no such thing. They said if I have a friend mixed up with some of the people in the pictures, then that friend—you—is in real danger."

A sigh escaped me. "Interrogation 101, Jason. The only danger I'm in is getting kicked out of the program. Just hang in there a couple more hours and it'll all be over anyway. There's still time." It might have been wishful thinking, or maybe I was just trying to convince myself, but saying it out loud did just that. I believed it. "I can do this," I said again. "I'm in the middle of the final competition right now. I just have to win. They'll see that I belong here."

Jason cursed under his breath. "I don't know. They made it sound like you were in a lot of trouble, man. Like, a lot! Like your life was in danger type of trouble."

"Jason, listen. I'm fine. I need your help, though. I'm going to pull that prank we talked about. The one at the station."

"You're *what*?"

"Shhh," I said. "Look, that's the challenge. I need to pull a prank. I need to cause a disruption. It's the biggest one I could think of."

"*We* thought of that one," Jason said. "Dude, that was supposed to be one we pulled together when we were old and didn't care about going to prison."

"This is a CIA camp, Jay. I'm not going to go to jail even if I get caught. But I need your contact."

A pause several beats long carried through the phone before Jason said, "Are you sure? Are you one hundred percent sure that you're in a CIA camp?"

I considered that for a second because there was a part of me that hadn't been sure a few hours ago. "They have 'Property of the CIA' etched into almost everything around the camp, Jason. One of the head instructors is a CIA interrogator. If you knew where to look, it would be obvious. Trust me. It's CIA. One hundred percent."

Jason paused for a moment. "Well, those suits that keep coming over here are excellent actors, man. You should see them. They had my mom crying, and the only reason they went away was because my dad called his lawyer."

"I just need them to not find out until three o'clock," I said.

"What happens at three?"

"The competition is over. If they come to question you again, don't tell them anything until three. After that, it's not going to matter. They'll either be impressed with me, or not. They'll either let me stay in the competition, or they'll cut me from the program."

I could literally feel Jason's frustration coming over the phone. "Okay, man. I'll call my contact. Do you have a pen?" I pulled a pen out of my pocket. "He's at a place called Rick's Waffle House."

"You get your fireworks from a kid at a waffle house?"

"Kind of." When he was done giving me directions, he added, "The guy's name is Kalvin, with a *K*, got it?"

"Yeah, I got it." Though I had no idea why it mattered how it was spelled.

"I'll let him know you're coming," Jason said. "He'll put whatever you need on my tab."

"Thanks, man. I owe you."

"Just remember," Jason said, "the train station prank was *our* idea. Do it justice."

I laughed. "Watch the news, buddy. I'll wave to the cameras."

I hung up and jogged back outside. Amara was where I'd left him, but he looked at me quizzically.

"What?" I asked.

"Cell phones are easy to listen in on, Matt." His voice was smooth and unemotional.

"You ... heard my call?"

"Not me," he said. He glanced up at the sky. "But you can be sure we are being watched. Graded. Scored. Maybe they can't hear us now, but snatching transmissions through airwaves," he shrugged, "even I could rig something to do that."

"How'd you know?" I asked.

"A guess," he said. "That, or I went through your things back at camp and found the phone in your jeans."

"Can no one be trusted at that place?" I glanced at my watch. "C'mon. If they heard me, then we don't have a lot of time."

CHAPTER 41

Rick's Waffle House was four stops away on the subway and had a tacky plastic waffle sculpture beside the entrance. A girl in her late teens greeted us as Amara and I pushed through the main doors. She had blonde hair that fell to her shoulders and she wore black pants that matched her short-sleeved shirt.

"Table for two?" she asked, brandishing a pair of laminated menus.

"We're here to see Kalvin," I said.

The girl sighed and rolled her eyes. "Kalvin?"

"Uh-huh." I leaned toward her. "Kalvin with a *K*."

The girl shook her head. "Are you kidding?"

I glanced at Amara. He looked like he was trying not to smile. I turned back to the girl. "No, I'm not kidding."

"Kalvin with a *K*?" She looked up at the ceiling and muttered something that sounded like a curse and then turned around and marched to a door a dozen feet away from us. She shoved it open and yelled, "Kalvin!" When there was no answer, she hollered again, "Kalvin with a *K*!"

There was a rush of footsteps, and a boy about a foot shorter than me with scraggly red hair and bony arms rushed out of the door. He glared at the girl. "How many times do I have to tell you not to say that name so loud?"

"You are such a dork," the girl said. "I can't even believe we're

255

related."

The boy pointed a finger in the girl's face. "I know that you close the restaurant early on days Mom and Dad aren't here. I'll tell them."

The girl laughed. "And I'll tell them what you're really doing in the basement when your "friends" stop by. I'm sure Dad would be really interested."

They locked stares for a minute. I was pretty sure they'd had that exact dialogue a dozen times.

There was a ding from somewhere in the dining area, and the girl jerked her gaze away. Then she turned to us. "This is Kalvin," she said, gesturing to the boy, "with a *K*." She rolled her eyes again and strolled back into the dining room.

Kalvin stared at us carefully.

"I, er …" I glanced at Amara, then back at the kid. "You're Kalvin?"

"I am," the boy said. "Why? Not what you were expecting?"

I shook my head. "No, you're just—"

"Short?" the boy snapped. "Is that what you're about to say? That I'm too short to sell fireworks?"

"Younger than I expected," I said quickly.

"And short," Amara added.

I shot Amara a look, and he shrugged.

The boy's hands became tiny fists at his side. "I am not short. I just haven't hit my growth spurt yet."

Amara laughed. "That's like saying, 'I'm not stupid. I just haven't learned anything yet.'"

"Oh, yeah?" the boy said. "Well, you two can find a different place to buy what you want."

He turned to leave, and I reached out and grabbed his arm. "Wait."

256

He spun around and punched me in the stomach. I pulled away from him, holding the spot where his tiny fist had jabbed me.

"You're not getting anything from me." He turned to leave and then stopped and jerked around. "And you can tell Jason that he can go somewhere else too."

He pulled open the door he'd come out of a moment before, and I coughed. "I don't think so, Kalvin."

He hesitated and then turned around.

I cleared my throat and pointed in the direction of his sister. "She's not the only one who could tell your parents what's in the basement."

Kalvin pointed a warning finger at me, opened his mouth to speak, and then snapped it closed. He pointed at Amara and looked about to speak again but instead just sighed. He glanced over his shoulder at his sister, who was carrying a tray of drinks across the dining room. "I hate sisters."

He led us back onto the street, around the side of the restaurant, and down an alley to a small staircase that led us into the basement. Fluorescent lights kicked on when the door opened, and a row of storage lockers lined the back wall. Kalvin marched to the one on the far left, unlocked the padlock, and lifted the door.

The walls of the locker were lined with enough fireworks to burn the entire building down. I recognized several pieces. There were M80s, flying spinners, ground spinners, snakes and strobes, rockets, ladyfingers, bottle rockets. But there were dozens of other pieces that I'd never seen, some so large they looked like the Air Force could drop them from planes. In the center of the room was a bare wooden table, and below it were boxes. A couple of them had no lids and were filled with neatly organized tools.

Amara whistled. "Not bad, Kalvin with a *K*. Not bad at all."

"Where do you get all this from?" I asked.

"Does it matter?" he asked.

I shook my head. "I'm just surprised you still have all your fingers."

He raised an eyebrow. "I know what I'm doing, and safety is my top priority." He waved his hand around the shed with the flourish of a magician. "Well? What'll it be?"

"Roman candles," I said. He reached under one of the shelves and pulled out a box of Roman candles and put them on the table. "More than that," I said. "A lot more."

"That's all I have," he said.

"Jason said you had crates of them," I said. I sounded whiny and instantly regretted it.

"Well, Jason exaggerates," he said. He pointed around the room. "I have other stuff."

I had no idea what other stuff might be as good as a Roman candle. I turned to Amara. "What do you think? Can you modify some of this stuff to make more Roman candles?"

He looked at me as if I'd just asked him if he knew how to tie his own shoes. I felt my face flush again.

Kalvin's face lit up. "A fellow pyrotechnician?"

"Hardly," Amara said.

"Just grab what you need," I said. "I want to get back."

Amara was as methodical as a world-class chef gathering ingredients for his next meal. He even smelled a few of the items the way you might test the freshness of an herb before deciding to make a purchase. A couple times he returned the items he'd inspected to a different spot from where he'd found them, and Kalvin, who obviously prided himself on the organization of his work area, would huff and move them back. I got the impression that Amara was doing it as a distraction, but even though I was watching him carefully, I didn't see why. By the end I decided he just wanted to mess with the little twerp. That made me smile.

"That's it then?" Kalvin asked when Amara had finished stacking items on the table. Amara nodded, and Kalvin made note of everything in a small binder and then pulled two black duffel bags from a box under the table and stuffed the items carefully inside.

"Jason said he'd pay for all this," I said.

Kalvin nodded. "I know. Must be nice to have rich friends."

I doubted this kid had any friends at all.

He nudged the bags toward us. "If you get caught with any of this stuff—" Kalvin shot us an icy stare, "you don't mention my name."

"Sure," I said. "Not a word."

As we made our way back to the station, I thought again about how Amara had purposefully messed with Kalvin by putting things back in places they didn't belong. The more I thought about it, the more I wondered if he hadn't stolen a few things while Kalvin had been distracted. I don't know why he would, since he could have put anything he wanted on the table. Still, it was the only thing that made sense. It didn't matter to me that he'd done that, but I wanted Amara to know that he hadn't fooled me.

"I saw what you did in there," I said.

Amara raised an eyebrow but said nothing.

"When you distracted him by putting stuff back in the wrong place," I added.

Amara smiled slyly. "I thought you might."

Aha, I knew it. I kept a straight face. "Not that I mind," I said, "but it wasn't really necessary, you know."

"No?" Amara asked.

I shrugged the duffel bag onto my other shoulder. "It doesn't matter. He was a little punk. He deserved it."

Amara nodded. "That's what I thought too."

Something in Amara's tone gave me a chill, but I decided to let it go. He was an intense guy and no doubt disappointed I'd seen him steal or, at least, that he thought I'd seen him steal. I wondered if theft was another skill the camp would teach. I smiled at the prospect. I'd already learned so much. I couldn't wait to put the stuff I'd learned to use. I imagined using some of the skills to torment my teachers or to get even with some of the school bullies. Before I realized it, I was smiling so big I almost laughed.

Amara was looking at me with a slightly scrunched face. "You're happier than I thought you'd be about that," he said.

I shook my head. "Honestly, I'm indifferent."

"You and Angie will get along well then," he said. "I still feel kind of bad when I have to do stuff like that."

I almost laughed but decided Amara wasn't someone I wanted to offend. Amara was more complicated than I'd thought. He'd deal with explosives and work to disrupt an entire transportation hub in the downtown core. But he'd have remorse for stealing from a little punk like Kalvin with a *K*? I wondered if all this spy stuff messed with where you drew the line between right and wrong. I shook my head.

The CIA was a good thing. Part of our government. They protected people. They protected the entire country. At least, I thought they did. I would have to do a bit more research on them when I got home.

CHAPTER 42

I was relieved to see that the bakery lights were out and the windows were covered with blinds when we got back. A striped black-and-yellow **CLOSED** sign was on the front door, and it seemed genuinely closed. We went to the side entrance, in an alley that it shared with a small three-story office building. Amara reached for the door without hesitation and pulled it open.

"They just left it unlocked?" I whispered.

Amara scrunched up his face. "Of course they did. Do you want to stand out here pounding on the door while the neighborhood notices you? Or do you want to walk in like you have every reason in the world to be here? Seriously, Cambridge, I'm really starting to worry about you."

"Oh, yeah, of course," I gestured him on. "Let's go, er, in ... I guess." My stomach knotted as we stepped through the door and into a small locker room, no doubt where employees locked up their personal stuff. There was a bathroom off to the right and racks of dry baking ingredients on the left. Straight ahead was a door with a small sign that read WASH YOUR HANDS. Amara strolled through the room toward the door on the other side as if he knew exactly where he was going and had every right to be there.

I, on the other hand, froze.

The worst thing I had ever done before this moment was a bit of vandalism—minor stuff, really, like when I'd used fertilizer to burn a swear word into the grass of the school football field, or when I'd used epoxy resin to permanently lock a teacher's car door. But here I was breaking and entering. I could get a criminal record for this. Worse, my dad would rip me apart. The thought made me want to puke.

"Coming?" Amara asked, his hand poised over the handle of the door that led farther into the building. He looked like he couldn't care less about the consequences. Like nothing mattered.

Pull it together, Cambridge.

We're in a CIA training camp. Nothing that happens today can be used against you. We're running a mission in broad daylight. The odds that we'll get caught are really high. The odds that we're going to be seen are one hundred percent. The goal was not to get caught, but if we did get caught, if the owners of the bakery showed up and called the police, or if we let off Roman candles and security nabbed us, well, we were with the CIA. They'd have us out and back in camp before I could say, "Get me a lawyer." I suddenly felt very foolish for being so nervous.

I smiled. "Yeah, I'm coming."

We stepped through the door and made our way into the kitchen. Huge ovens covered the far wall, and large mixing contraptions and metal bowls filled tables around the perimeter. A gigantic metal table sat in the center of the room and was polished to such a degree that, even with the lights off, the faint light that seeped into the room from the fogged glass windows reflected off the surface. Amara slipped the duffel bag off his shoulder and tossed it on the table.

"This is where I'll work," he said. "You can toss your bag up here." He tapped the table.

"And you can get it all done before"—I checked my watch—"one o'clock?"

- DISRUPTION -

Amara shook his head. "It'll probably be done by just a bit after two. I don't rush unless my life depends on it, and even then I might not. Rushing around explosives isn't smart."

I groaned. "Yeah, okay. Of course." I rubbed the back of my head. "But if you see a *safe* way to speed something along ..."

Amara nodded and then gestured to the door. My cue to leave.

I turned and pushed through the swinging door that led to the front of the store. Rylee and Juno were seated at one of the tables, examining a map. Yaakov was at another table, surrounded by wires, bits of plastic, and what looked like a dismantled radio.

"About time you got here." Angie's voice came from my right, and I spun around to see her perched at another table, chowing down on a plateful of pastries. She gestured to the glass display case that held dishes filled with the bakery's wares. "Eat if you're hungry. We don't get treats like this at the camp."

How in the world could she eat? My stomach was twisted in such a knot that the mere thought of food caused discomfort. I shook my head.

Rylee looked up from the map. "Amara?"

"He's set up in the kitchen," I said.

"Good," Yaakov said. "If he messes up in there, maybe we won't all be killed."

"Any trouble getting in?" I asked, glancing around the group.

Angie shook her head, then held up one of the pastries from her plate. "Easy as pie."

"The people just left when you cut the power?"

"Customers did," Yaakov said.

I glanced at Rylee and she grimaced and nodded to a door at the back of the room.

It took me a second to put together what her gesture meant. "Wait, so the workers are in there?"

"Don't be so dramatic," Angie said. "There were only two of them, and I don't think they were willing to share the space."

I walked over to the door and pulled it open. It was a bathroom and two bodies lay on the floor with actual flour sacks over their heads. Blood stained sections of the sacks, and there were red smears on the floor as well. The bodies were zip-tied at the wrists and ankles, and lay unmoving beside a toilet. I jerked around. "Did you ... kill them?"

Angie rolled her eyes. "Yeah, and then I tied them up, and covered their faces just in case they turned out to be zombies. C'mon, they're fine. At least half of that isn't even blood. It's raspberry filling."

"Raspberry—"

"C'mon, just close the door. We have to get the rest of this sorted out."

I looked at Rylee and she mouthed the word *psychopath* and shrugged as if she was shrugging away the quirky habits of an embarrassing family member.

"But they're fine, right?"

Yaakov shrugged. "They're not dead."

I couldn't believe how unaffected they all were. There were two bodies zip-tied to a toilet, and they didn't seem concerned at all. If something like that didn't bother Yaakov, I was in farther over my head than I'd thought.

I closed the door and pushed the image of the two bodies out of my head—or at least tried to—as I walked over to Rylee and Juno.

"Do you have the key areas mapped out?"

They nodded, and then Rylee spoke. "Listen, we really can't

understate how big this station is. It's huge. If we're going to make this work, if we're going to cause a real disruption, we're going to have to be really strategic." She looked around the room and then gestured at the map in front of her. "That means you guys are going to want to take a look at this."

We crowded around. The map had been colored with pink, green, and yellow highlighters. In addition there was a series of circles and *X*s with dotted lines trailing out from them, clearly indicating travel routes. It looked like something you'd find on the sidelines during a football game.

"Basically," Rylee began, "there are the inner-city trains, the commuter trains, and then we have the subway lines and the street cars. If we're going to cause any significant disturbance, we need to place the explosives—"

"Fireworks," I corrected.

"Right," Rylee said. "Fine, we'll need to place the *fireworks* in three different locations." She tapped the map of the subway. "Platform three on the red line. Platform four on the green line. And platform four on the white line. The panic from the commuters rushing out of these areas should ignite panic in the other platforms. Everyone's going to clear out. If we toss a few smaller explosives—er, fireworks—on our way out, it'll make things all the more effective."

When Jason and I had formulated the plan originally, we'd thought it would be great to put bundles of fireworks on the commuter trains. Right on top. If it was timed right, they'd go off just as the trains were leaving the station, and they'd carry a bundle of exploding fireworks through the whole station. I told the group, and their faces lit up.

"Awesome idea," Juno said.

Rylee nodded and bit her lip. "This could actually work."

I felt my smile spread.

"You seem awfully excited," Angie said, eyeing me suspiciously.

"You're not?" I asked.

She shook me off. "I'd be more excited if I didn't think our plan was super lame and we were going to get crushed by everyone else."

"We're going to do fine," I said. "We're going to empty that place." I turned back to Juno and Rylee. "That reminds me. Did you guys figure out how we're going to get away?"

Juno shrugged. "Like you said, it's going to be a madhouse. We just run out with everyone else."

Rylee nodded. "If we ditch through an emergency exit, or down one of the tunnels, any cop who spots us will know we were involved. But ..." She took out a pen and circled several places on the map. "These are the alternate exits if you're spotted and have no other choice."

"I hacked their system," Yaakov said. "I can set a timer to upload a virus that will erase the footage from the areas we'll be working in, but I'll wait until Amara is done so I have a better idea about timing." He tapped the screen of his laptop. "I've been watching the cameras in that station, and since we're hitting three places at the same time, there isn't really a time when security will be especially lax. The guards seem to just wander around."

"We might need a distraction," Juno said. "Something they'd all respond to if they're getting close to us."

"I like it," I said. "But nothing so big that they'll call the police early."

"I don't think we're going to have to worry about them calling the police," Rylee said.

"Why not?" I asked.

"Matt, there are two other teams in the city right now, all about to put into motion some kind of major disruption. The first thing each of them is going to do is call in a series of fake emergencies—"

"Or create a series of real emergencies," Angie injected.

"Sure," Rylee said, "or real ones, so that police aren't anywhere near when things go down." She looked at her watch. "For all we know, the other teams have already started their disruptions. If they go first and distract the cops even more, it could make things a whole lot easier for us."

Yaakov cleared his throat. "Maybe."

"Not maybe, Yaakov," Rylee snapped. "For sure. Chase and Becca are nuts, you know that." She glared at Yaakov. "If either one of them starts their disruption first, there won't be a cop left in the area."

Yaakov laughed. "I'm not debating the fact that they're nuts, Rylee. I just said maybe it would help us." He shrugged his shoulder. "But maybe it will make things a whole lot worse for us."

Rylee opened her mouth to argue, and then her expression changed, as if she'd just realized something she should have already known. "Oh, man, you're right."

Juno and Angie glanced at each other, then at me, both with the same puzzled expression. I shrugged.

"Care to share with the class?" Angie asked.

"We're at the largest commuter hub in the city," Yaakov said.

"And?" I asked.

"And," Rylee said, continuing for Yaakov, "this'll probably be a place that each Delta considers. For all we know, each team is already setting up."

"The more the merrier," Angie said.

"No," Rylee snapped. "No way. If there are multiple teams here, only one of them is going to succeed."

I cleared my throat. "Why?"

"Because the police will show up," Yaakov said, rolling his eyes. "Even if they're distracted across the city, they're going to hear about the disturbance, and they'll respond. The chance of us implementing our plan if another team goes first will be ..." He shrugged again. "Let's just say it'll be unlikely. Plus, who would get the credit? The counselors would have to somehow figure out who caused which disturbance." He bit his lip and muttered, "Maybe I shouldn't delete the footage."

"There's something else we're not considering," Juno said. "If we knew where the other teams were going to pull their disruptions, we'd do something to make it harder for them."

"And they'd do the same to us if they knew we were here," I said, speaking the obvious.

Rylee nodded. "It could be something as simple as calling in a bomb threat for the station."

Yaakov pointed to a box in the corner of his computer screen. "I'm monitoring emergency services right now. If anything comes up about the station, I'll know. So far, nothing."

Rylee pointed at the computer screen. "Have you seen anyone else from camp?"

Yaakov rolled his eyes. "Yeah, Rylee. I saw Becca and Chase, both of them setting up major operations, but I thought it wasn't worth mentioning."

Rylee fixed him with an icy stare.

He cleared his throat. "No. I haven't seen anyone from the other teams. But it's not like they wouldn't blend in. I probably wouldn't see them. But ..."

"But what?" I asked.

"But I'm pretty sure someone else was trying to hack into the cameras after we got here."

"Are you sure?" Angie asked.

Yaakov looked at Angie the way a babysitter looks at a kid who has just asked "why" for the hundredth time. "How about this, Angie?" Yaakov said. "You trust me when I talk about computers. And when you talk about psychotic breaks or," he gestured to the pastries on her table, "emotional eating, I'll trust you."

Angie smiled, and then in a blink, she snatched up the fork from beside her and threw it across the room. The fork impaled the back of the chair beside Yaakov and made him shriek. The rest of us stood motionless while Yaakov looked nervously at me, then Angie.

"I am not," Angie said through clenched teeth, "an emotional eater."

"Riiiiight," Juno said. "You're not really all that emotional at all."

"Apologize," Angie said, eyeing Yaakov. Her voice oozed with warning, and she picked up a spoon and flipped it in her hand.

Yaakov swiped his hand across his forehead. "Okay. I'm sorry. I shouldn't have said that."

Angie glared for a moment and then abruptly smiled and went back to her pastries.

"Okay," I said after I was reasonably sure Angie was done throwing utensils, "how do we make sure we beat any other team that might be here?"

"There's only one way," Angie said happily. "We have to be first."

CHAPTER 43

By two pm, we were all getting anxious.

"C'mon, Amara!" Rylee yelled toward the kitchen. "We're running out of time."

Amara hadn't responded to any of our urgings, except the one time Juno had poked his head in the kitchen to see the progress and was instantly struck by a burst of fire I assumed came from one of the Roman candles. Though I'd never seen a Roman candle shoot only one blast. He never responded to Rylee's shouts either, but I bet if she'd put her head in the door he'd have shot something at her.

I paced for another ten minutes and was about to risk injury by going into the kitchen to tell Amara it was time to go, when he stepped through the doorway. He had both duffel bags slung over his shoulder. I sighed, relieved.

"About time," Rylee said. "What were you doing in there anyway?"

Amara glared at her with a *what do you think I was doing?* look and then tossed the duffel bags onto one of the tables. "Making it so this plan works," he said.

Juno rubbed his hands together. "I never get to mess with explosives. At least not ones big enough for what we're doing."

Amara unzipped one of the bags and pulled out nine cylinders, each one about the size of a large water bottle. They were built, it seemed, from scraps, glued and taped together without much thought for how they looked.

"It looks like something Frankenstein would create," Angie said, practically reading my mind. "If Frankenstein were five years old and his kindergarten teacher told him to make a papier-mâché tube from the corpses of other papier-mâché tubes."

Amara took the cylinders, put them end to end, and screwed them together. When he was done, there were three cardboard tubes that looked a lot like those poster tubes kids in art school carry around all the time. In fact, because of the colorful mosaic scraps, the tube looked exactly like something a kid in art class would have.

"I asked for Roman candles," I said. "Those don't look like Roman candles. They look like ... well, I'm not sure what they look like. Will they work like a Roman candle?"

Amara shook his head. "Roman candles are for four-year-olds on Halloween, Matt."

"Four-year-olds?" I muttered. "You played with Roman candles when you were four?"

He held up the tube and tilted his head, examining it the way a jeweler might examine a ruby. "This is better. A lot better. If you want, we can call it a Roman grenade."

"Oh, I like that," Angie said. "Has a certain ring to it, don't you think?"

"Grenade," Juno said, a smile spreading across his face. "Now we're talking. Blow the place up and we're sure to have a disruption."

"I didn't want a bomb," I said. "We're not trying to hurt people."

"I know," Amara said. "This is entirely non-lethal. But if you get hit by any of the blasts, they're going to sting."

"Stinging is fine," I said. "Just tell us how to set it off."

He held up one of the tubes and pointed to one of the segments.

"You saw me put them together. They come apart just as easily. When you unscrew them, the friction sets the charge. Just separate and put the pieces wherever you want. Then get out." He licked his lips. "It's that simple."

"How long do we have?" Rylee asked. "After we unscrew the pieces, I mean. Is it just a couple seconds like a grenade?"

"One minute and twenty-seven seconds," Amara said.

"One minute and twenty-seven?" Angie snickered. "Not twenty-eight, or twenty-six?"

"It's one minute and twenty-seven seconds," Amara said. "That's the longest delay I could give with the supplies I had. But that should be plenty of time to separate the segments, get them in place, and get out." He turned over one of the other bags, and a dozen fist-sized cardboard balls tumbled onto the table.

"What are those?" Juno asked. He reached out, plucked one from the table, and tossed it from one hand to the next.

"I heard you talking," Amara said. "You wanted something on the roofs of the trains." He gestured to the small bundles. "Just give 'em a twist," he picked one up and pointed to the thin line along its center, "and then toss it onto the train."

"Very cool, Amara," Juno said, "very cool."

"Same amount of time?" Rylee asked.

Amara shook his head. "A little less, so separate your segments first; then, as you're heading to the exits, toss them onto the trains or anywhere you want to toss them."

"Fine." I looked around the group. "Yaakov, you're going to stay here. I want you to record what happens so we have proof, if we need it. But if another team somehow gets in there and goes first, I want you to wipe out everything."

He nodded.

I stood over the map that Rylee and Juno had made. "Amara," I began, "you and Angie take this area." I pointed to the area shaded pink. "Rylee, you go with Juno and hit the yellow area. And I'll get the green area."

I smiled. "Everyone good?"

"That's it?" Angie asked. "That's your pep talk before the big game?"

"I expected a bit more too," Juno said, smiling.

"Very funny," I said. "We're setting off Roman candles." Amara drew in a breath, and I turned and nodded. "Sorry, Roman grenades. Point is it's not like we're setting out to win the World Cup or anything."

"The what?" Amara asked.

"Seriously?"

He shrugged, and I turned to Yaakov. "Still nothing on the news about any of the other teams? No major disturbances?"

He shrugged. "There was a fire about fifteen minutes from here, but it was mostly contained to one building. I guess it could have been part of another team's disruption, but I doubt it. Probably just a coincidence."

"They'd burn down a building to cause a disruption?" I asked. "Isn't that kind of ... severe?"

"It wasn't them," Rylee said. "They're waiting. It's like a big game of chicken. They probably think we're waiting too." She turned to me. "Maybe we should wait."

"No!" The word came out with more force than I'd intended. I glanced down at my watch to avoid the quizzical stares from my teammates. There was no way we were waiting. Jason had said the FBI was coming for me. If they'd traced the call, they might be at the station already. We didn't have time to wait. Not another minute.

"C'mon. Let's do this."

Three minutes later, we were in the alley behind the bakery, tubes in hand. I looked at my watch. "Mine says two nineteen." The others checked their watches and made adjustments accordingly. "At two forty-five, we set off the fireworks. That should give us all time to get to our spots and decide the best place to put the segments."

They all nodded.

"Then," I continued, "get to the bus. It's not much of a lead, but hopefully it'll be enough." I glanced at my teammates. "Got it?"

"Got it," they said together.

We split up and headed for the station. Nerves rattled in my stomach, and I kept looking over my shoulder and toward darkened sections of the building, half expecting men in suits to emerge, guns drawn, and take me away. None came, and as I stepped into the station, Roman grenade tube in hand, my nerves went out the window. This was a prank. Just a prank, and I'd done dozens of these.

Plus, I wasn't going to get caught. I wasn't even going to be seen. I'd blend in with the bustle of the traveling public, and Yaakov would delete any security footage of me ever being here. This would be the best disruption the camp counselors had ever seen. When the smoke settled, and everyone arrived back at camp, they might know the truth, but it wouldn't matter. I'd be welcomed into the group with open arms. They'd see that I was a good agent, or operative, or whatever they called kids working for the CIA. I'd be a spy. A real, honest-to-goodness spy.

It wouldn't matter that I wasn't supposed to be at that camp, or that my dad had done something, probably illegal, to get me on the list. It wouldn't matter that I'd kept my mouth shut when I figured out the truth about the camp.

It wouldn't matter, because I was going to win this competition and it would all work out.

It had to.

Because if I didn't win, and they didn't welcome me back ... well ... I'd be in a lot of trouble.

Suddenly my anxiety was back, and I thought I might hurl.

CHAPTER 44

For the first few minutes, I tried really hard not to look suspicious. Thing is, when you're trying *not* to look like you're up to something, it almost always makes you look like you *are* up to something. But at first I couldn't help it. Every time someone looked at me, I'd look away, usually down at my feet. If I saw a security guard, I turned about-face and walked in the other direction. All I was doing was drawing attention to myself, and that just made me act more and more peculiar.

I stopped at a pair of vending machines and caught my reflection in the glass covering the display.

Get it together, Matt. This is your chance. Stop blowing it.

I felt my wallet in my pocket and remembered the cool fake ID I had for my Swedish alter ego, Gunnar Konstantan. I quickly made up a story about how I was on a summer exchange program. I had the colorful tube that looked like a poster tube, so I just added the fact that today was art project day and I'd made a papier-mâché tube. I even decided that my host family lived at Rick's Waffle House a few stops down the line and my dorky host-brother was Kalvin with a *K*. I smiled and genuinely felt better.

That's it, Matt, you're just an art geek from Sweden living at a waffle house. Not a kid about to pull the prank of the century. Not a soon-to-be CIA spy.

My smile widened. For the second time I relaxed, and this time it stuck.

I was about to turn around and head to my section, which was on level four near the green-line-platform, when something caught my eye. Through the reflection on the vending machine, about a dozen yards over my right shoulder, I saw her. Becca Plain. I resisted the sudden urge to duck for cover and, instead, kept my eyes on the reflection.

She walked like a girl on a mission, albeit with a slight limp, straight to a magazine kiosk where she browsed a rack of fashion rags. Then she glanced over her shoulder toward me. At first I thought maybe she'd spotted me, and I nearly sprinted for cover. But just when I shifted my weight to the balls of my feet, one of Becca's teammates wandered over and stepped up beside her to examine the same publications. Another second passed, and they both headed for the stairs.

I counted to twenty before I followed her. Not because I wanted to put some distance between us, but because I wanted to see if her other teammates were around. Sure enough, when I got to fourteen, two other members of Team Hyena headed for the same stairwell, and then another two came from the opposite end of the station and also headed for the stairs.

Were they planning something here at the station, or were they in transit? They had a driver, so why would they go anywhere by train if they could go by bus? They must've been planning something here. Unless a getaway would be easier by train, for whatever they planned to do. They were all together, after all. If they were planning something here, wouldn't they spread out, like my team?

Too many questions. I had to follow. Maybe I could sabotage them or even just distract them long enough for us to get our disturbance underway.

I wove through the crowds with my cardboard tube clutched against my chest. When I got to the stairs, I stepped behind a group of girls who had their arms filled with bags from department stores I'd never heard of.

At the platform, I ducked behind a pillar.

It was a single-track platform about a hundred yards long, with large, tiled columns that ran the length, right down the middle. There weren't any construction workers on the platform, but large tarps hung from scaffolding along a section of the wall, opposite the tracks toward the far end. Becca and her team were down there, too, near the tracks. I realized that if I could get to the scaffolding, I could duck behind the tarps and have a pretty great spot to watch them. I wouldn't be close enough to hear them, but if they started doing something, I'd at least see it.

At first, I moved between the posts, keeping out of their line of sight. I was halfway there, and I checked my watch. 2:33 pm. I had twelve minutes. A buzzer from overhead sounded, and then an echoey, distorted voice announced a train's arrival.

A burst of cool air whipped around me, and then a second later, a horn reverberated down the tunnel, and the train rolled to a stop at the platform. The doors hissed open, and I glanced around the pillar I was standing against. Becca's team was in one of the cars, standing in the doorway. Becca was gesturing with her hands, then at her wrist, and then she waved her hand down the track, as if to say, *Go on without me.*

Her team stepped all the way into the train, and a moment later, there was a loud *beep* and the doors closed. As the train rolled away, Becca headed the rest of way down the platform and pushed through the door to the ladies' room.

This was a waste of time, I told myself. Her team was clearly in transit. They'd probably finished their disruption somewhere else in the city and were en route to wherever they had decided to meet up with their driver.

I checked my watch. No time to waste. If Becca wanted to cause a disturbance in the girls' bathroom, so be it. It wouldn't be enough to stop what we were doing. Plus, I'd gotten the distinct impression that Team Hyena had set their plan in motion long before they got to the station.

Suddenly someone grabbed my arm, pulled me back around the pillar, and then shoved me hard, so the back of my head smacked the tiles.

Instinctively my hands shot up to my head, and the Roman grenade clattered to the floor and rolled along the platform. I blinked away some of the haze from the impact, only to be punched in the stomach.

Hard.

I gasped, trying to catch my breath. Finally, my attacker came into view.

"A-Alexis?" I blinked some more, staring down at the girl I had told clearly that she could not be part of this competition. "What—"

Her foot shot up before I even realized what was happening and caught me right between the legs. Pain exploded through my body, and I dropped to my knees. Someone moved on my right, and I looked up just in time to see Rob's face. He had a wicked sneer, and I barely had time to register who he was before his fist hammered into my face, knocking my head back into the tiled pillar behind me.

I groaned and slumped back.

"Wh-what ..."

"What are we doing here?" The voice was on my left, and I squinted up to see the third member of their little gang, Duncan. "Is that what you were going to ask?" he asked, leaning over me. "It's simple. The plan was for you to include us. Remember? You're the one who deviated. You're the one who lied." He and Rob hauled me to my feet by my arms and led me, staggering, to the cordoned-off construction area, and before I could gather my senses enough to call for help, they shoved me behind a flap of tarp. I tripped on a section of scaffolding, and my face hit concrete.

A second later Rob, Duncan, and Alexis were beside me again.

"We had it all worked out, you know," Rob said. "You would have come in second. Second still advances, Matt. That was the plan all along. But, no, you had to listen to your team."

"What are you guys talking about?" My head pounded like someone was taking a hammer to it, and something warm ran down the back of my neck. I licked my lips and tasted blood.

The area behind the tarp was quite wide, and a section of the platform wall had been demolished, exposing a series of metal pipes. There were a number of gaps in the sections of tarp covering the scaffolding, so I could see out onto the platform. My tube was in the hands of a boy who couldn't have been more than seven years old, and he was using it as a sword to torment a girl who was either his sister or his babysitter.

I looked at my watch. 2:37. I had eight minutes.

"What a total rookie." I recognized the voice easily. Chase ducked under the tarps and strolled up behind Alexis, holding a half-eaten cinnamon pretzel in his hand. "How in the heck did you become a Delta?"

I *am* a Delta, I remembered, and being a Delta meant I could cut any team member, at any time, for any reason, and they'd be out of the program. I pointed at Alexis, Duncan, and Rob. "You three are cut from the program effective now." I straightened and tried to push back up to my feet, but Alexis lunged out and kicked me in the stomach, and I slumped back against the metal frame of the scaffolding.

"Y-you're cut!" I said, coughing. "You know the rules. You're out of the program. Leave. Now!"

Rob and Alexis chuckled and shook their heads while Duncan gave me a *you can't be serious* look.

Chase laughed. "What an idiot. How can you still not know what's going on?" He glanced around at the others, then down at his watch. "I mean, sure we didn't really try to *beat* you during the Capture the Flag competition. But that was part of a bigger plan. You were given more credit than you deserved, that's for sure." He shook his head. "Clearly our source is an idiot." He waved his hand as though he were swatting at a fly. "But these three ..." He laughed again. "They were just for fun. Just to see if you'd fall for it. It was so easy I actually thought you might have been playing along with a plan of your own. But, no. You were just that stupid."

I didn't know what he was talking about, and my expression must've shown how confused I was, because he leaned over and spoke clearly. "These three are on my team, you stupid weakling. You can't cut them."

They weren't on my team? How did I not know that? Chase was right: I was an idiot.

Chase slipped the bag off his shoulder and tossed it to Alexis. "Set it up. And take care of Becca. I don't know what she's doing in there," he nodded at the girls' restroom, "but I don't want her messing up our plans."

She nodded, clutched the bag against her chest, and then she, Rob, and Duncan slipped through the tarps and jogged down the platform.

I cleared my throat and pushed myself to my knees. I wanted payback. Where was the rest of my team? Yaakov had to have seen what was happening on the cameras. I looked up at the ceiling and spotted a camera, but it was pointed at the platform.

"Looks good, doesn't it?" Chase said. He had a section of the tarp pulled back, clearing a view of the platform.

I used one of the bars of scaffolding, pulled myself up, and looked out onto the platform just as Alexis took a yellow OUT OF ORDER pylon out of her bag and put it in front of the girls' bathroom door. There were dozens of passengers lined up on the platform now, and I considered shouting out to them for help. If I did that, though, I might stop Chase, but I sure wouldn't impress the CIA. They didn't want babies. No, if I was going to make this last event count, I had to do it on my own.

"Looks like the real thing, don't you think?"

I forced a laugh. "If you think disturbing people's ability to use the toilet is going to get you a win, you're dreaming."

Chase just shook his head at me. "Oh, that pylon will do more than that."

I took another look at the pylon just as Alexis slapped an OUT OF ORDER sign on the door and went inside; a couple seconds later, Duncan and Rob did too. I wondered if Becca was even still in there. For her sake, I hoped not.

"What do you think?" Chase asked. "Is Becca gonna fight her way out?"

I didn't speak. If she was in there, it would be three against one, and Becca was injured. It didn't take a rocket scientist to figure out she didn't have much of a chance.

"What's in that pylon?" I asked.

He opened his mouth to speak and then nodded back through the tarp. "And they're out. Guess Becca wasn't as tough as I thought she was."

The trio jogged back to the scaffolding.

"When that thing goes off," Chase said, "just imagine the *disruption* it will cause."

"What do you mean, when it goes off?" I glanced back at the pylon and then at my fellow campers. "Are you saying that's a … is that a bomb?"

Chase shook his head. "Pathetic."

I peeked through the slits in the tarps. The young boy who'd picked up my cylinder was still there, but he was now in a tug-of-war with the girl he'd been taunting. She pulled and twisted while the boy held tight to his end and pulled and twisted as well. Then, with a mighty heave, the boy and the girl stumbled to the ground, each clutching a segment.

"One minute and twenty-seven seconds," I said, reminding myself how much time I had before the segments went off. It would be early. Earlier than the rest of the team, but hopefully not by much. The boy stood up and angrily kicked one of the segments down the platform and then started screaming at the girl for wrecking his toy.

"What?" Chase asked. When I didn't answer, he turned to the others. "What did he say?"

"He said 'one minute and twenty-seven seconds,'" Duncan answered.

Chase scowled at me for a beat and then grabbed my wrist and slammed it against one of the bars of scaffolding. I'm not sure where the plastic zip-tie came from, but it was around my wrist in a flash, and I was secured to the metal bar.

I jerked my arm back, and the plastic band bit into my wrist. "Hey!"

Chase spun me around so that I was facing the wall and then zip-tied my other wrist so both hands were now behind my back. I was about to swear, when he shoved something soft into my mouth. Alexis handed him a piece of duct tape, and he pressed it over my lips. "Quiet now," he said. "Wouldn't want you warning anyone." He reached into his pocket and pulled out a small device, about the size of a pack of gum. "Tell you what I'll do: I'll give you your minute and twenty-seven seconds. Because that's about how long it will take me to get out of the building, but then I'm going to push this button." He held up the device, which had a small, round black button in the center. "That ought to give you a chance." He laughed and then strolled away like he didn't have a care in the world. As if he didn't have a detonator in his pocket and he wasn't a couple minutes away from setting off a bomb on a train platform.

A burst of wind signaled that another train was coming into the station, and a few seconds later, it arrived with a squeal and a gasp of air before the doors opened and people started streaming in and out. Rob, Alexis, and Duncan turned and jogged over. I tried to call after them to reason with them, but it's incredibly tough to be heard when your mouth is duct taped and you're worried about choking on a sock. Sheesh, I hoped it wasn't something worse than a sock.

That's when Amara's Roman grenade gave its first pop.

CHAPTER 45

There was a couple-second delay from the first pop to the second. But then it was like someone had opened fire with a machine gun. Screams and explosions happened farther down the platform too. Somehow, one of the segments must've made it down there.

Passengers screamed and ran for cover. I thrashed against the bars of the scaffolding, pulling and twisting like a maniac. Something sliced into my palm, and I glanced back. The very tip of a screw jutted out from the scaffolding bar like a thorn. I rotated my body and slid the plastic zip-tie over the barb, sawing back and forth. Over and over. More than once I slipped and cursed as the screw jabbed into my hand or wrist. Finally, the tie snapped, and I spun around and sawed my other wrist against the same spot. It was a lot easier when I was facing the right way, and in a couple seconds, the tie snapped.

I jumped through the scaffolding and onto the platform and was immediately knocked back by a woman screaming and running for the exit. The train was still on the tracks too, which was good since it meant no one was getting run over, but bad because the last car had filled with dozens of people ducking for cover, and they were pretty much lined up with Chase's pylon bomb.

Amara hadn't been kidding that his invention was a lot better than a typical Roman candle. It was a steady stream of tiny missiles. Some of them screeched, and others ricocheted off walls or the ceiling—or people—and each left a trail of smoke in its wake. I was hit at least half a dozen times before I managed to stand up again.

I considered heading for the exit. I even took one step in that direction, but I just couldn't bring myself to leave. Becca was not going to survive in the bathroom if that bomb went off, and while the train car might protect some of the people from the sting of the Roman grenade blasts, I had my doubts it would help against Chase's bomb.

I had to do something. Now.

"Move!" I shouted as I rushed down the length of the train. The smoke from the thousands of blasts made it tough to see, and I kept slamming into people or tripping over those who had already stumbled. I imagined the rest of my team were probably well into their disturbances on their platforms, and I bet Chase was sauntering out the main exit as everyone else stampeded around him. He probably had his finger on his button at that very moment. The thought almost stopped me in my tracks, but somehow I forced myself forward.

I hit the wall at the end and snatched up the OUT OF ORDER pylon from in front of the restroom. I sprinted the dozen steps to the edge of the platform and heaved the pylon down the tracks as far as I could. I thought it might explode when it hit the ground, but it didn't. It just bounced against the tracks and settled a good fifteen yards down the line.

I went to the last train car and yelled, "There's a bomb, get out of the station!"

I don't think anyone in there really saw me because the smoke was so bad by then, but they sure heard me. They screamed and poured out of the train shouting things like, "There's a bomb!" and "We're under attack!" as well as curses and cries for help.

I rushed over to the girls' bathroom and shoved the door open.

"Becca!"

I followed the groans to one of the stalls and opened the door. Becca was on the ground, bleeding from her nose and mouth. They'd really done a number on her. I grabbed her by the arm and pulled her to a sitting position.

"C'mon," I said, "get up." I tried to pull her up, but she just slumped back, her eyes fluttering. I opened the toilet and reached into the bowl and scooped out water—I hoped it was just water—and threw it in her face. I only had to do it twice before she sputtered and started coming around.

"Get up!" I said again, pulling her arm. "The whole place is going to blow up any second."

That seemed to get her attention a bit more. She made it to her feet, and I threw one of her arms over my shoulder, and together we scrambled to the door.

The colored blasts from the Roman grenades pelted us as we headed down the platform. Every step gave me hope that we might make it out, and each step seemed to bring Becca back more and more until we were almost jogging. I shouted at others to run, to get outside, and half a dozen times, Becca and I both had to stop to heave a few cowering or injured travelers to their feet and get them moving again.

At first, I was a bit surprised that Becca cared enough to stop to help, but then I realized she probably needed my help to get out, and if I was stopping, she didn't have much of a choice. Plus, there was a very real possibility she was just a regular CIA operative, and not necessarily a psychotic one. Chase and his group—now, they were a different story.

It was a small bomb, I told myself. The pylon wasn't that heavy, and it wasn't that big. It couldn't do a ton of damage. Plus, I'd thrown it far enough down the tracks. We clambered up the steps to the second level. It couldn't cause that much—

BOOM!

CHAPTER 46

I only knew I'd been unconscious because I didn't remember falling down, and yet there I was, face down on the tiled floor. I couldn't have been out long. Amara's fireworks were still sputtering, though not nearly to the extent they had been. The main lights were out, no doubt disabled by Chase's bomb, and the emergency lighting cast an eerie glow through the smoke. As I pushed myself to my knees, I realized there weren't any screams anymore. The occasional figure dashed past me, but I'd been out long enough that most of the people had made it out. Becca was gone too. She'd just left me there.

I used the wall to pull myself to my feet and nearly toppled again when a sharp pain exploded at the back of my head. I reached back. My hair felt sticky. I followed the wall to find my way through the haze to the stairs, up to the next level, and out the exit.

The sunlight felt like a fresh blow of a hammer to my skull, and I slumped against one of the outside walls. There were people everywhere. Hundreds of them, most covered in thick dust like me, some limping or pressing cloths against bloody injuries. I expected to see droves of emergency vehicles: police, fire, ambulances. I wouldn't have been surprised to see some kind of military presence, even. But although I could hear sirens in the distance, there was only a single fire truck on the scene.

I took a moment to catch my breath. I had to get as far away from the station as possible.

"The bus!" I glanced at my watch. 3:15. I swore and then turned and looked down the street toward the alley where I was supposed to meet the bus. It was gone.

I straightened and hobbled down the outer wall of the station through the frazzled and dusty mob. I made it to the corner of the building just in time to see the bus pull into an intersection a hundred yards away.

All I could think was that I needed to get on that bus. I needed to get away from the station. Our disturbance might have been bigger than I'd intended it to be, but Chase had outright lost his mind. I needed to tell someone what he'd done. I stepped off the curb and staggered across the street.

Behind me someone yelled, "Hey!"

I turned and spotted a security guard. He was eyeing me as though he recognized me. I didn't see how he could've. I turned back and kept going. I could make it to the bus if I could just get their attention. They'd stop for me.

"Stop!" the voice yelled again. It was closer now, just over my shoulder. He sounded angry. I wondered if he'd seen me on the security cameras or if he'd seen me acting weird on the main platform and thought I was responsible. I *was* responsible, at least partially, but I wasn't about to let some rent-a-cop stop me. I willed my legs to move faster.

The man yelled again, but this time, it was more of a generic yell and not really any words. I glanced over my shoulder just in time to see him dive at me. Enough time to see him, but not enough time to move. He tackled me to the ground, and pain exploded all over. I rolled, and he rolled too. I tried to get up, but he got up first and tackled me again. I saw the curb coming straight at my head, but I don't remember hitting it. I don't remember anything really. Just the security guard tackling me for a second time, and the curb. I definitely remember the curb.

After that, everything went black.

CHAPTER 47

I woke up lying on a soft mattress. For half a second, I thought I was home. I wondered if my mom would call me to breakfast or if Jason would be calling to hang out.

It was the scent of antiseptic cleaner that jolted me into full consciousness. I jerked upright into a sitting position and winced when I tried to pull my hand to my face to shield my eyes from the harsh fluorescent lights, because something hard bit into my wrist. It took a minute for me to realize what I was looking at when I glanced down at my hand.

"Handcuffs?"

A dizzying wave of nausea forced me onto my back, and I counted to twelve before I thought I might not puke. I hurt. Every part of me. My head felt like a team of soccer players had used it for a practice game. I tried to reach for it, only to have the handcuffs dig into my wrist again. There were bandages on my wrists too, and with my free hand, I felt around and realized there were bandages around my head as well.

It came back slowly. First the summer camp. Then the CIA. Then, finally, Chase and what must've been his psychotic break. He'd really tried to blow the place up. He actually wanted to kill people. Didn't the CIA do any psychiatric screening of the kids they let into camp? I thought about my team and how Angie was clearly unstable. Then there were Rob, Alexis, and Duncan. They were nuts too.

Maybe psychiatric tests don't work on kids.

The door to my room opened, and two police officers dressed in dark blue uniforms walked in.

"You're awake," the first man said. He was short and chubby and had a flat face that made him look a bit like an angry, overweight dog. "Good."

He moved to one side of my bed while his partner slipped over to the other. His partner was young, maybe mid-twenties. He had a narrow face and close-cut hair.

"What's your name?" Flat-face demanded.

I tried to focus. What was I supposed to do in a situation like this? I had to talk to someone in the CIA. I had to tell them that Chase had gone crazy. Camp Friendship was a secret, wasn't it? I remembered Jason and how the FBI had all but figured out who I was anyway. They'd be here soon. I could be uncooperative with these officers, or I could be direct and just tell them I needed to speak to someone in the CIA. That would probably speed things along a bit.

"Should we call you Gunnar?" Flat-face asked.

I realized the chubby officer had my wallet. I shrugged.

"You don't look like a Gunnar Konstantan from Sweden."

I sighed. My head hurt. My body ached. For all I knew, Chase had gotten away and was blaming the whole thing on me. I needed to hurry this along, so I settled on being direct. "I need to speak to someone in the CIA."

The two officers laughed.

"The CIA?" Flat-face asked. He turned to his partner. "Did you hear that? The CIA."

"We have ourselves a genuine spy," the younger officer said. "A

Swedish one, at that, only I didn't hear any accent when he spoke." He raised his eyebrows as if he'd just pointed out a mistake.

"So, you would like to speak to someone in the CIA?" Flat-face asked again. "Not a lawyer? Not your parents? Just the CIA?"

Definitely not my parents, I thought, but didn't say. "The CIA," I repeated. "It's important."

"Obviously," Flat-face said. "It must be very important if you want to talk to the CIA. We don't usually get requests like that unless it's very serious." He leaned over my bed smelling of sweat and coffee, and I had to try very hard not to gag. "Did the CIA tell you to do it? Did they hire you to try to blow up the station?"

"*What?*" I shook my head and just about passed out from the pain that exploded behind my eyes. After a couple breaths, I added, "I didn't do that. I stopped it."

The younger officer raised his eyebrows. "If *that's* what you think 'stop' means, you need a new dictionary."

"I tried to stop it. I tried to get everyone out before—" Stop talking, I told myself. Just keep your mouth shut about anything that happened at the station. "CIA," I said again. "I need someone from the CIA."

For the next couple hours, the officers tried to get me to talk. When I wouldn't, they'd switch tactics and try something else. They'd leave for a while and then come back and pepper me with questions. Sometimes they'd be friendly; other times they'd yell and get right in my face. It was annoying more than it was intimidating. These guys were amateurs compared to Butler. I smiled at the fact that I'd managed to survive his interrogation. That had to count for something once the CIA got here and had to decide what to do with me.

"Something funny?" Flat-face asked.

I wiped the smile off my face.

"People were hurt today, Gunnar. A lot of people." He pointed a stubby finger at me. "We have you on the security tapes. You're the one we see carrying that exploding tube. You're the one we see throwing that bomb onto the tracks."

Yaakov, you idiot. Why didn't you erase the ... I let out a slow breath. He probably did erase it. He erased the footage from the tracks he was supposed to erase. I wasn't on the right track. I had followed Becca, and because of that, they had me on camera.

"But we know you weren't working alone. So just give us some names and—"

"Enough," I said, surprising myself with my defiance. "You both are giving me a headache. I'm not intimidated by either of you. I won't be answering your stupid questions. For the hundredth time, I want to speak to someone from the C – I – A." I emphasized each letter.

The officers left, and a little more than an hour later, the doctor came in. She was young and had chin-length brown hair and red-rimmed glasses. It was a pretty nice change from the nurses who had come in from time to time during the interrogation. They'd all looked like they could be very close relatives to Flat-face. From the same litter perhaps.

The doctor scanned my chart and then sat down on the edge of the bed.

"How are you feeling?"

"I hurt," I said.

"Anywhere in particular?"

"Everywhere." I reached up with my free hand and touched the side of my head. "But especially my head."

She shone her little penlight in my eyes, one at a time. "You're lucky to be alive."

"Yeah, I know." I jerked lightly on my handcuffed hand. "Real lucky."

She studied me for a moment. "You don't seem nearly as worried as I would be if I were you."

That made me feel pretty cool. Here I was, handcuffed to a hospital bed by police who thought I was some kind of insane-Unabomber-type psycho, and I had a smoking-hot doctor telling me she thought I was brave. She was saying that, wasn't she? I felt my smile widen. The crazy thing was that once the CIA showed up, I had a good shot at being a hero, too. My friends back home would never believe it.

Things were looking up. Chase was a freaking psychopath, but I'd stopped him, and I was sure the CIA would make him disappear. It didn't even matter if everyone found out I wasn't supposed to be at the camp and that somehow my dad had weaseled me onto the roster. I belonged there now. I was going to be a CIA operative. Agent Matt Cambridge. I was going to be James freaking Bond. Well, not really, since he's British, but I was going to be the American version of James Bond. I tried to think of an American equivalent of James Bond and couldn't. They really need one of those.

"You're smiling?" the pretty doctor said. "I don't think I could be as collected as you if I were facing the charges they've levied at you."

"Let's just say that when the truth about what happened gets out, I won't be in any trouble at all."

"So you didn't blow up the station?"

I shook my head. "If I hadn't been there, it would have been a lot worse."

Shut up, Matt!

"But you know who did it?" she asked. "And the other attacks around the city too?"

I nodded. "Oh yeah, I—wait. What do you mean attacks *around the city*? You mean the one at the station, right?"

She studied me for a moment and then reached across my bed to grab the remote control. She pointed it at the small TV mounted against the opposite wall. "There were attacks at a few places," she said, flipping through the channels. Every channel seemed to be playing the news, and each had scenes of destruction and panic, people crying, buildings on fire, and crowds huddled outside of buildings. A few of the scenes were of the station, but many weren't.

"The university was evacuated because of anthrax," the doctor continued.

"What? An anthrax scare?" I wasn't sure exactly what anthrax was, but I knew it scared the heck out of people and it was pretty deadly. Jason and I had wanted to have a long weekend once and considered filling an envelope with flour and sending it to the school with the word *Anthrax* on the inside. But we decided, on the off chance we got caught, we'd get in less trouble if we called in a bomb threat instead.

"Not a *scare*," the doctor said. "It was real anthrax. There were a few exposures. Those people might die."

My jaw dropped. That didn't make any sense. Chase was the one who'd lost his mind. He was the one trying to kill people, and his team had been at the station. Hadn't they? Maybe only some were, and the others were doing crazy things in other parts of the city. Becca and her team might have been responsible too. I mean, they must've put their plan in motion before getting to the station. They certainly hadn't looked like they were in any hurry, and by then, they only had a few minutes before the three o'clock deadline. But *real* anthrax? It had to be Chase.

Becca was crazy, but not that crazy.

Something on the screen caught my attention as the doctor flipped through the channels, and I jerked my cuffed hand, trying to point. "Wait," I said. "Go back." She flicked back a couple stations. "There," I said. I only recognized the sign at first. The giant plastic waffle was partially melted and charred, but it was definitely Rick's Waffle House. Kalvin with a *K*'s house.

"Do you know that place?" the doctor asked.

It was a coincidence. It had to be. I mean, the kid did have an entire storage locker of fireworks. Those things are dangerous.

"Do you know that place?" she asked again.

I nodded slowly. "I don't get it. Chase wouldn't have gone there. He wouldn't know that place. And that means ..." It came to me all at once. Amara hadn't been trying to steal anything. He'd been rigging something to go off in that room. He knew explosives. He'd have known the fire would take the building down, but he'd done it anyway. Why would he do that?

"That means what?" the doctor prodded. When I didn't respond, she added, "It hasn't been released yet, but they're saying that place was part of the attack. It was one of the first targets."

"They are?" I asked. "They think it's one of the first attacks?" I jerked my head around to the doctor. "Wait a minute. How do you know? How do you know any of this stuff? If it hasn't been released, then where are you getting your information?"

Her expression turned to ice. She tossed the clipboard to the foot of my bed, stood up, and shrugged off the white lab coat. There was a gun on her hip.

She walked over and opened the door, and two men wearing dark suits marched in. One of them closed the door behind him, set the lock, and then put his back against the door while the other man closed the curtains in the room and then took a position beside my bed.

"What's going on?" I said, looking frantically between my gun-strapped doctor and the new dangerous-looking men in the room. "Who are you guys?"

She turned and looked at me through narrowed eyes. "My name is Agent Knox," she said. "That is Agent Chen, and the man by the door is Agent French."

Agent Chen was tall and lanky but looked mean. He reminded me a bit of Bruce Lee, only older and with less hair. He sat down on the small chair beside my bed and opened a laptop. Agent French had dark hair cut really short and was about six feet tall. He wore a scowl that made him look really angry, like he wanted to hurt someone. Like he wanted to hurt me.

"Agent?" I asked. "Then you're not a doctor?"

She shook her head. "No, Gunnar, I'm not a doctor. I'm with the Domestic Operations Division." She paused and then added, "CIA."

CHAPTER 48

"**Y**ou're CIA?" I should have been able to relax at that moment, but instead, a wave of embarrassment washed over me. I'd been so cool a moment ago, and probably would have told her everything if she'd kept prodding me. She probably thought I was just some stupid kid who couldn't keep his mouth shut about national secrets.

She nodded. "That's right. And I want you to tell us what happened out there, or we turn you over to the half a dozen FBI agents waiting just outside the door."

I jerked my head to the door. "The FBI is out there? Why?"

Agent Knox sighed. "Look, kid. We don't have time for stupid questions. A train station was blown up today. A school was exposed to anthrax. An entire section of the city was without power for about two hours. It was chaos, and estimated damages are in the tens of millions of dollars. And best we can tell, you had something to do with it." She glared at me. "We have footage of you heaving something onto the tracks, and then a minute later, the tunnel explodes."

"Look," I said. "I was following the rules. I was only going to cause a *disruption*. It was Chase, that crazy lunatic. He lost it out there. I don't know how to explain it. He's been kind of nuts all along, but come on, who tries to blow up a freaking train platform?"

Agent Chen was typing as I spoke, and I got the impression he was writing every word I said. I had to be careful. I bet Chase had already blamed me for everything, and they were trying to decide who they'd believe.

"So you were told to cause a disruption at the train station?" Agent Knox asked.

I shook my head. "No. The station was my idea. It's a prank a buddy and I had been planning for years."

"Jason Cole?" Agent Knox asked.

I sighed. "Okay, I shouldn't have called him. I know cell phones are prohibited at the camp. I'm sorry about that. But before you kick me out of the program, please, just look at what I accomplished."

Agent Knox raised an eyebrow. "And what would that be?"

"I planned and executed an amazing disruption. I identified Chase's psychotic break, and his crazy plan to blow the place up. I intercepted the bomb and threw it onto the tracks so no one would get hurt. Then I cleared the platform." I was going to mention that Becca had helped me, but after I got her out, she'd left me unconscious on the floor, so she wasn't getting any credit for this. "I deserve to be at the camp," I said. "I deserve to be a CIA operative."

Agent French had his hands in tight fists, and he kept looking at me like I'd just farted really, really loud. Agent Chen just kept typing with a face that didn't change. I bet he was a really good poker player.

Agent Knox rubbed the back of her neck.

"I'm going to show you some pictures. You tell us if they're the ones responsible, or if you know them."

I felt my brow furrow. "I know exactly who's to blame. I told you—"

"Just," Agent Knox cut in, "look at the pictures."

I shrugged. "Fine."

Agent Chen tossed a yellow folder onto the bed, and I opened it up.

"Dalson?" I asked, holding up the first picture. "How could he be responsible? He runs the whole camp." I flipped quickly through the next dozen or so pictures. "Half of these people I've never seen," I said, "and the other half are counselors at the camp. How could they be responsible when the challenge was for the campers?"

"Because," Agent Knox said, speaking very slowly, "all the campers are ... kids."

I wasn't sure if that had been a question or a statement, so I just nodded.

"Keep flipping," she said. "There are some youth in there, as well."

After another half dozen adult pictures, there were some of the campers. I recognized a few from just spotting them around the grounds, or during activities, until I hit Juno's pictures. "Juno?" I asked. "He's on my team. Why would you even suspect anyone from my team?" Agent Knox didn't answer, and I kept flipping. I pulled out Amara's picture, as well as Yaakov's. "Both of these guys are on my team." I shook my head. "You have pictures of my team in there, and not one of Chase's team?" I shoved the folder away with my free hand. "You've already talked to him, haven't you? I don't know what Chase told you, but he's lying. He's responsible. He's probably responsible for the anthrax too."

"And the fire at the waffle house?" Agent French asked.

I felt my face heat up. "Maybe." It wasn't a lie. Not exactly. I didn't *know* if Amara had done it. Chase had all but admitted he'd followed us, and for all I knew he'd gone into the basement of the waffle house after we'd left, to see what supplies we'd gotten from Kalvin. He could've set the place on fire as punishment for him helping us out. Actually, as I thought that scenario out, it sounded entirely possible. If that wasn't what happened ... if Amara *had* been responsible, what did that mean?

That he was as crazy as Chase? That Rylee was wrong, and it had been him, not Angie, who was the team psychopath?

"He's lying," Agent French said.

"About what?" I asked. That was probably the wrong thing to say, since it sort of implied that I had lied about something.

"About everything," Agent French snapped back.

I opened my mouth to speak, but Agent Knox held up her hand. "You're good, Matt. If you're telling the truth, you're quite brave, and you saved a lot of people. If you're lying, you're a sociopath."

"You guys really don't know about the camp?" I asked. "You don't know about Camp Friendship?"

"Camp Friendship?" Agent French asked. "You have to be freaking kidding me."

I looked at Agent Knox, and fully intended to double my efforts to explain myself, but something in the way she looked at me sent my stomach on a downward slide to my toes. It was as if she was watching a puppy about to be put down. She didn't have the slightest idea about Camp Friendship. She didn't know who Dalson was, or Mr. Smith. She didn't have a clue about any of it.

The morning's events played out in my mind again, and it hit me again how I'd been congratulated in the dining room after my interrogation with Butler. How they said he hadn't broken me even though he most certainly had. I'd spilled my guts. I'd told him Camp Friendship was a CIA camp for kids, I'd told him my real name ... I'd told him everything. It had been a passing thought at the time, but now it was an amber flashing sign in my head. The only reason they'd congratulate me on not breaking was because in their mind I hadn't. Because what I'd said hadn't been true.

When Dalson had played that particular scene, the one where I shouted that I was part of a CIA camp for kids, the campers, especially those in my team, had cheered. Cheered and laughed.

I swore and muttered under my breath. "It's not a CIA camp, is it?" If that were true, if it was all a lie, then what kind of camp did that make it? And what about Butler? There had been no misunderstanding that he was one of the head CIA interrogators. But maybe that's why his presence was so awe-inspiring to the other campers.

There was a knock on the door, and Agent Knox hesitated a moment before she stood up and dusted her hands together. "I'm not sure what's going on here," she said. "I'm not sure if you're crazy, or if we've stumbled onto a very, very dangerous situation. It's not my call to make. We need a professional to tell us that."

Agent French opened the door, and there he was. Standing there in a three-piece suit, his face bearing a couple days of stubble, looking very similar to how he'd looked in the underground interrogation room.

I didn't mean to speak at that moment, but the realization of what kind of situation I was in overwhelmed my senses. The word just fell out of my mouth.

"Butler."

CHAPTER 49

Agent Knox looked between Butler and me. "Do you two know each other?"

"Yes," I said.

"No," Butler said at the exact same time.

Agent French closed the door and stood in front of the doorknob.

Butler gave me a quizzical look. "I'm afraid we've never met, young man."

That did it. His insistence that we hadn't met was the final bit of information I needed to fully appreciate how very wrong I'd been about everything I'd experienced in the past three weeks. There was no reason to lie about it unless it was something he didn't want the CIA to know.

"His name," I said, "is Robert Ingleton. He goes by Butler when he interrogates people. I know because he taught me counter-interrogation techniques at the camp."

Butler blinked and then forced a smile. "Of course I did." He rolled his eyes at the other agents in the room. "Because I frequently teach ten-year-olds."

None of the other agents laughed. Agent Knox, especially, seemed to be weighing the situation carefully. Butler acted like he was more confused than any of them though. He kept a smile on his face, but his eyes said, *What are you doing?*

Once he put it together, once he realized that I really was Matt

Cambridge, that I had somehow ended up at their secret camp despite having no business being there, he'd pull out all the stops and I wouldn't have a chance.

I pointed at my interrogator with my free hand but directed my voice to Agent Knox. "He's going to figure it out in a second," I said. "He's going to realize that I had honestly thought I was in a CIA camp for kids. He's going to realize it, and he's going to do everything he can to get you three out of the room."

That did it. Butler's eyes widened for a fraction of a second. He recovered instantly and became utterly stone-faced. I would've missed the hint of realization if I hadn't been watching him carefully.

"How does he know that name?" Agent Knox asked.

Butler gave a shrug. "No doubt one of his compatriots has crossed paths with me. Doesn't bode well for the company he keeps and what we can expect to learn from this kid, now does it?"

"Yes," I said. "We have crossed paths. Last night when you interrogated me." I gestured to the folder Agent Knox had shown me. "Dalson, the man in one of the pictures you showed me, he and Butler are friends."

"I think I'm going to need some one-on-one time with our suspect," Butler said. "If I could have the room, please."

"Do not leave," I said to Agent Knox. "I told you he'd ask for alone time. I said it, right? Now he has, and it's because I wasn't supposed to be at that camp. He's only just realized it."

"You say he interrogated you last night?" Agent Knox asked. I nodded, and she added, "Prove it."

"Indulging a suspect's lies is not how I run an interrogation," Butler said. He was stern, but something in his voice shook, and I just hoped Agent Knox heard it.

"He gets to speak," Agent Knox said. She nodded at me. "Tell us something about him."

"Yes," Butler said. "Please do. I'd be very interested in hearing what you have to say about me."

I opened my mouth to speak but stopped. What could I say? Could I talk about how he'd treated me? The things he'd asked me? That wouldn't convince anyone, let alone a CIA operative. Everything that happened in the interrogation room could be explained as a complicated scenario that I'd dreamed up.

Butler took a seat in one of the chairs by the bed and leaned forward. And that's when I saw it.

"Look at his lip," I said. "You see that cut? After the interrogation last night I hit him. I head-butted him when he cut the straps holding me to the chair."

Knox and the other agents eyed Butler suspiciously, but I could tell they weren't convinced.

Butler stood up. "Impressive. You spot a cut on my lip that I got playing catch with my son, and you twist it into your story. How very industrious of you." He turned and faced the door. "If you won't allow me to interrogate the suspect on my own, I'll be on my way." He took a step toward the door, but Agent French didn't move. "If you'll kindly move," Butler said.

"His shins!" I said as I replayed what happened after I'd split Butler's lip.

"Oh, I've had enough of this," Butler said.

"After I hit him with my head, I shoved his metal cart at him. I hit him in the shins. He hobbled around. I bet there's a mark." I turned to Agent Knox. "How could I know that unless I'd done it?"

"Enough!" Butler snapped. He didn't take his cold gaze off me, but when he spoke, it was to the others in the room. "I'll be leaving now. I have no intention of further indulging the lies of Mr. Cambridge." He turned to the door. "Agent French, you will step aside, or I will see to it that you are reprimanded."

"How'd you know his name?" Agent Knox asked.

Butler turned and exhaled tiredly. "Agent, you introduced him when I walked in."

"I did no such thing," Agent Knox said. "I was planning on doing so. But I never had a chance." She turned to Agent Chen. "Isn't that right?"

Agent Chen tapped his computer and then nodded. "That's right."

"And yet you just called him Mr. Cambridge," Agent Knox said. "How did you know his last name?"

Butler pointed at the chart at the end of my bed. "I saw it on the chart."

Agent Knox picked the chart off the bed and glanced at it. "Matt's wallet had ID for a Gunnar Konstantan. That's who the hospital staff thought he was." She tapped the board. "That's whose name is on this board."

Butler shrugged. "Then I must've heard it from one of the other agents looking into this case. What difference does it make, Agent?"

Agent Knox looked at me. And I indicated at Butler's legs with my eyes.

"Lift your pant legs, sir," Agent Knox said.

"I will not." Butler swallowed, and a bead of sweat rolled down the side of his face.

"Roll up your pant legs, sir, or I'll have Agent French do it for you."

"This is outrageous, Agent Knox." Butler scowled. "I came here at the request of the Agency. I will not let some child dictate how I am treated. I will report your actions here to your superiors."

Agent Knox pointed at Agent Chen. "Everything we say and do is being recorded, sir. If you pull up your pant leg and there are no marks, you will be given a copy for your report." She spoke with such authority I didn't know which one had a higher rank, or even if there was such a thing as ranks in the CIA. "Now," she continued. "Pull. Up. Your. Pant. Leg."

Butler looked at me and sneered and then relented. Both shins were skinned, right where the trolley had hit him.

"This proves nothing," Butler said. He pointed at Agent Knox and was about to say something else. Probably another threat, or maybe he was going to tell her how he'd skinned his knees playing a pick-up game of basketball or something, but Agent French grabbed Butler's outstretched hand, spun him around, and pressed him into the door before twisting his arm behind his back and handcuffing his wrists.

Then French opened the door and led Butler away. Agent Knox and Agent Chen followed, leaving me in the room, alone.

* * *

Over the next several hours, Agent Knox and Agent Chen came into my hospital room repeatedly and asked me one question after the next. They brought in printed pictures of the images I'd sent to Jason. I identified everyone I could, including my teammates. After all was said and done, I must've told the entire story of my time at Camp Friendship a dozen times, frontward and backward. It was exhausting. And the more I told it, the more obvious it became that the CIA had nothing to do with the camp, and the more embarrassed I became at having misread the situation so badly.

Each time I thought it was the last time, and then they'd come back and ask more questions. When they returned for what must've been the hundredth time, Agent Chen took his position behind his computer again. Then Agent Knox removed my handcuffs, pulled up a chair to the edge of the bed, and took a seat.

That was different. They'd never taken my cuffs off before.

"It's been hours!" I said. "How much longer are you guys going to make me do this?"

"We're almost done, Matt," she said. Her voice was softer than it had been before, and the muscles in her face flexed like she was worried about something. "I think you're telling the truth. I think you saved a lot of people today. That was a brave thing."

I sighed, but didn't really feel any better. I rubbed my wrists. "Thank you for believing me. Did Butler admit it? Did he tell you what kind of camp I was in?"

Agent Knox pulled out the yellow folder of pictures again and tossed Mr. Dalson's photo on my lap.

"Mr. Dalson," I said again.

"His name is Robert Hader. He worked for the CIA up until about a decade ago, when he quit and dropped off the grid. He suddenly popped back up about five years ago, working for a multinational communications corporation. His passport would be flagged every now and again, but it wasn't until your friend Jason Cole uploaded his picture, along with a dozen other high-interest targets, that the pieces fell into place."

"What pieces?" I asked. "What are you talking about?"

"We suspected that Hader had met with some pretty bad people over the last decade. There's some bad blood between him and the Company, and it was suggested he might take his skills and switch sides."

"Switch sides, how?" I asked.

"We thought he was visiting terrorist training camps and offering consulting services to some of the major criminal types around the globe. He had inside information on how to avoid law-enforcement and intelligence-gathering organizations like the CIA."

"So," I began, "he was helping the people you guys were trying to stop."

"That's what we thought," Agent Knox said. "But now that we know a bit more, it seems he was more cunning than we gave him credit for."

She stared at me for several awkward seconds. It was as if she expected me to understand something now that she'd explained that much, and there was a part of me that did know what she was going to say, but I couldn't bring myself to say it out loud first.

She pulled out a picture of Alexander Bratersky and put it on the bed. "This is Mikhail Sokolovsky, son of Boris Sokolovsky, a member of the ROC."

ROC. I'd heard that before. Juno had said that Bratersky was a member of the ROC, but I hadn't figured out what that meant yet.

"Russian Organized Crime," Knox said. I swore. "The Russian mafia," she added. "Not a nice man." She took out a picture of Juno. "Junosuke Tagai. I'm not surprised he used his real name. I'm sure he's proud of it because he's the son of Kenji Tagai, a top-level yakuza." Amara's picture was next. "This is the son of Nkoyo Okereke; she's a South African freedom fighter." She took out Yaakov's picture next. "This is Haim Eldad. He's the son of the Israeli telecommunications mogul,

Alex Eldad. There's long been suspicion that Eldad had ties to various organized crime rings in that region." She flipped Angie's picture over next, followed by Rylee. "These two," she said, "we're still looking into. Their pictures don't come up on the regular sources, but it's just a matter of time."

"Are you saying they're all terrorists?" I asked. "It's a camp for training terrorists? Not CIA?"

She shook her head. "Not terrorists, Matt. Well, not only terrorists. There are a number of campers and counselors in those pictures who have ties to terrorist organizations, but most are just tied to the criminal underworld. From what Butler said, they run these camps as training zones to give the kids of top-level criminals an education. Then they go even further. The best teams from each camp are used as criminals for hire. It's an opportunity to build a reputation while aligning yourself with one of the most secret and well-funded criminal organizations we've ever encountered."

I leaned forward. "Who would want to hire a bunch of kids?"

Agent Knox's eyebrows lifted. "Imagine all the places a kid could get into that an adult might not. Or imagine the kind of information a kid would get access to that an adult would never be able to. Plus, it would be easy for a kid to be overlooked during a major crime spree."

"Like today," I said.

Knox nodded. "Like today."

"So if I had won, I'd have had to do other missions," I said. "They'd have used me to commit crimes?"

"And you'd have been paid for it," Knox said. "At least that's what Butler said."

She hesitated, and I could tell there was something else she wanted to say.

"What?" I asked. "What is it?"

"Well, Matt, it turns out your team *did* win. I know you said you tried to stop Chase, but by throwing that pylon onto the tracks, you, apparently, got credit for the bombing. Butler was here to try to get you *out* of trouble. They want you back at the camp."

I laughed. "That's not going to happen."

Agent Knox didn't smile.

"Wait," I continued. "It's not going to happen, right? You can't make me go back in there now that I know they're all a bunch of criminals." I tried my best to steady my breath. "Can you?"

CHAPTER 50

"**M**y parents will never go for it. The whole reason my dad put me in that camp in the first place was to get me away from bad influences." I shook my head at the irony.

Yeah, great job, Dad. You kept me away from friends who liked to play harmless pranks and threw me in with a bunch of criminals.

"Speaking of my parents, you guys have known who I really am for a while. How in the world have you managed to keep my dad out of here?" I glanced at the door. "I bet he's dying to tell me how disappointed he is."

"We haven't called your parents yet," Agent Knox said.

I looked at her and felt my mouth gape. "What do you mean? They know about today, don't they?"

Agent Knox shook her head.

"Why not?"

"We're just waiting until we have a better picture of the whole event."

A better picture. I quickly went over everything I'd told the agents about my experiences at Camp Friendship. The one part they'd kept going back to was how I'd managed to get into the camp in the first place. That's it. "You think my dad's one of them."

Agent Chen glanced up from his computer but didn't speak.

"Look, if you knew my dad, you'd know he wouldn't do anything criminal. No way. He's as straight and boring as a piece of lumber."

"And yet he's the reason you were at that camp in the first place." Agent Knox straightened in her chair. "Butler doesn't have an answer to that question either, Matt. He has no idea how you managed to get onto the roster."

"My dad's not—"

Agent Knox held up her hand. "I believe you, Matt. We've done a pretty extensive background check on your whole family, and boring is about right. But we're doing a check on the company he works for. Sledge Industries *is* part of the organization, and if we spoke to your dad, and he suddenly started acting differently at work, well, it might shine a spotlight on you, and that might not be very good for anyone."

"So, no one at Camp Friendship knows I wasn't supposed to be there?"

"That's what Butler's told us," Agent Knox said, "and I'm inclined to believe him."

"You're inclined to believe the guy who has basically been a double agent for who knows how many years?" I flopped back onto the bed. "He's like a genius manipulator. He's probably lying to you."

"He's one of the best interrogators, Matt." She shook her head. "And, yes, he managed to keep his affiliation with your Dalson a secret, but he's not an operative, Matt. He's an academic, an expert in psychology. Believe it or not, guys like him don't do well when facing down treason charges or public vilification. He has a family. He did what he did for money and because he thought he'd get away with it. He has a lot to lose right now, and his only option is to cooperate. He knows this. Believe it or not, we *can* trust him."

Butler has a family? I tried to picture it and couldn't. What would his kids be like? They'd probably make Chase look like an angel.

"Look, Matt, if you don't want to go back to the camp, you don't have to."

"Great," I said. "I don't want to."

Agent Knox took a breath. "Hear me out. Butler said your team won. He said that now you and your team will get real missions. You'll be dealing with actual coordinating members of this organization. Dalson's organization."

"You mean Hader," I said. "Not Dalson. You keep calling him that, but that's not his real name, right?"

"Keep thinking of him as Dalson," Agent Knox said. "Less likely you'll slip up if you only think of him as Dalson."

"I won't slip up," I said, "because I'm never going to see him again. I'm not going back."

"But if you did go back," Agent Knox said, "you'd be able to learn how communications are made. We'd be able to follow those communications back to the source and get real intelligence. Intelligence that would bring Dalson and the whole organization down."

I shook my head. "I'm just a kid."

"You were just a kid today, too, Matt. But you saved dozens of lives." She licked her lips. "You'd be one of us," she said. "If you did this, you'd be a real CIA operative. It's what you said you wanted all along, right?"

"I'd be a spy?" I asked. That's exactly what I wanted, wasn't it? It didn't feel quite the same now that it meant doing something actually dangerous.

She nodded.

"And I'd just be going back for the last two days of the camp?"

"That's it, Matt. Two days. Give or take."

316

"Give or take what?" I asked.

She shook her head. "We're not asking you to stay there any longer than the next two days. But we need to know who the people are who coordinate the missions they're sending kids on. That means that *technically* you'd be staying undercover until you get your first mission. I don't know when that would happen, or *how* it would happen for that matter. It could come via phone, or by email, or by some other code we haven't thought of."

"And that'll be it?" I asked. "Nothing else?" I pointed at her. "And I'll really be a CIA spy?"

She nodded. "Yeah, Matt, you'll be one of the youngest in recent history. Besides," she continued, "if you don't do this, there's a good chance the only option for you and your family is witness relocation. That means leaving your whole life behind. It would mean your parents would have to leave their lives behind too."

"And just doing two more days means we wouldn't have to do that?" She nodded.

It's two days, I thought. Just two days. I spent three weeks there already, so what's two more days? Besides, I kind of wanted to see Chase's face when he found out I'd won.

I contemplated what going back would mean. I don't think I spoke for the better part of half an hour. It was a lot to take in. My teammates were all criminals, or at least their families were all criminals. It explained a lot. But I still didn't see them as criminals. They were friends.

Agent Knox didn't pressure me for an answer. She waited until I was ready to speak, and when I'd finally reached a decision, she genuinely looked like she'd accept any answer I gave her.

I nodded. "I'll do it."

Agent Chen tapped a key on the laptop, closed the screen, and then left the room without a word.

"Chen is the agent in charge of logistics," Agent Knox said. "We needed to hear you were on board, but now he's got to make some magic happen. You need a story for why you're being released. He'll be the one who comes up with that." She gathered up her papers. "You made a brave decision, Matt. Don't worry. We'll be right beside you the whole time. You won't see us, but we'll be there."

"I want training," I said as the agent took a step for the door. She stopped and turned around. One eyebrow rose. "Training," I said again. "You know how stupid I looked out there this summer?" I blew out a breath. "I want real spy training. I know this might not last long, but that's one of my conditions."

Agent Knox smiled. "Done, kid. No problem. When you get back home, I'll arrange some private tutors for some of the courses you'll need to be a quality spy. I'll set that up for you personally."

"Okay," I said. "Let's do this."

CHAPTER 51

Everything happened in the morning.

I'd only been asleep for about twenty minutes when Agent Knox woke me up. It didn't matter; I was overtired by that point, and my stomach was in knots over what I was about to do. Still, there was a plan, and I needed to hear it.

Agent Chen had come up with a very simple story, which was good, since the only lesson I learned getting beaten up by Butler during my interrogation session was that all fake stories must be simple, and layered with more truth than lie. Mine went like this:

The security guard who had tackled me at the station had done so because he was working in the surveillance room at the time of the explosions and had seen me throw the pylon onto the tracks. While Agent Chen got rid of the footage, Butler sat down with the guard and somehow convinced him that he hadn't seen what he thought he'd seen. I'm not sure how he did it. Maybe some interrogation technique, maybe hypnosis, maybe he injected him with a drug that made people forget stuff.

Next, Agent Knox spread the word that, indeed, I was Gunnar Konstantan from Sweden, and that I had simply been in the wrong place at the wrong time, and I was not at all responsible for the bombing at the station. The police and FBI hit the streets again, following up leads and searching for those responsible.

Butler, Agent Knox explained, wasn't difficult at all. Once everything was out in the open, there was nothing he could do but deal, and the deal was that he would help bring the organization down. If anyone asked how I'd gotten away from the police, I was to say, "Butler helped." And leave it at that.

"Have you ever heard the expression, 'Those who can't do, teach,' Matt?" Agent Knox had asked. "Butler is a prime example of that expression. He teaches operatives how to handle themselves in interrogation settings, but after twenty minutes and a couple of threats, he folds like a piece of origami."

Butler seemed smaller to me after that.

Getting me out of the hospital and back to the camp was also pretty easy. Agent Knox had given me a wallet that I was to say I'd stolen from another patient. I was supposed to use the money in the wallet to get a taxi back to camp. They'd put microscopic trackers on me and promised they'd be watching from a distance. All I needed to do was finish out the next two days.

As for actually getting out of the hospital, that was the easiest part of the whole thing. I'd imagined that they'd plan some kind of diversion, and then I'd jump into a laundry cart that would be pushed by a bribed orderly. I figured a car would be waiting to whisk me away from a back exit or at the bottom of a fire escape or somewhere similar. But I guess that stuff only happens in movies, because it wasn't like that at all.

Not even close.

With all the destruction in the city, the hospital was overrun with patients, and the doctors and nurses were overwhelmed. I ate the breakfast the candy striper brought, got dressed, and then did exactly what Agent Knox told me to do: I walked out. No one tried to stop me.

No one even noticed me. I wasn't even trying to be sneaky about it.

Once outside, I walked over to the taxi stand and got a cab. Wave after wave of exhaustion hit me during the drive, but I couldn't bring myself to sleep. I kept going back and forth, one second so excited I was actually a CIA spy heading out on my first real mission, and the next, I wanted to tell the driver to turn around and take me back to the hospital. Back to Agent Knox so I could tell her I'd changed my mind, that I wanted the witness protection option. But while I had a back-and-forth argument with myself, the minutes ticked by, and before long, it had been just over an hour, and the taxi was heading up the driveway to Camp Friendship.

The experience of driving up that gravel stretch for a second time is difficult to explain. I'd gone to Universal Studios with my parents when I was younger, and I remember getting to tour a movie set. Things looked totally real on that set. The trees, the buildings, even the people. But none of it was real. It was all just a veneer. A fake exterior to impress tourists. That was how the camp felt to me now. Nothing I saw was as it really was. It was all just an intricate distraction.

I paid the cabbie and made my way down to Team Grizzly's section. There were campers everywhere, each scampering around like they'd just been assigned the world's most important task. I made it halfway through the section before anyone really noticed me.

"Captain?" a younger girl asked. The three campers with her jerked around at her words and stared at me, openmouthed.

"Yeah," I said without slowing down. "Sorry, I don't have time to stop."

After that, almost everyone I passed noticed me.

"Sir!" another girl blurted out. "You made it back?"

"Uh-huh," I said, picking up speed.

There were sighs of relief and kids shouting my name. It was all very uncomfortable, and I wondered if maybe losing a Delta in an event meant that everyone on the team had some kind of punishment. The crowd of kids following me only grew as I jogged the rest of the way to the cabin. I glanced over my shoulder as I climbed the steps to the door and cringed. There were at least twenty campers smiling and calling out to me.

I turned away, shoved open the door, and slammed it shut behind me.

"Captain?" Angie stood up from her bed and eyed me carefully. "It *is* you!"

Juno laughed and clapped his hands. "I told you he'd make it back."

Rylee stepped up and bit her lip. "We've been worried."

"What happened?" Amara asked. "And how'd you get away from the police?"

I pressed my back against the door and stared at my team. I had expected that seeing them again, knowing what I knew about them, would make being in the same room with them uncomfortable. But for some reason, it didn't. I thought about that for a second, and I realized that I'd always found them intimidating, and being around them had never been comfortable. The only difference was that now I wasn't entirely clueless.

That Juno was the son of a yakuza crime boss or that Amara's mom was some South African freedom fighter didn't make them any more intimidating than they'd already been. I did wonder, though, about Rylee and Angie, though I figured Angie was the psychotic daughter of someone really nuts. An escaped mental patient from a hospital in Europe, no doubt. It wouldn't have surprised me if her mom or dad had a nickname like *the Berlin Psychopath* or *Sociopath Steve.*

I snapped out of my daze and realized my team was staring at me. "Sorry," I said, "it's a long story." I plopped down on my bed. "I'll tell you about it when I get up."

"Just give us the CliffsNotes version," Rylee said. "We know we won; we just don't have any idea how."

They weren't going to let me sleep, at least not without some answers. "All right," I said, thinking fast. "The CliffsNotes version, huh? I got blown up by Chase's bomb, got tackled by security when I was running away from the building, and got hauled to the hospital, where the freaking FBI showed up because they thought I was the bomber. Then Butler came just in the nick of time and convinced everyone I was who I said I was: a kid on a foreign exchange in the wrong place at the wrong time. It's a good thing I took all the fake IDs I'd made for my Swedish counterpart, because I technically sabotaged Chase's plan; but if we won, I must've gotten credit for the bombing."

Juno nodded his head at me. "Nice."

"Butler?" Rylee asked. "You're kidding. I can't believe they sent in Butler to help you out. I mean, we won, so maybe you're more valuable than an average Delta, but Butler?"

I closed my eyes and then snapped them open and pointed at my teammates, who were still crowded around my bed. "You guys remember those three campers? Rob, Alexis, and Duncan?"

They all nodded.

"Your little lackeys," Juno noted.

I harrumphed. "Well, they're not on our team at all. They're impostors. They were working with Chase all along. I want you to spread the word: if they step one toe off the path while they're in our section ..." I looked around at the faces again and drew back my lips. "Hurt them."

"I'm impressed," Angie said. "I didn't think you'd ever tell us to hurt a trio of eleven-year-olds."

"They're not *regular* eleven-year-olds," I said. "And they deserve it."

"Chase planted those little brats?" Rylee asked. "I knew I should have objected more when I saw you talking to them. I knew something wasn't right."

"Sleep," I said, settling back into my bed. "I need some. Bad."

I was tired. Exhausted. All I wanted was a couple hours of sleep. Then I'd deal with all of this. Just a couple hours.

My eyes had been closed for maybe ten seconds when the door to the cabin crashed open. I was too tired and too sore to jump to attention but did, miraculously, find the strength to roll out of bed and stand. Though Ms. Clakk was already halfway across the room when I did.

"Cambridge," she said in a much-too-pleasant tone, "you're back. I heard you were but wanted to see for myself."

"I'm back, ma'am," I said.

"Decided to take a tour of the city while you were out, did you?"

"A tour of the hospitals anyway, ma'am."

"Since you pulled off a win and made me look good, all is forgiven." She slapped my shoulder and then looked around the cabin. "Put on one of your team shirts and get moving. You're to be outside doing your best to look like campers enjoying the last day of camp."

"Last day?" I asked. "I thought tomorrow was the last day."

"Keep up, Cambridge," Clakk said with a sigh. "Tomorrow you guys are shipped out first thing. Today's the last day that matters." She snapped her fingers. "All of you. Get out there!"

CHAPTER 52

We weren't out of the cabin for five minutes before Chase wandered up the path toward us. He didn't stop walking, but as he passed us, his eyes narrowed and he bared his teeth. "We're not done, Cambridge," he said, seething. "I'll get you for what you did. I promise you I will."

Part of me wanted to throw back a snappy comeback, but another part of me wanted to puke on my shoes. Chase was certifiable. Really nuts. He'd tried to blow up a train station. If he said I was going to pay, I had a feeling that's exactly what was going to happen.

"Stop being such a baby, Chase," Angie said. "You lost, fair and square. You're clearly not Delta material."

Chase didn't turn around. He just dropped his chin and kept trudging down the path.

We came to the archery range and spotted Dalson talking to a woman near one of the targets. Instinct told me to stop, turn, and go the opposite direction. But as soon as I stopped, Dalson looked up, spotted me, and signaled me to come down.

"Good luck," Rylee said as I stepped off the path and headed to the range.

"Mr. Cambridge," Dalson said with a grin that looked entirely sincere. "Good timing."

He gestured to the woman on his right, and it took me a minute before I recognized her. The camp accreditation lady. The one I'd met the very first day in the parking lot. I tried to think of her name.

"Ms. Sani," I said.

The woman nodded. "I was hoping I'd run into you, Matt." She grimaced and gestured to my face. "I heard about your accident when I was reviewing the first aid logs. How are you feeling?"

I shrugged and wondered what the logbook said about my injuries. "I'm fine. I'm sure it looks worse than it feels."

She smiled. "Glad to hear it." She waved her hand around the camp. "So? How was your camp experience?"

"Matt was captain of one of the teams this year," Dalson said before I could answer on my own.

Ms. Sani's eyes widened. "Really?"

"More than that," Dalson said. "He led his team to victory."

"Is that a fact?" Ms. Sani said. "Then you had a good time, Matt? You'll be back next year?"

I laughed and blurted out, "Not unless my parents hate me."

Dalson's eyes narrowed for a fraction of a second.

Ms. Sani smiled. "Then you didn't have fun?"

I cleared my throat. "It was, um, better than I expected, but I'd have more fun at home with my friends."

Dalson put his hand on my shoulder. "He's still got a bit of an attitude, but I think, deep down, he's had a wonderful experience. It's what we strive to give our campers here at Camp Friendship."

"Yeah," I said. "It was wonderful."

Ms. Sani smiled. "I'm sure it was, Matt." She turned to Dalson. "I'll get the last bit of paperwork from my car and meet you back at your office."

When Ms. Sani was on the path, Dalson turned me around. "Not bad, Matt, not bad at all. Your scores were impressive, of course, but you did an excellent job making people underestimate you this summer. I don't know how you came up with the plan to both cause a disruption and sabotage Mr. Erickson's team, but it was out-of-the-box thinking like that that got you the win. The city will be cleaning up that mess for months."

Dalson nodded knowingly and then reached into his pocket, pulled out a small cell phone, and handed it to me. "Here's your reward. You earned it."

The cell phone was small and black and had a touch-screen display.

"Keep it handy," Dalson said. "Your team's numbers are already programmed in. When you get a mission, you set the rendezvous location and carry out the plan."

The CIA was watching, I reminded myself. I wondered if they were close enough to hear what we were saying. It was my chance to get a bit more information and show the real CIA that I was a capable spy.

"It's just me?" I asked. "I don't have to report to anyone else?"

"Ms. Clakk is your advisor," Dalson said. "Any questions or concerns go to her, but you don't need her permission."

"And the call," I asked, "the one I get with the missions? That comes from ..."

"The Agency, of course. We are the middlemen, Matt. We handle payments, as well. Our fees are taken off the top, but don't worry; your share will be deposited into accounts we've set up for you."

I shook my head. "Of course. I knew that. I just wanted to make sure." I bit my lip. "And the missions. What sort of things should I be prepared for?"

He slapped my shoulder. "I wouldn't worry about that, Matt. After your display at the station, I'd say you're ready for anything they'll throw at you."

Great, I thought. That narrows it down. So blowing up a train station filled with people is the upper limits of what I might be expected to do. Just perfect. At least they're not going to make me do anything really crazy.

Dalson checked his watch. "Good luck, Matt. I'll be curious to see how you do with real challenges."

As he headed back up to the path, I muttered, "Yeah, me too."

CHAPTER 53

Buses left the camp first thing in the morning, and we arrived at the Sledge Industries parking lot a couple hours later. There were cars waiting for my team.

"Thanks for the most interesting camp yet, Matt," Juno said. He held up his phone, which looked identical to mine. "I can't wait until our first mission. It's going to be great."

"Yeah," Yaakov said, "who'd have thought I'd win the Delta challenge the first time I was ever picked. My parents aren't going to believe me."

Angie nudged Rylee. "I guess we all owe you a thank-you, as well. You put the team together."

Rylee tilted her head. "But Matt agreed, clearly." She turned to me. "Thanks, Matt. I don't think I could have handled going to another one of those camps."

"You and me both," I said.

"It was nice to be trusted," Amara said. "You're not like other Deltas, Matt. I'm looking forward to working with you again. And I don't like working with *any*one."

Juno took a step back and gasped dramatically. "No! But you're such a people person, Amara."

The others laughed, and even Amara smiled.

It had only been a few weeks since my dad had dropped me off, but it felt like months. I guessed that was why my discomfort with my team felt so, well, comfortable, even though they were all a bunch of criminals, or at least criminals in training. My dad hadn't intended me to be sent to a camp for criminals; there was just no way. I knew that as well as I knew anything. But his goal—to make me less of a trouble-maker—had worked.

I was different. The camp had changed me, and not into a criminal. I wasn't interested in pulling pranks anymore. It seemed so childish compared to what I'd just been through. I wanted to work for the CIA. I wanted to stop people like Chase.

"See ya when I see ya," Juno said as he strolled to his car.

The others said their good-byes and then walked off to their rides too. I wondered how much farther all of them had to go. I knew Juno was headed back to Japan, and Amara to Africa, but I wondered about the rest of them. They could be headed anywhere.

I heaved my bag onto my shoulder and glanced toward the alley where my dad had dropped me off. The lights to his Honda blinked and I made my way over. I threw my bag into the back seat and slid into the front for the drive home.

Dad grabbed my chin and turned my face to his. "What happened to your face?"

I shook my head. "I slipped down a ravine during one of our hikes. It looks a lot worse than it is."

He nodded and then looked at me for an uncomfortable minute. "I know it's only been a few weeks, but you look different. And not just because of all the scratches and bruises."

I shrugged. I felt different too. But I wasn't really sure what I should, or *could*, tell him. He started the car and pulled onto the street.

"How was it?" he asked finally.

I shrugged again. "Better and worse than I expected it to be."

He nodded as if that made perfect sense. "Did you have time to think about what you did at the assembly?"

I stopped myself from snickering. The assembly seemed like a million years ago, and honestly I hadn't given it much thought at all. But what I'd done *was* stupid. It was thoughtless and juvenile. It seemed like something Chase would do, only he'd use poisonous gas. I wasn't proud of it anymore, that's for sure. I was embarrassed about it.

"I'm sorry for what I did," I said finally. "All I can do is promise it won't happen again."

My dad pulled up to a stop sign and glanced at me. "You know, you look like you actually mean that."

"Yeah, well," I began, "let's just say it's not something I'm proud of anymore."

We didn't speak for another couple blocks, and then he put his hand on my shoulder and gave it a squeeze. "I'm proud of you, son."

We turned onto our street, and I spotted Jason leaning against the basketball pole in my driveway.

"Your mom's waiting to see you," my dad said. He nodded at Jason through the windshield. "Don't be long."

It was only a bit after eight in the morning, and I'd never known Jason to get up before noon on summer vacation. I gave him a nod when I got out of the car and gestured to the street. He walked his bike beside me without saying a word until we were nearly a block away from my house.

"What I tell you," I said, "needs to stay just between us. Okay?"

He nodded.

"I'm serious, Jason. This is literally my life we're talking about. You can't tell anyone. Not a single person."

He held up his hand. "I promise, dude. You know I don't blab about important stuff. Do I need to remind you of all the secrets I already know about you? Or all the secrets you know about me that you could tell if I ever broke my word?"

I shook my head. "I know. I just want you to really understand, that's all."

"I get it."

Once I started talking, everything just sort of fell out of me. I'd wanted to tell someone for so long that it was just such a relief to have Jason to talk to. I told him everything. I even told him about every time I'd gotten beat up and about crying when I was strapped to the chair getting interrogated by Butler. He didn't laugh even once, and when I was done, he just rubbed the back of his neck and kept muttering the word *unbelievable* over and over.

I let out a long sigh and felt about a million times better.

"This is crazy, Matt," Jason said after a couple minutes. "Just crazy. I mean, when I saw the news about the station and how someone had blown the place up, I didn't know what to think. I thought maybe Kalvin gave you the wrong stuff or something. It looked like a war zone out there."

"I know," I said. "I was there."

He nodded. "But you're a hero, Matt. You saved people. You saved a *lot* of people. And now you're a CIA agent. You're like double-oh-seven. Only cooler because you're a kid. If you help shut these criminals down, you'll be, like, a full-fledged spy." He shook his head at me. "What are you going to tell your parents?"

"Nothing," I said. "Absolutely nothing. I'll let Dad think he sent me

- DISRUPTION -
to a strict camp, and that I've learned my lesson. I'll keep out of trouble." I lifted my shoulders and shrugged. "Our pranks just don't seem that important anymore."

"I know what you mean," Jason said. "After seeing what went down at the station, I'm not really interested in doing that kind of stuff anymore."

That surprised me. Jason lived for pranks. I actually thought he'd love the fact that he'd been questioned by FBI and CIA. But the way he was acting, I believed that his pranking days were over.

Jason drew in a deep breath and stood tall. "I'll help you. Whatever you need. Maybe you could even ask them if I could be your partner."

"You're my best friend, Jay," I said. "I'll ask them, and if they say no, I'll still want your help."

He held out his fist, and I bumped it with mine.

"So when do you think these criminals are going to contact you to give you your first mission?"

I shrugged. "I dunno. A week? A month maybe?"

The phone in my pocket vibrated, and I pulled it out. The screen was lit up with the name *Alpha* written across the display.

I blinked. "Or right now."

- END -

3

And please check out these other titles
by **Steven Whibley**.

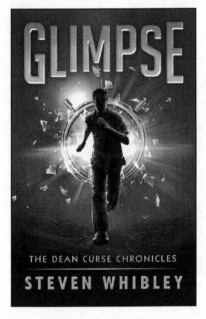

Dean Curse avoids attention the way his best friend Colin avoids common sense. Which is why he isn't happy about being Abbotsford's latest local hero – having saved the life of a stranger, he is now front page news. Dean's reason for avoiding the lime-light? Ever since his heroic act, he's been having terrifying visions of people dying and they're freaking him out so badly his psychologist father just might have him committed. Dean wants nothing more than to lay low and let life get back to normal.

But when Dean's visions start to come true, and people really start dying, he has to race against the clock – literally – to figure out what's happening. Is this power of premonition a curse? Or is Dean gifted with the ability to save people from horrible fates? The answer will be the difference between life and death.

GLIMPSE, BOOK 1
THE DEAN CURSE CHRONICLES

ISBN 978-0-9919208-0-8 / PB
ISBN 978-0-9919208-2-2 / HC

Fourteen-year-old Dean Curse is still having horrifying visions of the soon-to-be-dead. But after saving his sister, he sees it for the gift the mysterious society intended it to be.

So far, Dean's ability has cost him a few broken bones and a standing appointment at group therapy. But those are small sacrifices compared to the lives he's saved. But now, Dean – and his best friends, Colin and Lisa – are forced to make hard decisions that could get them in serious trouble with the law. They have less than twenty-four hours to decide if a few wrongs really can make a right.

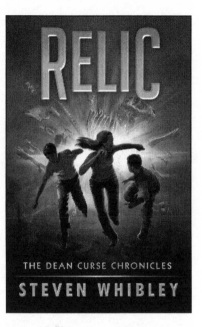

RELIC, BOOK 2
THE DEAN CURSE CHRONICLES

ISBN 978-0-9919208-4-6 / PB
ISBN 978-0-9919208-5-3 / HC

WWW.STEVENWHIBLEY.COM

The time has come: Dean Curse and his two best friends will soon meet the other members of the society who share his gift of premonition. They're so excited to finally get a formal welcome that they don't even mind that the timing means they miss the opening day of the city's premier event: the annual Abbotsford air show.

But what is supposed to be a relaxed meet-and-greet with their new team, quickly becomes a race against the clock. Dean, and every other member of the Abbotsford sector, are hit – at the same moment – by a particularly horrifying vision of death which prompts members of the *Congregatio de Sacrifico* from divisions all over the country come to help. One thing is clear: they have 24 hours to stop what is sure to be the most catastrophic event the city has ever seen.

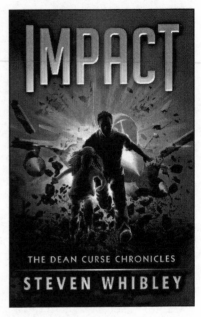

But as desperate seconds tick by, Dean, Colin and Lisa become more and more convinced the disaster is going to be caused by someone within their own new-found ranks. It's going to take every ounce of determination and bravery for Dean and his friends to find the answers before it's too late – but how do you stop someone who already knows the tricks of the society's trade?

IMPACT, BOOK 3
THE DEAN CURSE CHRONICLES

Coming in 2014

ISBN 978-1-927905-00-5 / PB
ISBN 978-1-927905-01-2 / HC
ISBN 978-1-927905-02-9 / EBOOK

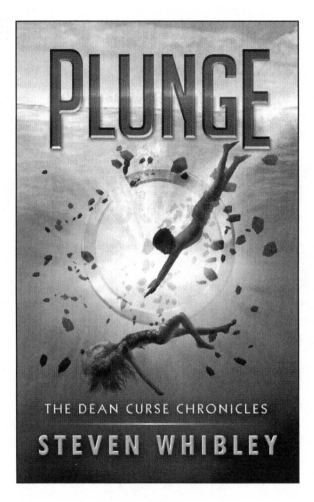

BOOK 4

RELEASE DATE TO BE ANNOUNCED

VISIT:

WWW.STEVENWHIBLEY.COM

FOR MORE HEART-POUNDING ADVENTURES CHECK OUT THIS TITLE:

CITY OF THE FALLING SKY by JOSEPH EVANS

ISBN 978-0-9572912-0-1 / EBOOK
AVAILABLE ON AMAZON ASIN: B005E8YZ2M

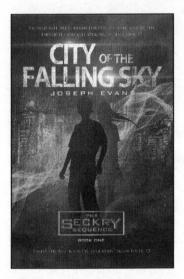

When Seckry Sevenstars is forced out of his village by the greedy Endrin Corporation and relocated to the daunting metropolis of Skyfall City, he harbours resentment for the company and vows to get them back one day for taking away his home, his school and his friends.

Fortunately, the marvels of the city do a good job in distracting Seckry from his anger and homesickness, and it isn't long before he's competing at Friction (the city's most popular multiplayer video game), slurping awe-inspiring multicoloured milkshakes, and getting butterflies on his first date.

Then, when a mysterious email asks Seckry to break into the headquarters of the Endrin Corporation and steal a container full of worms for a hefty sum of money, his anger resurfaces, and he can't resist the revenge he promised himself.

Alone at night, Seckry creeps through the sewers whilst wondering what experiments Endrin might be doing on the worms, and emerges into the silent complex. But the worms aren't the only thing that he finds. Staring at him through the darkness, with wide, innocent eyes, is something that makes Seckry's heart almost stop.

A girl.

She's shaking, petrified, and has no recollection of who she is or what she's doing there.

Floodlights bleach the area and Seckry has no choice but to grab a hold of the girl and escape with her.

Suddenly the question of what Endrin were doing with a few worms becomes the last thing on Seckry's mind. What were Endrin doing with a *human*?

WWW.THESECKRYSEQUENCE.COM

Made in the USA
San Bernardino, CA
09 December 2018